FLAT
WHITE
FATALITY

For baristas everywhere

Books by Emmeline Duncan

FRESH BREWED MURDER

DOUBLE SHOT DEATH

FLAT WHITE FATALITY

Published by Kensington Publishing Corp.

FLAT WHITE FATALITY

Emmeline Duncan

Kensington Publishing Corp.
www.kensingtonbooks.com

ISBN: 978-1-4967-3344-3 (ebook)

ISBN: 978-1-4967-3343-6

First Kensington Trade Paperback Printing: June 2023

10 9 8 7 6 5 4 3 2 1

Printed in the United States of America

Chapter 1

It is a truth acknowledged by coffee aficionados that nothing is ever as good as your first cup in the morning. But as I tested the new batch of our newest blend, a light roast we'd jokingly dubbed "Concrete Blonde," and the name stuck, I decided sometimes your second cup could be life changing.

Just in case, I poured myself a third cup.

Still perfect.

One of my baristas, Kendall, grinned as he wiped down the espresso machine after making a mocha for a customer. "Do you and that coffee need to go get a room?"

"Based on my developing level of commitment with this coffee, I'm thinking marriage."

Kendall poured his own cup and sniffed the coffee to test the aroma in a coffee snob–approved fashion before taking a sip. His usual low-key vibe felt comforting, like nothing could shake him, not even world-class coffee. Although I knew he was the sort of guy who cares deeply but approaches life pragmatically. It's one of the reasons I love having him as a barista. Barely anything fazes him.

And Kendall brews a mean cup of coffee.

Except I should say "kind cup of coffee," since he's not mean unless provoked. Even then, it's less cruel and more principled.

"Okay, I understand why you had a dopey look in your eyes while you drank this," Kendall said.

We chatted about how to brand it until the calendar on my phone beeped an alert. "I have to motor," I said. From the half smile that flashed on Kendall's face, he'd gotten the joke. I unlocked my bike from its spot chained up behind the Ground Rules cart and headed out.

But I paused before leaving the Rail Yard. The cart, with its teal awning and accents, has a retro-throwback feel that I love. And now, it was time to check on the next phase of the Ground Rules plan for world coffee domination.

When I left the cart, I swung by the Button Building, aka the micro-restaurant development that would eventually house the first brick-and-mortar Ground Rules shop. The shell of the building was up, but it would be a while before the interior was fully built out. But as I chatted with the contractor and architect and walked with them through the space that would eventually be our shop, I felt like I could see the future.

And the future was going to be well-caffeinated but also light and airy with big windows, white subway tiles, a long bar made of reclaimed oak perfect for patrons to sit at while lingering over an espresso, a handful of café tables, and polished concrete floors. Plus, an order window from the street as a nod to our coffee cart roots that would hopefully attract commuters, dog walkers, and people on the go.

I swapped my borrowed hard hat for my bike helmet and cycled toward the Ground Rules headquarters.

When my business partner, Harley Yamazaki, and I had rented space in SE Portland for our roastery, I hadn't known how perfectly it would work out. The area was ideal: we had plenty of room to set up the roaster and store coffee beans as they degassed. Plus, storage space for our bagged coffee during the brief time between packaging the beans and sending them out into the world. The location was an easy bicycle ride from the Rail Yard and central. Like we were in the heart of the city, sending out our coffee to all six quadrants of Portland and the world beyond. (Yes, six quadrants. As we say, we like to keep Portland weird.)

Our neighbors in the building looked like a true Portland mix of people passionate about their businesses. A gym. A seamstress specializing in bespoke and repurposed clothing. A woodworking shop that made custom furniture and, when their door was open, made the hallway smell faintly of pine dust.

But, most importantly, a video game development company named the Grumpy Sasquatch Studio was next door to the roastery.

We hadn't been in the building for very long when I took coffee to our next-door neighbors, who were rarely grumpy, even when everyone was stressed during deadlines.

I'd met Bax—actually named Lukas Evans Baxter but no one called him that—the co-owner of the studio, and even though I didn't realize it, the universe had clicked a puzzle piece into the landscape of my life. 'Course, it took me a while to know it.

Then, a while back, Bax asked me to do motion-capture work for his new video game in production. It turned out I'd partially inspired the basis for the game. Bax acted all starry-eyed when he told me about the concept. It involved some sort of urban fantasy world with a magical blonde who righted wrongs and solved mysteries. She didn't back down from anyone.

I couldn't say no, even though I'd been tempted because: I'm busy working on world coffee domination. So, after a brief negotiation, I'd started dressing up in motion-capture gear a few afternoons a week. My small but reliable roster of fantastic baristas kept my coffee cart chugging along when I was in Grumpy Sasquatch Studio, wearing what was basically a black onesie with sensors on it, acting out scenes and choreographed movements that the game designers were using to render me as a video game character. Yesterday, after working with a choreographer, I'd done a series of fighting moves, and she was scheduled to come back periodically over the next few weeks.

Yesterday was also supposed to be my first payday. But it hadn't shown up, so I needed to stop by the studio's office manager to troubleshoot the problem.

When I entered Grumpy Sasquatch Studio, I turned to the short hallway leading to a handful of private offices, including the office manager's domain. But Bax's office had its own gravitational pull, and I had to pop my head in.

He was still dressed in his typical workday unofficial uniform of jeans and a T-shirt, today covered with a charcoal cotton sweater. But I knew he'd mix up his attire later today with the rest of his crew.

Bax glanced up as I entered. His face softened from focused to a smile. "How's the Button Building looking?"

"Like someday, it will be a real coffee shop!"

We chatted for a moment, then I walked over to Elaine's office, which felt like a different world compared to Bax's. His office has personal touches. A photo of his son on his desk. Framed video game posters on the calm green walls, and a couch under the window.

Elaine's office is all business. Her desk faces the door, and there's a hard wooden seat for visitors, giving it the feeling of a principal's office. One wall has file cabinets, and a second has a console table in institutional gray. The only personal touch is a small succulent on the corner of her desk. Elaine matches the ambiance, and she always dressed in what I term motherly business casual. She favors capris year-round and loose tunics in classic colors versus most of the office's dress code of jeans and graphic T-shirts.

I knocked on her doorframe, as the door was open, even though she was meeting with Noah Parkes, one of the "sasquatches" I now worked with sometimes. If I had to guess, I'd put his age in his early thirties. He was intense when he worked, but he also joined the weekly office no-drop bicycle rides, meaning the group never leaves a rider behind. I'd seen him spring into action and fix flat tires with a calm efficiency and sense of humor as he got the group ready to restart.

"Oh, Sage, come on in. We're done here," Elaine said.

Noah stood up from the wooden chair. "So, it's all taken care of?"

"Yep, you can head back to work," Elaine said. She sounded like a bone-weary mother dealing with a horde of teenagers.

Noah nodded at me as he passed. "See you in a bit!"

It was my turn to slide into the hardback chair, which wasn't comfortable enough to make anyone want to linger. Like Noah, I left the door open, implying this wasn't too sensitive of a conversation.

Elaine handed me an envelope. "The payment problem was a bit of a miscommunication. We set everything up for automatic payment, but everyone's first and last checks are always hard copies."

I tucked the envelope into my messenger bag. "That makes sense." We had the same process at Ground Rules. How I got paid didn't matter to me; I planned to funnel all of my motion-capture payments into my avocado toast fund (which some people prefer to call a rainy day fund).

"I'm not sure where the confusion came from. Maybe because it feels like you've been here forever, even if you only recently became an official employee. I've been paying your coffee invoices for forever, it feels like," Elaine said. Her words felt bland, and I wondered what she was truly feeling, deep inside. And I wondered if Elaine intended her comment about me being around to be a criticism since it felt slightly judgy. But she also looked like she needed either a nap or a week away on a beach with a book and no responsibilities. So maybe I was reading more into an off-hand comment than I should.

And the studio had been one of Ground Rules's first corporate accounts, and since they were next door, one of the easiest to service.

"Are you excited for today?" I asked.

A frown slid across Elaine's face before a more neutral look covered her face. She forced herself to smile. "It's not quite to my taste, but I'll join everyone, of course. It's certainly a creative celebration."

"Ah, so today's not quite your cup of coffee?" I said.

My joke didn't change the expression on Elaine's face, but a laugh sounded from the doorway behind me. "That's our Elaine," Lindsey Barlow, Bax's business partner, said. "One of the things I love about our company is how welcoming we are with diverse viewpoints. And the event today is optional for everyone, of course. But by not participating, you'll miss out on some killer snacks."

"Oh, hi, birthday girl!" I said.

Lindsey had opted for a vintage-inspired shirtwaist dress with a matching cardigan to celebrate her annual celebration of another orbit around the sun. As long as I'd known her, she'd embraced natural hair, and she'd recently taken to box braids with dark purple beads at the end. She's always stylish in a way I'd love to be. Although it's hard to bring an A-game clothing sense to a job that involves regularly taking unexpected baths in coffee.

Lindsey smiled at me. "Thank you! If you're done with Elaine, I have a few things to go over before starting the festivities. I need her usual help cutting through bs to keep this place moving smoothly."

"I cede the floor," I said and stood up. As I shuffled past Lindsey, I got a whiff of her perfume, which featured notes of cinnamon and cherry.

"See you on the flip side," Lindsey said and shut the door softly after I left.

So I chilled on the couch in Bax's office until it was go-time.

Chapter 2

For once, I wasn't the only person at Grumpy Sasquatch Studio dressed in a goofy costume.

Everyone here had changed from their usual office attire into duck costumes. It was part of a team-building game involving us waddling around town, solving scavenger hunt clues, and, presumably, cementing solid work friendships. As we walked around Portland, people would hopefully know we were playing a game. However, I suspected they'd think we were hard-core University of Oregon fans showing our love for the Ducks.

Me being part of the team builder felt amusing, but hey, I even had an official Grumpy Sasquatch paycheck in my bag. It still felt weird to be an employee, considering I was dating the co-owner. But he'd been so persuasive, and I was enjoying the motion-capture work.

Speak of Prince Charming. Bax paused beside me. He grinned at me, and I felt a bit warm inside. "Aren't you the cutest duckling in the room," he said.

Lindsey walked up. She's about an inch shorter than Bax, with a rangy build and an ever-present mischievous twinkle in her eyes.

"I'll get this started in a minute. I assume you have a partner in crime picked out?" Lindsey said.

Bax nodded his head at me. "I'm partnered with the coffee angel," he said. Bax wore the hood of his duck costume up and looked absolutely ridiculous. But the costumes, which were basically onesies, looked silly on everyone. Thankfully, the October day was brisk, 'cause the onesies would've been murder in the summer heat, which extends into late September.

A voice spoke from behind us.

"How do I look?" From the Australian accent, I knew without looking that Robbie Kayle had spoken. I turned and held in a laugh.

Robbie had somehow found a white goose costume and emerged in it, butterfly-like, from a cocoon of ducks.

A couple of people chuckled. A few people stared with expressions I couldn't quite decipher. But I thought I also caught a mix of annoyance and indifference.

"Looks like one of the groups will be a mixed fowl matchup," Lindsey said. "Hopefully, it doesn't lead to fowl play."

"You mean worse than the rubber chicken Robbie left in your desk drawer this morning?" someone asked.

Of course, Robbie had tried to pull a prank on Lindsey for her birthday.

"I wanted to partner with Sage," Robbie said. She put her arm around my shoulder, giving me the whiff of coconut, bananas, and a nutty scent I couldn't quite place. At 5' 6", Robbie was about five inches taller than me. She was slightly overdue to get her blond roots touched up, showing light brown hair underneath, but it worked with her carefully styled beach waves. Everything about Robbie seemed purposeful. Including her upscale jeans and trendy wardrobe with a touch of surfer chic sourced from hip and higher-end shops that, I assumed, her programming job helped her afford.

Robbie must have also been thinking about hair. "What shade of blond do you aim for? Sunflower? Champagne?" She touched a lock of my hair where it rested on my shoulder. I'd blow-dried my hair this morning and left it down for once instead of pulling it into a ponytail.

"This is my natural color, although I did play around with dyeing it darker when I was a teen."

"Really," Robbie said, like I was lying about not bleaching my hair.

"It's one perk of having two blond parents." Hair wasn't the only thing I'd inherited from my parents. Neither are particularly tall, and both have blue eyes. But that's where their similarity ends, as my father lives by a strict moral code, and my mother is amoral at best, if not the villain of her own life story. Although I'm sure if you asked her, she'd assume she's the hero.

One of the other programmers, Wyatt Tornsey, stepped up to Lindsey. His duck hood was around his neck, so I could see his spiky brown hair that always stood on end. Kat and a couple other members of his work team followed along behind him, like birds of a feather flocking together.

Wyatt handed Lindsey a box with a silver ribbon wrapped around it. "This is from the dev group," he said. "Kat found it, and we all agreed it was the perfect gift."

"You guys didn't have to buy me anything," Lindsey said. But she looked delighted as she untied the bow. Lindsey opened the gift to find a tiara with rhinestone stars. She laughed, put the box down, and carefully settled the tiara over her braids.

"It's the closest thing we found to a crown," Wyatt said.

"I love it!" The tiara sparkled in the overhead lights.

"It's your birthday. Why are you the one staying in the office?" Robbie asked.

"The birthday gift I'd planned is the acknowledgment I'm the puppet master, and you're all going to play the game I spent the last few weeks organizing," Lindsey said. "And Sage made me dairy-free brownies. I can't leave because I can't stop eating them."

Bax laughed. Lindsey looked at him, and they shared a silent moment that showed their decades-long friendship.

Robbie sang out, "Why was she born so beautiful? Why was she born at all? Because she had no say in it, no say in it at all!"

Everyone stared at Robbie. Her song sounded vaguely familiar, and my brain whirled as I tried to place it.

"Okay," Kat finally said.

"It's the Australian birthday song. You've heard it before, right?" Robbie said.

"I've read about it before," Wyatt said. "It went semi-viral when an Australian didn't realize how unique the lyrics are if you're not expecting it."

"One of the birthday songs in Russia has the lyrics, 'and I play the accordion for all to see. It's a pity that (my) birthday is only once a year,'" Kat said.

I noticed the accent that frequently shaded Kat's voice.

Robbie snorted.

"Is there a story behind the Russian song?" Lindsey asked. I sensed the subtle rebuke directed toward Robbie in her voice. I wasn't the only one who'd noticed the occasional animosity Robbie sent Kat's way. I'd yet to see Kat react; she'd always acted like she hadn't noticed. But I suspected, deep down, Kat cared.

"It's from a movie about Gena the crocodile," Kat said. "It involves accordions."

"Interesting, we'll need to talk about this more later," Lindsey said. She got everyone settled into teams. Raoul and Addison had already partnered up, while Wyatt Tornsey and Noah Parkes had decided to work together.

"I'll join Wyatt and Noah," Robbie said. "They'll need my help."

"You're welcome to join us, Kat," Raoul said. He'd done the math and realized Kat was the odd duck out.

"Or us," Bax added.

As they talked, Robbie made eye contact with me. "You baked something for Lindsey? That's a mistake. I'd never become the staff baker."

"I'm sure you could find a way to turn it into a great practical joke." Would anyone be brave enough to eat something Robbie had made? One of my favorite aspects of running my own coffee company is that experimenting with flavors is part of the job. However, there's a reason I buy my pastries from a beloved local shop.

"True, think of the jokes! But no, being the person everyone turns to for cakes turns you into the office mom. No one will take you seriously professionally, but they'll act pissed if you forget their birthday. It's not worth it. I'd rather keep these guys on their toes." She blinked. One of her green eyes looked slightly red and watery.

"You okay?" I asked.

"Stupid contact lens." She smiled, but it felt like one of the log videos shown on TV during the holidays. It looks festive, but there's no warmth to it.

But maybe I'm biased since I can never decide how I truly feel about Robbie. I want to like her. But something inside tells me to keep up an invisible wall between us.

"Luckily, I'm just here as a favor to Bax. And baking is fun. I mean, there's a reason I didn't start a bakery, but it's nice to be able to make something special for Lindsey for her birthday." Especially since she had some food issues and avoided dairy.

Lindsey clapped her hands. "Okay, everyone! You have your teams, and I will give each of you a clue to start. You will visit eight destinations total, and the first person to visit all eight and arrive at the final spot will win. You won't be working on the clues in the same order, so don't think you can just follow another team and try to pip them at the end."

"What's the prize?" Robbie asked. "A raise?"

"Don't you wish you knew," Lindsey said. "So may the best flock win!" I groaned at the pun, then thought I saw a flash of annoyance in Lindsey's eyes as she glanced toward Robbie, then looked away.

"You ready, team?" Bax asked Kat and me.

"I have been ready since the day I was born," Kat said.

I wondered if she'd meant she'd "been born ready."

Robbie started blinking hard as she stood with Wyatt and Noah.

One of her eyes began to water. "Give me a minute," she said and bolted to the bathroom. She shoved her way past my business partner, Harley, who was beelining my way.

Harley rubbed her shoulder and stared at Robbie's retreating back. "That's rude," Harley said.

"Deal with it, Princess," Robbie said. Her hand covered her left eye.

"We'll work on the first clue, and I'll text you how to find us!" Wyatt called after Robbie. Wyatt and Noah glanced at each other, and Wyatt's easygoing mood from earlier seemed to have turned into a wary slouch.

Harley walked up to me, still rubbing her shoulder. Harley operates at her own high-energy frequency, but today she felt sedate. More down than usual.

"You okay?" I asked her.

"I was going to tell Lindsey 'happy birthday' and ask if you'd gotten the proposal ready for tomorrow."

"Yeah, it's all printed and locked in my desk. Do you want to see it?"

"Nah, I trust you. Have fun."

Harley headed in Lindsey's direction. My business partner still looked like a shadow of her usual self. I wondered if I should stick around and see what was going on.

"You ready, team?" Bax asked.

"Sure." We walked to the door, and after a final glance at Harley, who was standing with Lindsey and Wyatt, we left.

Chapter 3

"So, what's the first clue?" I asked Bax, and he held out the slip of paper so Kat and I could read it. The words were printed in a red chalkboard font.

"'What blows in the wind and drops in the fall?'" Kat read the clue out loud. "What does this mean? A waterfall? Water droplets?"

"Or fall like autumn," I said. "Like a leaf."

"The Red Leaf," Bax said, referring to a low-key diner a few blocks from the studio. "I bet that's our first destination."

We walked down the street, passing by a house converted into a pisco bar, and a handful of warehouses and offices. The funky hat manufacturer on the corner had a small storefront with a display of weekender and bucket hats and baseball caps, all with hand-sewn embellishments. A few weeks ago, I'd picked up a gray cloche with a black felted leaf from them.

On the major thoroughfare, we walked past a low-slung mini–strip mall with three businesses, all painted a terra-cotta orange, to the ramshackle café on the corner. The Red Leaf had a couple of tables in a covered outdoor area and green-striped awnings. The teal WE SERVE GROUND RULES COFFEE sign in their window ensures my on-going loyalty. Their breakfast burritos had long ago earned Bax's undying devotion.

In Bax's defense, they manage to fry the bacon for the burritos perfectly. It stays crispy even when surrounded by potatoes, cheese, and scrambled eggs. And their vegan breakfast burrito is shockingly good.

A waitress waved at us as we walked in. She seemed to live in the diner, as I'd never seen it open without her presence keeping the morning flow in check.

"Hiya, ducks! We've been watching for you." She pulled an envelope out of her apron and withdrew a card from it, which she handed over to Bax.

He read it, then gave it to me.

Kat read it out loud over my shoulder. " 'Your task: take a photo of your group drinking a full glass of water. After all, it's important to stay hydrated! Text your photo to base camp to get your next clue.' What's this base camp?"

"Lindsey," I said. "We need to text the photo to her."

"Then why didn't she say so?"

"Poetic license."

The waitress had already poured us three glasses of water with no ice, which she set up on the retro dining table with padded red seats. She stood next to the table.

"Thanks for doing this for us," Bax told her as we sat down.

"It's not a problem! This is fun! And you've been good neighbors for us over the years," she said. "Want me to take your photo?"

We held up our glasses, and she snapped a photo with Bax's phone, then handed it back to him.

"Good luck with your game! I'll see you next week for your usual round of breakfast burritos."

"You can count on it," Bax said. He tapped at his phone while Kat and I took sips of the water.

Bax's phone beeped. He laughed and showed us the screen. "We need to send a photo of the empty glasses to get the next clue."

"Hydration is important, y'all," I said. "Bottoms up."

"It's weird that no one else has arrived," Kat said.

"We're not doing the clues in the same order." Bax adjusted his duck hood. "Remember, Lindsey said we'll all have the same end-point but will take separate journeys."

"I guess starting the hunt out with a full glass of water isn't the worst way to get started," I said.

"Although it feels a bit anticlimactic. But maybe I only feel that way 'cause I downed my water bottle a few minutes before leaving the office," Bax said.

I looked at Kat. As soon as the weather had started to turn colder, she'd begun wearing hats. Today's was a military green cotton beanie that matched the green in her plaid shirt peeking out from under her duck costume, which was partially unzipped at the neck, with the hood down. She'd pulled her brown hair into a thick side braid. She'd always fit into the sasquatches without standing out, and I wondered why, since now she felt like the most unique sasquatch I'd met, other than Bax.

"Kat, you were born in Russia, right?" I asked.

"Yes, near St. Petersburg. We moved to the United States when I was a teen."

"That must have been a challenge." I'd traveled quite a bit, but I'd never been to Russia.

"My English was not good when I arrived. But after working in a McDonald's for a year, I was able to follow conversations with my high school classmates and leave the ESL program for regular school taught in English."

"And you went to Oregon State University?"

"Yes—go, Beavers!" she said. "I should have found a beaver costume since now I look like a University of Oregon fan."

"C'mon, you two, drink up." Bax had already downed his water.

After texting Lindsey a photo of our empty glasses, we received the next clue.

"'If adventure is what you seek, take a look, I'm a . . . blank,'" Bax read aloud.

"Crook?" Kat asked.

"Book," I said.

"The nearest library is outside our game zone," Bax said. Showing her background in video game development, Lindsey had set a perimeter of eight blocks in any direction from the office. A small red structure popped into my mind.

"But there's a Little Lending Library just around the corner," I said.

We trooped outside and promptly came across two ducks and a goose as we waddled down the block. The goose wore a yellow-and-green-striped hat over her long blond hair. Dollars to donuts, it was a Socceroos hat supporting Australia's national team.

"Hey, Wyatt, Noah, Robbie," Bax said.

"Bossman," Wyatt said with a nod. "Coffee genius. Kat."

Robbie shook her head. "Are you still trying to solve your first clue? We made the mistake of listening to Noah for our first clue and went the wrong direction, but we're back on track."

Noah started to speak. "I swear I thought it was the place on—"

"Hush! Don't help them out if they haven't gotten that clue yet!" Robbie glared at Noah like he was trying to give away state secrets.

"Remember, this is supposed to be a team builder," Bax said. His tone was mild, but I could hear the rebuke layered inside.

"And our team is going to win. You're going to wish you'd paired up with me!" Robbie's tone was light, and she flipped her hair playfully over her shoulder.

My phone beeped, and I glanced at it. A text from Sophie, aka my newest barista. Her profile picture showed her grinning at the camera, holding an iced coffee. A cascade of curly red hair flowed over her shoulder in perfect spirals. If fabulous hair was a competition, Sophie always brought her A-game and a cheeky smile.

I read her text. *Some dude came by asking questions about you.*

A slightly sick feeling swirled in my stomach, and I started to type out a question asking for more information. But a second text popped up, this time with a photo. I stared at the man in a baseball cap for a moment. He was partially in shadow, but I could fill in the details of his face from memory.

My former boss, Mark Jeffries. Sophie had snapped it from the Ground Rules cart in the Rail Yard, based on the background. Mark is the owner of Left Coast Grinds, a rival coffee shop and roastery. Both Harley and I had worked for Mark in our university days. Harley had stayed with him after graduation and worked her way up from barista to roaster under Mark. Even though she'd learned a ton, she'd despised working for him. It didn't help that Mark had taken credit for some of her blends and roasts, including an espresso roast that had won big at the regional championship. Mark had a small chain of cafés sprinkled around the city and distribution in the regional grocery store chains, plus various coffee shops and restaurants carried his beans. But, I was proud to say, Ground Rules had been steadily chipping away at his empire as we'd carved out our own niche.

Which didn't answer why he was sniffing around my cart.

I hid a smile. Maybe Mark wanted professional advice.

That's Mark. What did he ask? I texted back.

First, if you'd be in. He ordered a pour-over and asked what you were like to work for and how busy we were. It felt sketch, so I didn't really answer him, Sophie texted back. I could picture her acting vague but friendly with a big smile.

Thanks for telling me. Why was Mark sniffing around now? Did he know about Ground Rules's meeting tomorrow with a distillery that wanted to partner with us?

"Earth to Sage!" Robbie's voice interrupted my thoughts.

I glanced up. Robbie raised her eyebrows as she looked at me. "Do you think your little trio will beat us?"

I grinned, although I felt a flicker of annoyance inside. "Today is supposed to be fun, remember? Whoever wins will get bragging rights and whatever Lindsey has arranged. Still, it's not like it will matter tomorrow."

"Don't bet the farm on that," Wyatt said.

Robbie's turn was lightning fast as she glared at him.

My phone dinged again, but it was Harley this time. *Leaving work a bit early. Headache. I will be better by tomorrow for the meeting, I swear! Even if I have to load up on every painkiller known to humankind.*

I quickly texted back. *Feel better. Let me know if you need anything.*

"Everything okay?" Bax asked.

I glanced up. Everyone was looking at me. "Harley's closing up the roastery early. Nothing big."

"Do you need to go? I know tomorrow is important." Bax sounded concerned. Ever since we'd started dating, he'd gotten to know Harley through me, so he had to know my business partner would've only gone home if it was serious. Harley works hard to make sure our coffee beans are roasted to perfection, and she does the grunt work of packaging them for sale. I've told her we should find an assistant for her, at least part-time, so she doesn't burn out. But for now, she insists she can do it herself.

"Nah." I shook my head. "I'll double-check everything to-night for my meeting tomorrow, but I don't need to go into the office now."

"You must be tired of having to pull Harley's dead weight," Robbie said. Her tone was light.

I glared at her. "Ground Rules would be nothing without Harley."

"Like I said, team builder, fun, paid time to slack off and have fun," Bax said.

"We'll keep that in mind, boss. Team, let's move on," Noah said.

"We'll see you at the finish line," Robbie said.

"Maybe we should've created teams of people who don't work together," Bax said as we walked away.

"I think this is a fun idea," Kat said. "And I'm glad you invited me to join your team."

"Hey, here's the Little Lending Library," I said. We stopped at a wooden box painted barn red with white trim, a pitched roof, and a glass door showing the motley selection of free books inside. Anyone could take, or leave, a book.

We found the task on an index card in the Little Lending Library and took a selfie of us holding books. After texting it to Linsdey, we received a clue that led to the cheese shop (where would I brie without you?). After sampling some cheddar and rating it, we stood outside the shop with our next clue.

"'What kind of bar is kid-friendly?'" Kat read out loud.

"Sports bar? Vegan juice bar?" Bax said.

"Soup?" Kat said.

"Where did you find a soup bar?" Bax asked. He sounded a bit excited, like the idea of bellying up to a bar with a variety of soups sounded like a fun time.

"Grocery store?" Kat said, and Bax almost deflated.

I thought about how Lindsey's clues like to play with words. Riddles, but not impossibly difficult ones.

"Soap?" I said. "Is there a place with specialty soap bars nearby?"

"I know! Chocolate," Bax said. "Which I only thought of because you said soap."

"That's an obvious transition," I said, and Bax laughed.

"Niko found out the hard way that fancy soaps don't taste good when he mistook some for chocolate and didn't ask before biting into it," Bax said, referring to his elementary school–aged son.

"That happened to me once," Kat said.

"That's so rough for kids."

"It was last year," Kat said.

I paused, trying to figure out if Kat was serious. I suspected she was joking, but her face was straight.

"I bet Lindsey means the Jamulet Patisserie a few blocks away. She loves their truffles."

"Their cakes are legit, too," I said.

As we walked in the direction of the patisserie, we waved at a couple groups of sasquatches dressed as ducks who were also on the path of the scavenger hunt. They looked like they were on their way back to the office.

Jamulet is on a major road, with a small parking lot and large garden behind it. You enter through a short, dark hallway with glow-in-the-dark stars to a wide-open space filled with light.

We emerged from the dark to come face-to-face with a sea of living dolls.

Chapter 4

One of the dolls looked at us, took a sip of her wine, and turned back to face the bar. The dolls were all gathered in front of the swanky wine-bar side of the patisserie.

Some looked like classic porcelain dolls in gingham dresses, while a couple were dressed as Raggedy Ann. One lone doll was dressed as Sally from *The Nightmare Before Christmas*. Their costumes were perfect, like serious cosplayers who value quality.

"Why are people doing this on a workday?" Kat asked. "It's barely lunchtime."

"Yes, doll costumes are clearly evening wear," I said. "Keep in mind you're waddling around town dressed as a duck."

"I don't waddle. I prance," Kat said.

I realized she was making a joke and laughed. Her sense of humor had finally clicked for me.

There was a sign that said DUCKS and pointed to the back room of the patisserie. We walked past the display case of cakes, truffles, and assorted sinful deliciousness, then weaved a path through the dolls. About half looked traditional, with gingham dresses over stiff petticoats and skin made up to look porcelain. There were a couple more Raggedy Anns, while a trio was definitely a nod to an anime I didn't recognize. The girl dressed like Sally caught my eye again; the stitches she'd drawn on her face were both over the top and perfect.

I hummed a couple lines from "This Is Halloween" as I followed Kat and Bax into the back room.

"Of course, you three were the first to arrive," Lindsey said from a table in the middle of the room. She was surrounded by trays of mini-desserts and Spanish tapas-style snacks, including my Jamulet Patisserie favorite: bacon-wrapped quail eggs. A silver teapot sat by her elbow, accompanied by a dainty teacup and saucer.

"We're first? Is this the end the of the scavenger hunt?" Kat asked.

Elaine, the studio's office manager, walked into the room. Her round face was twisted into an uncharacteristic scowl. She hadn't changed into a duck costume and wore the same blue tunic and black capris with clogs as earlier.

"No, this is the midpoint refueling stop," Lindsey said. "Grab a plate, and the waitress will be by shortly for your drink order."

"What if someone who arrives after us skips the snacks and leaves before we finish stuffing our faces?" Kat asked. She added a couple of slices of ham to a plate, along with some olives and a goat cheese tart.

"I thought of that. I'm keeping track of who arrives when and will ensure you get an appropriate head start." Lindsey motioned to a pink legal pad beside her.

I put together a plate of snacks, including a wedge of tortilla española, a salmon crostini, and two of the quail eggs. Bax followed me, loading up his plate with one of everything from the savory side of the table.

"Lindsey, thanks for the invitation, but I'm heading home," Elaine said. "I'm not feeling my best."

"Okay, Elaine, but I'm sorry you're missing out on the fun," Lindsey said.

"Next time," Elaine said. "Usually, I'd be all for helping you make a work event like this successful."

Elaine headed toward the door like she couldn't get out of the patisserie fast enough.

"It's too bad the whole group isn't here for the snacks," Bax said.

"I thought this would be a fun way for me to check in with everyone and actually talk to people in small groups. The food at the finale will be lit, and you'll be able to talk to everyone." Lindsey refilled her teacup.

The waitress stopped by, and after ordering a hazelnut latte (Kat), an espresso (me), and a regular cup of coffee (Bax), she started to turn away.

"What's the story with the dolls? Is that a bachelorette party or something?" Bax asked the server.

She turned back. "They show up occasionally to hang out, drink wine, take photos, and disappear, only to reappear a few months later in full glory." She left.

Lindsey and Kat got up together to look at the display case of tarts and fancy desserts, even though we already had a selection on the table.

I glanced at Bax. "I'm glad Kat's with us. I feel like she's coming out of her shell."

"She's hilarious once you get on the same wavelength. And she's one of the best programmers I have, if not the best. She excels at seeing coding problems before they happen."

"Robbie seems low-key mean to her," I said.

"I think that's just Robbie trying to prank her," Bax said. "Robbie pranks everyone."

I'd seen Robbie's pranks in the office. She did silly things like switching people's coffee cups. Once, she'd changed the office Wi-Fi to "Bathroom Camera Network." But the way she talked to Kat felt different to me.

"It feels like more than a prank to me."

"I'll keep my eye on them and ask Lindsey to keep an eye on the situation, too. I wouldn't be surprised if Robbie was jealous."

"Are you saying she wants to be the top duck, err, goose?"

"Always. But our games require all of us to work together as a team for success. No lone ducks here."

I laughed. "But sasquatches aren't known for roaming in packs. They'd be much easier to find if they did."

"I'm guessing that's why Lindsey sourced a bunch of duck costumes instead of sasquatches. Plus, she found a great discount."

"Will this become a yearly event?"

"I sincerely hope not. I'm never wearing this costume again." Bax rubbed the back of his neck like the duck suit was irritating him. "Unless you want to dress as ducks for Halloween."

"I'm sure you'll think of something better," I said. Bax had decided we needed a couple's costume, but he'd yet to select a theme. I'd said I'd wear almost anything, as long as it wasn't skimpy.

Lindsey came back, quickly followed by the server carrying our coffees. The waitress set Kat's latte down in front of an empty chair, then handed over my espresso with a shot of sparkling water. She handed Bax's coffee over last, along with a small carafe of cream.

"Where's Kat?" I asked after the server left.

"Bathroom." Lindsey added a dark chocolate truffle to her plate. "You know, sitting by all these desserts is dangerous. But I can only eat like two of the truffles 'cause the rest of the desserts have milk. Plus, I've already devoured half of the brownies you baked. I keep telling myself that future Lindsey would like to have a couple, but my present self is a glutton."

"It is your birthday," I said.

"True. If there's any day to indulge, it's today."

Bax had been steadily demolishing a plate of finger foods and re-filled his plate. "Have I ever told you how I met Lindsey?" he asked me.

I shook my head.

"Our high school teachers were fond of making us sit in alphabetical order, so I spent half of my classes next to Lindsey. We're lucky our teachers didn't let us choose our own seats, else we might not be here now."

"And I was suspicious of this weirdo that kept getting assigned next to me, but then I realized he was a good study partner."

"Although Lindsey's always been better at math than me."

"And coding. But any drawings I can make look like a kindergartner's scribblings compared to your sketches."

Bax looked faintly embarrassed. But I'd long known that, while he'd muddled through the computer science of his unlikely double major alongside art, the storytelling and visual graphic sides of the video games were where he excelled.

"I remember those nights working on our first game when we were both in school and during our first jobs. Who would've thought we'd be here all of these years later?" Lindsey said.

"I never doubted it," Bax said. His optimism and her pragmatic approach made for the perfect partnership. Their skills complemented each other, just like Harley and me.

Kat hadn't come back, and nature called, so I headed to the bathroom. Inside the women's room, I found a Sally doll crying at one of the sinks.

"Are you okay?" I asked her.

She didn't say anything as she glanced at me. She'd wiped off part of her makeup, revealing a red butterfly rash across her nose and cheeks.

"I'm fine," she muttered before bolting out the door.

Okay, then. I guessed this wasn't the right time for interspecies commiseration. Or maybe it was hard to take a duck offering sympathy seriously.

I took care of my own business, and when I returned to the table, Kat was back, and she'd been joined by six additional sasquatches in duck costumes. I smiled at Lila, the marketing intern who joined the weekly office bicycle rides, who smiled back.

"Which coffee drink should I order?" Lila asked me.

"Do you like sweet coffee? They use real hazelnuts in their house special hazy latte."

Then two ducks and a goose walked in, all scowling.

Robbie, Wyatt, and Noah.

When Robbie saw the assortment of Sasquatches-in-duck costumes, her scowl deepened.

"I told you guys that you suck at this." She walked away from Wyatt and Noah and took a seat at the end of the table. "I have the worst teammates for this. They're way too mundane."

"You're the one who . . ." Noah's voice trailed off when Bax held his hand toward him.

"Remember what I said? Teambuilder. Fun."

Robbie stood up. "Whatever, I'll win this on my own." She stalked out.

There was a pause for a moment. One of the ducks asked Lindsey, "She knows she needs the next clue from you, right?"

Lindsey raised her cup of tea. "Who needs a hot, cozy beverage? I'm partial to their Moroccan mint green tea blend, and I've heard their London Fog Latte is legit."

"Can we order another plate of salmon crostini?" someone asked.

"Is there anything without dairy for me?" Wyatt asked.

"I'll tell the server to bring the selection of nondairy snacks and desserts I ordered especially for you, Wyatt." Of course, Lindsey had planned around everyone's food allergies. Although Wyatt's was easy for her since it overlapped with her own food issue.

The party atmosphere picked back up, although Noah and Wyatt looked straight-faced as they murmured together at the end of the table.

Bax stopped by and talked with Noah and Wyatt, then returned to Kat and me. "You guys ready to move on?"

"You need to take a picture with me to finish this task," Lindsey said. My group posed with her, and one of the other ducks, Raoul, with dreads sticking out of his hood, took a photo. Lindsey texted Bax our next clue so no one else could overhear. Kat and I followed him out the door, unintentionally imitating ducks in a row.

Three clues later, I assumed we had to be on the home stretch. The clock was about to hit four, and it felt like we'd been walking for hours.

"We have to be nearing the end," Bax said as we entered the

joint building our businesses shared. We walked down the center hallway in the direction of Pump It PDX, aka the gym at the end of the building, which was blasting upbeat music. We'd guessed the clue "A ghost's favorite workout? Deadlifts!" referred to our fit neighbors.

"Unless we were supposed to go to the pop-up shop down the street with all the Halloween costumes," Kat said.

The door to the roastery was slightly ajar, but the lights were off, which made me frown. If Harley was here, she'd have the lights on.

And Harley would never leave the door unlocked, let alone open when she left. She was way too protective of her roasting equipment and the beans degassing, getting ready to make perfect little cups of coffee.

"I need to check this out," I said.

"We're here with you," Bax said. He patted my shoulder.

"Is this part of the game?" Kat asked.

"Absolutely not." I felt like the final girl in a horror movie as I took a deep breath. I metaphorically stood taller and showed command presence, aka a "you don't want to mess with me, else you'll regret it" attitude.

Bax followed me as I walked inside. As I flicked on the light, my nose caught a coppery scent that didn't belong, overtaking the usual notes of roasted coffee beans.

My stomach roiled as the scent triggered a memory, even before seeing the giant white goose sprawled on the floor next to the roaster. A figure in black knelt over her.

The figure screamed and wheeled around. Harley, dressed in black jeans and a black raincoat. Her dark hair swished around her shoulders.

"Sage, I'm so glad you're here. I just came in to pick up my charger and found her like this."

I forced myself to walk forward. Robbie's eyes were open, but she wasn't seeing anything. Not anymore. A trickle of blood had soaked into the dark roots of her blond balayage hair.

"Is that . . . ?" Bax's voice trailed off.

Kat said something else in a language I didn't understand, but I understood the horror in her tone.

My hands felt shaky as I dialed 911. But my voice was steady as I said, "We need an ambulance and the police." I told the operator the roastery's address and explained how to find us.

I turned to see Bax and Kat leaning on each other, looking sick. Harley stood next to them with her head in her hands.

"You three should go wait in the lobby next door," I said.

My whole body felt deflated, but I also wanted to panic. Or close my eyes and pretend this wasn't happening.

This wasn't the birthday celebration Lindsey had planned.

Chapter 5

Bax, Kat, Harley, and I sat on the couches in the front reception area of Grumpy Sasquatch Studio, with a police officer standing by the door to the communal hallway. The illustration on the door felt wrong. Too happy, despite the mock scowl on the sasquatch's face. We still wore our duck onesies, and Harley had her black raincoat curled around her. My body kept shifting between shivering with cold and feeling like the duck suit was causing me to roast. Harley had her arm over her eyes like the light hurt.

Two people in suits showed up, including one man I recognized.

Of all the police officers in Portland, Detective Will had to catch this crime scene?

I'd first met Detective William E. Will back when he'd investigated a crime at the Rail Yard when Ground Rules first opened. I knew a couple things about him: he was sharper than he appeared, and he liked to ask questions that made one feel unbalanced.

Like the first time I'd met him, he was still very square. Everything about him felt like it was built on right angles: his build. The muscles of his shoulders. His jaw. Even the dimple in his chin. I suspected his view of the world was equally full of right angles. Even when things were circular.

Detective Will paused for a brief moment when he saw me.

"Ms. Caplin," he said.

"Detective."

"I take it this is Lukas Evans Baxter, Katerina Kaslov, and Harley Yamazaki?" His gaze shifted across Bax, Kat, and Harley a few times.

"That's correct," I said.

At the same time, Kat said, "Yes," in a tiny voice. Harley blinked against the light like it was hurting her, while Bax nodded.

The detective's gaze took in all of us again with a questioning look. "What's with the duck outfits?"

"Team builder," I said.

Detective Will shook his head slightly like he was checking to see if my comment made sense and had decided no. His usual straight facial experience took back over. "We'll need to talk to all of you individually."

Bax nudged my arm. "Should we wait for Jackson?" he asked. Bax was referring to my older half brother, Jackson Hennessey, who, after graduating law school, specialized in child advocacy and, sometimes, keeping me out of trouble.

"Jackson would say yes," I said. "We should call him."

"Good thing he's on his way. I already texted him."

Some of the weight on my shoulders lifted slightly, but I knew it was there, ready to press back down. "We'll talk to you once our lawyer gets here," I said.

"We just need to know what happened today," Detective Will said. This made me realize we should wait until my brother arrived before being interviewed. And if Jackson didn't want to sit in with Kat and Harley, we should find someone for them.

"We just had a scavenger hunt," Kat said. Her voice was still tiny, like an echo of her usual tone. "It wasn't a big deal."

"Kat, we'll tell the whole story once our legal representation is here." Bax's voice had a slight note of authority in it, the one I'd heard him use in the office—aka, his low-key version of command presence. I'd heard notes of it earlier when Bax had subtly reprimanded Robbie. Bax was chill until he felt like he needed to step up.

Robbie. My arms felt cold again, and I shivered. Bax wrapped an arm around my shoulder, and I rested my head briefly against him, then straightened up. I needed to stay strong, at least for now. Detective Will stepped into the hallway for a moment with a uniformed officer. I watched him through the glass door, through the Sasquatch logo, until a familiar face marched up.

Like always, my brother was scowling. If you didn't know Jackson, you might think he was perpetually angry. When really, he had one of those faces that always looked annoyed. But when you get to know him, you see the heart behind the façade. When he finished law school, my brother had plenty of options, including a few lucrative job offers, but he'd chosen child advocacy. Jackson wanted to be a voice for those who are rarely listened to. He'd eventually opened his own practice. My brother knew enough about the criminal justice system to give me advice. Even if he mainly interacted with the juvenile court system and family court. If this turned into legal charges, he'd call someone on our behalf.

But I knew it wouldn't. There's no way the police could seriously suspect one of the three of us. We'd been together all day. Even though she hadn't been with us, there's no way Harley would hurt anyone, let alone kill someone.

None of us were killers.

But, before today, I would've said that about everyone I knew in the building. Yet Robbie's body was still lying a few hundred feet away.

Detective Will walked back in. "I'd like to start with Sage Caplin. Is there a room we can borrow?"

Bax pointed across the room. "Feel free to use the conference room."

I squeezed Bax's hand for a second before letting it go, and followed the detective and a second police officer across the office to the conference room, with Jackson at my side.

The detective settled at one side of the table, facing the door, and I slid into the seat across from him. The other officer stood by the door.

Detective Will did that thing where he looked like he was analyzing my face again. Then he looked at the prints on the walls of classic video games, including some old-school Atari games, along with a few anime prints. "So, what exactly is this place?"

Jackson nodded at me, so I said, "It's a video game development company." After briefly explaining what they did, I mentioned a few of their games, ending with, "Many people know their biggest hit, *Dreamside Quest.*"

Detective Will's eyes widened slightly. "I know that game. My son loves it. Who would've thought the people who made it live in Portland?"

Son? I pictured Detective Will with a square child who looked like him but at one-half the size. I held back a smile.

"So, what's with the duck costumes?"

It almost physically hurt to not tell the detective this was the current rage, and he should buy his own version to fit in at his local pub. "We had a combined scavenger hunt–team builder today."

"What's this about a scavenger hunt?" Detective Will eyed me, giving me the feeling he was reading more than I was saying. But I wasn't sure he'd picked up the right translation guide for the unique language I spoke.

I glanced at Jackson, who nodded an okay my way.

"It's Lindsey Barlow's birthday, and she's one of the co-owners of Grumpy Sasquatch Studio," I said. I explained how she'd turned her annual day of clicking one year older into a combined team builder and party. "I don't know how Robbie ended up inside the Ground Rules Roastery since Harley said she'd gotten there right before us."

"Your . . . roastery"—he said the word like it tasted weird on his tongue—"wasn't one of the stops on the scavenger hunt?"

"No—well, not as far as I know. But if Lindsey decided to use it, she never asked me, and she would've. Plus, Harley never would have left it unlocked and unattended. She'd never risk anyone messing with the equipment. Some of it's expensive to replace. For example, coffee roasters start at twenty K, and ours cost more. We're serious about keeping our equipment safe." The memory of Robbie crumpled next to the roaster made me shudder.

"Harley?"

"Harley Yamazaki, my business partner. You saw her out there." I explained how Harley had spent the morning packaging a batch of our Puddle Jumper blend that was done degassing. Meaning it was ready to be sold to consumers at a couple of local grocery stores. "She was also stressing out about a business meeting we're having tomorrow and went home today with a nasty headache."

"Hmm." The detective's eyebrows twitched like he'd just discovered something important.

Jackson touched my shoulder, and when I looked at him, his eyes told me to shut up.

Argh. Now the detective had to think Harley was a suspect, no matter how improbable. A headache didn't mean guilt, after all. I didn't mention their literal run-in earlier today. If only Harley hadn't found the body.

"Do you have any idea what happened?" Detective Will asked.

Jackson nodded at me, but I could swear his eyes said, *Choose your words carefully.*

I glanced at him, hoping he would feel the honesty pouring out of me. "I have no idea what happened or why someone decided to hurt Robbie."

"Any insights? I seem to remember you notice things."

"Robbie is . . ." My words faltered. I took a deep breath and powered on. "Robbie was unique. She was smart. Social. She almost had an over-the-top Australian heartiness. Like if you took all of the stereotypes and rolled them into one energetic bundle."

"Australian?"

"Yeah, Robbie said she was from Sydney originally, I think, but she went to university somewhere in the States." Now that I thought about it, Robbie had always been vague about her past.

"That's interesting."

"I have no idea why. I don't know much about Australia. But

there's no way university here is cheaper, especially as an international student." Talking about something other than what I'd seen made me feel grounded, at least for a moment. It removed me from the horror of finding someone who could've been me dead in Ground Rules.

Was there any chance someone had been after me? Someone looking for a blonde and didn't realize Robbie was too tall to be me? But why would anyone want to attack me?

"Who has keys to your office?" Detective Will asked.

"I'm wondering that, too," Jackson murmured into my ear like he was dispensing legal advice.

"Let me think," I said. "Harley, my business partner, has a set, of course. I keep a spare set at my dad's house."

"At your dad's?" His voice sounded off. Like he thought I was lying.

I felt my forehead furrow as I looked at him. "Are you saying that keeping an extra set of keys at a police officer's house sounds sketchy? It seemed like the safest backup to me." My father, Christopher Caplin, was with Portland Police's Cold Cases Unit, although I suspected he was on the verge of retiring.

"Anyone else?"

"No. None of our baristas have keys to the roastery, just to the cart. My uncle Jimmy should have a set, although I'd be surprised if he's ever used them."

"Uncle?"

"Jimmy Jones." Great, now my poor uncle was probably going to be visited by our favorite neighborhood detective.

Detective Will leaned back in his chair. "Remind me. Who were you were partnered with during the scavenger hunt?"

"Lukas Baxter and Kat Kaslov."

"Two of the people out there, waiting to be interviewed?"

"That's correct."

"Tell me about the scavenger clues."

I pulled out my phone and read him a few examples. He motioned like he wanted me to hand over my phone. I turned and held my phone to my chest.

"I'm not giving you my phone," I said.

"Not without a warrant," Jackson said.

Detective Will glared at my brother, who gazed impassively back, then slid one of his business cards across the table to me. "Can you text me a few of the examples? Including the clue that led you here?"

"I'm fairly sure the clue was for Pump It PDX, the fitness studio down the hallway. But I could be wrong, as we never made it there to find out."

"And you found Harley Yamazaki in the roastery with the victim."

"Harley said she'd just gotten there. I could tell earlier in the day she wasn't feeling well, and if you look at her now, you can tell she has a migraine."

"Do you have anything else you'd like to ask my client?" Jackson asked. "She's had a rough day."

"We're done for now, but I might have more questions later. Ms. Caplin can leave for now."

For now. Like I was going to end up being a criminal mastermind.

"If you decide you need to talk to Ms. Caplin again, call my law office and make an appointment," Jackson said. He stood up, so I followed suit. Jackson walked back outside with me to where Kat, Bax, and Harley were waiting. A uniformed officer still stood with them.

A thought entered my brain and wouldn't leave. If Harley had come in and found Robbie in the roastery, could they have argued? Harley wasn't violent, but if she'd found Robbie sabotaging something in Ground Rules or setting up a prank, she would've been angry.

If only I knew why Robbie had been in Ground Rules. And more importantly, how did she get inside?

"Mr. Baxter," Detective Will said and motioned to the conference room.

Bax paused by me. "I'm going to head out," I told him in a quiet voice, but I was aware of Detective Will listening by the conference room door. "I have something I need to take care of."

"I'll text you when I'm done. I'll see if Jackson will sit in on all of the interviews."

"Good. See you soon."

Detective Will looked slightly annoyed when Jackson followed Bax.

"You're not talking to my clients without me," Jackson said.

Kat looked at me. "How was it?"

I glanced at the uniformed officer, who was clearly listening in. "Not bad. Just be honest. And brief. And listen to Jackson."

As I walked out of the door, I pulled my phone out of the pocket of my bag. I walked past the police officers in the hallway. Seeing the cluster of people by the Ground Rules entrance made me feel sick. Death didn't belong in Ground Rules.

I texted Harley. *We need to meet, no matter terrible you feel. Tav in one hour?*

And then I called my dad, and it went to voice mail, so I left him a message. Then I focused on the big guns and texted my uncle.

Chapter 6

Visiting the Tav always feels a bit like coming home. I basically just needed to hear a refrain about how everyone knew my name blare as I walked in the door. Part of me calmed down for the first time since I'd seen Robbie's body.

Maybe it was the lingering notes of ale in the air and the aroma of French fries from the kitchen.

Or it could be because my cousin Miles was behind the bar, and he could be loud when he wanted to be, like now. His "Hello, Bug" practically echoed against the original stained glass windows on one wall of the Tav. Then bounced off the vintage booths to one side and rebounded through the bar stools lined up in front of the polished bartop that smelled of citrus cleaner.

Miles had managed the Tav for as long as I could remember. Sometimes, I felt like he was part of the Tav like he'd been born here. Or maybe he has a portrait of himself, Dorian Gray–style, hidden in the bar's back room, somehow tying himself to the never-changing feel of the bar. He's technically my mother's cousin and about twenty years older than me. But no one in my family was overly particular about labels. Family was family.

As I headed to the bar, my eyes returned to the series of five stained glass windows that showed the parable of the lady and the tiger. The center window shows the princess. The person looking at the windows is the lover, being punished for daring to lift his eyes to her. He needs to decide which door to choose—the tiger, which leads to death, or to the beautiful young maiden, whom he will wed—or be separated from his love forever. The princess knows which door leads to death, and which to a new life. I always think of the tiger as being our own personal demons, while the maiden is a new normal. It's up to each person to decide which journey to take. The windows are a bit ironic in a dive bar that's continued to persevere in a neighborhood that was once full of abandoned warehouses, flop houses, and a rollicking heroin trade, but has since gentrified into art galleries, condos, high-end boutiques, and upscale restaurants. But maybe it just shows the Tav has charted its own path, weathering the storms that have been thrown at it with a shot of whiskey and a sort of hipster attitude of "well, we were here before you'd even heard of us."

"Is the man around?" I asked Miles.

"Uncle Jimmy just stepped out, but he said he was coming back. Want a drink?"

A minute later, we both had lemonades, and Miles propped up the bar from the inside while I'd settled on a mahogany barstool. Just comfortable enough to keep someone at the bar for a few drinks, but not so cozy you'd fall asleep.

"So, what's wrong, Bug?" Miles asked.

I filled him in on the day's events.

"This deserves corn dog nuggets," Miles joked, but I could see the genuine concern in his eyes. He started to turn but wheeled back around. "Wait, are you talking about the Australian programmer who worked for Bax?"

"Yeah. Blond. Pretty." Memorable. She was the sort of person who acted like she was always the star of the ensemble.

"Also kind of fake," Miles said.

I blinked. "That's unkind." Although a snarky voice in the back of my mind chimed in and said that Robbie always did everything she could to stay in the limelight. Maybe she'd been afraid that she'd fade away into nothingness if she weren't the center of attention.

"I caught her making out with a dude in one of the back booths last week. He had a bicycle-and-compass tattoo in a place that you shouldn't see in a public bar." Miles pushed the sleeves of his navy hoodie up to his elbows, showing off a tattoo on one forearm of a small skeleton with a heart. In my world, Miles had always had the tattoo. But he refused to talk about the meaning, although I knew it hinted at a long-ago heartache.

"Oh?" What was Robbie like away from work colleagues? She'd known me as her boss's girlfriend, so I'd seen a different side of her than, clearly, Miles had seen.

"I'm guessing they came from the Thorns game, 'cause she came in bragging about how one of the players is the star of the Australian national team. They got a couple of drinks and headed toward the back, and a few rounds later, they were a bit too intimate for public. Robbie tried to argue with me when I told them to either leave or sit on opposite sides of the booth, and I had to threaten to ban her. She flipped to charm, then."

"That's weird," I said. But I'd seen that strategic flip in Robbie before.

"Bax's crew is usually better behaved," Miles said. "Well, at least the ones I recognize."

"That's good." Bax had held his company holiday party at the Tav last year, and ever since, a chunk of his sasquatches had turned into regulars. A few of them lived in the neighborhood, called the Pearl District, which was full of condo and loft-style apartments, coffee shops, cafés, and a handful of high-end restaurants. The Tav feels like the last standing dive-bar oasis in the neighborhood.

My phone beeped with a text from Bax. *Please come stay here tonight.*

"Someone's having sleepovers?" Miles teased me.

"You can read upside down?" I asked as I texted Bax back. *Of course.*

"You can't?" Miles said. "It's a useful skill."

"I bet you read a lot of drunken mistake texts to exes."

"To be fair, I see people make all sort of drunken mistakes, and, for you, Bax isn't one."

"Plus, I'm sober. Unless there's something you're not telling me about this lemonade."

"It came out of the soda gun. I'm not sure there's any real lemon in it, let alone alcohol."

I looked at the yellow liquid in my pint glass.

"I'm kidding. The ingredient list includes lemon concentrate alongside corn syrup."

Harley walked herself in, moving slowly and still looking like a shadow of herself. She pointed back toward our usual booth, and I nodded. She dragged herself toward it, and Miles poured a glass of water for me to take her.

"Call me if you need me," Miles said.

"As always." My cousin always feels like the human equivalent of a warm cup of cocoa on a cold night.

The Tav had been picking up, and the bar felt about half full, with most of the crowd mingling in the front. A couple of guys were standing by the jukebox, arguing about which songs to choose. Anyone could tell them an afternoon like this was prime time for classic rock. Then slip into harder music as the night went on and slide into the last call with classic country tales of woe.

I carried our drinks past the jukebox, into the back of the Tav, to our usual booth under slightly dimmer lights. Harley was sitting with her arms folded on the table, providing a pillow for her head.

"Water delivery," I said. "Do you need an Advil or anything? I have some in my bag."

Harley slowly straightened up and blinked against the dim lights. "I already took some."

"Is it helping?"

"A bit. I'm positive I'll feel bright-eyed tomorrow. I'm heading home and popping a sleeping tablet as soon as I get home."

A note of doubt underlaid Harley's positive words. Fingers

crossed she felt better since I needed her professional opinions to-morrow even though I could schmooze and handle the relationship side of the meeting.

Harley picked up her water but then paused. "Today has been a nightmare."

"I thought you'd headed home?"

"I did but realized I'd left both of my phone chargers behind. I decided heading to work was easier than popping into a Fred Meyer to buy a new one. My phone is my only alarm clock, and I don't want to be late tomorrow morning."

I was about to tell her I could handle tomorrow solo if she still felt terrible, but I caught a glimpse of a man with white hair in the mirror on the far wall, and he was striding our way. My uncle Jimmy. He's technically my great-uncle, and he'd believed in Ground Rules from the beginning and invested in us.

"One moment. My uncle is about to join us so we can tell him what happened," I said.

"How'd you know that?" Harley asked.

I didn't answer as Uncle Jimmy slid into the booth next to me. "Hi, Bug. Harley. So what's this about a murder at the roastery? Is it a rumor?"

Harley flinched at his words and buried her head in her hands again.

"It's true." I jumped into the story, giving him a longer version than the condensed edition I'd told Miles.

We were quiet for a moment. Uncle Jimmy looked at the ceiling like he could read something in the old-school box planks above our heads. Harley looked disturbed, like a mix of sadness, distress, and headache was battling inside her. I felt guilty when I realized part of me was relieved I wasn't personally a murder suspect this time around. But I could still see the danger Robbie's death posed to everyone around me, including the company we were building. Plus Robbie deserved justice.

"I can't deal with this. Not now," Harley said. "All I want to do is panic. I can't even scream because that would cause my head to split in half."

"Go home and sleep and we can talk more tomorrow," I said. "I'm sure the police will want to speak to you again. Wait, one question. Did you lock the roastery before you left this afternoon?"

"Of course I locked it. And there's no way I would've let Robbie inside alone. I wouldn't have trusted her if I'd been there."

"I wonder how she got inside," I said. "Was the door unlocked when you got there?"

"No, I came in from the street entrance. The lights were off. I wish I'd just let my phone run out of juice and stayed at home."

Which would mean I would've found the body. I looked at Harley, and she looked down. "Let me rephrase. I wish this had never happened."

"We'll talk tomorrow. I hope you feel better."

"Me too." Harley left, looking almost drunk.

"Do you need a ride?" I asked.

"I'll be fine."

Why hadn't Harley turned the lights on when she realized the door was open, even if she felt sensitive to light? If I'd found the door open, it's the first thing I'd do to make sure no one was hiding inside.

"What's this about Robbie and trustworthiness?" my uncle asked.

The booths around were starting to fill. I imagined Robbie here after a Thorns game, probably decked out in an official team jersey and effortlessly applied makeup.

"Robbie liked to play practical jokes on people. Usually silly stuff, but Harley isn't the sort of person who likes to be pranked. She would've flipped if anyone messed with our equipment." The idea of Robbie tinkering with our equipment was slightly terrifying since she could've damaged something that would be a pain to fix. We'd need to check the equipment carefully before using it again.

"Can you think of any reason this Robbie would've gone into Ground Rules?" Uncle Jimmy asked. An echo of Detective Will asking the same basic questions sounded in my mind.

"She had no reason to be in there. The only reason I could see Robbie going into our roastery would've been to play a prank, but I don't see why. She purposefully stuck golf balls to my motion-capture suit once, but it was silly and not malicious." It was slightly obnoxious since Wyatt and I had to spend time getting the suit back into working order, but it hadn't damaged anything.

"Have you thought of anything else? Why her, and why there?"

"Robbie had blond hair, so maybe someone thought she was me. But I can't think why. She was taller, so I don't think anyone who knew me would've mistaken us. But it's not like anyone would hire an assassin to go after me."

"You assume they meant to kill Robbie."

His words felt important.

"You're right. It could've been an accident. It looked like Robbie fell and hit her head. Maybe she was startled or something. Maybe she was on her own in there."

"Or someone was trying to scare her and went too far."

His words made me shiver. "But why in the roastery?" I asked.

"Can you think of anyone who'd be after you?"

I shook my head. "No. You know I'm not any sort of criminal mastermind. Who'd want to hurt me?"

"Or who'd want to hurt what you represent," Uncle Jimmy said.

"Do you really think anyone my mother wronged would come after me? I mean, would they even know about me? We've been down this route before, and it wasn't a revenge plot. Let alone think I'd make a good target?"

One perk of being the daughter of a notorious grifter is knowing people might sometimes look at you like you, too, are poisonous. And it's always possible that one of my mother's enemies will come for me. But the possibility felt remote these days. I hadn't heard from my mother for ages, and the last contact had been a short phone call. I hadn't seen her since I was thirteen. She'd dumped me in Portland and split, leaving me to figure out why she'd left me at a homeless shelter with only the business card for the Tav. According to Miles, I'd looked like a grumpy, slightly dirty fairy when I'd eventually made my way into the bar. He recognized me and set me up with a lemonade in one of the back booths while calling for reinforcements. Uncle Jimmy had introduced me to the father I hadn't seen since I was a toddler by the end of the day. And my life had stabilized, although it'd been rocky at first.

"I'd say good point, but my main goal is for you to stay safe," Uncle Jimmy said. "So keep your eyes open, okay?"

"Always."

"You hungry?"

We chatted over a couple of club sandwiches, accompanied by fresh-cut fries. I went all out and had a second lemonade. Uncle Jimmy offered to give me a ride home. Based on the expression in his eyes, it was the sort of offer I couldn't say no to, even though I would've been fine biking home. Especially since taking off the bike's front wheel and wedging it into the trunk of Uncle Jimmy's pristine-but-at-least-a-decade-old BMW is always a challenge, even if the quick-release wheel is simple. And my uncle isn't the type to want to get his hands covered in bike grease.

As Uncle Jimmy drove me across town, I said, "The police know you have a set of keys to the roastery."

"If the detective wants to talk to me, he can call my lawyer." Uncle Jimmy sounded like this wasn't a big deal in his world, and all I could do was hope he was right. But the police sniffing around, even if there wasn't anything to find, made a paranoid feeling settle deep inside me.

Maybe it was because my grifter mother is a wanted criminal. And all I wanted was to live life by the rules that felt right, emotionally, to me. And doing my best to make the world a better place has always been a part of that plan. It was like when my medieval philosophy class in college talked about Aquinas. We'd spun off into a discussion of caritas—a sense of charity—and how building up other people and our communities can be considered an act of love.

Building my coffee business was my own tiny slice of caritas. I tried to give back in various ways, partially fueled by Ground Rules. Someone dying felt like the opposite of everything I wanted to build.

Uncle Jimmy left me and my now reassembled bike on the sidewalk in front of my brother's house. Jackson's close-in east-side neighborhood has a unique feature compared to most of Portland: most of the houses don't have driveways intersecting the sidewalk, although they do have alleyways with garages running behind the homes. Like they try to keep a pretty façade to the world and take care of the gritty side of life out of view.

Maybe the day was affecting me more than I realized.

Uncle Jimmy's parting goodbye rang in my ears. "Stay out of trouble, Bug."

Besides the porch light, Jackson's four-square house was dark as I tucked my bike into a corner of the front porch. Bentley, my brother's dog, didn't greet me, so I glanced at the hook by the front door. His red leash was gone, so he was out sniffing the neighborhood with my brother.

After scrubbing bike grease off my hands, I headed up two flights of stairs. I rented the attic suite of Jackson's house, although I hadn't been spending a ton of snoozing nights here, even if most of my possessions still called this home. During Bax's custody time, I tended to spend a few days here to give him and his son time alone, but they'd started inviting me to stay over more and more as time went on.

And later this year, Bax would have his son full-time for six months when his mother went on a twice-delayed research trip, so I could feel an incoming shift looming.

It didn't take me long to toss my favorite sweater, moto jacket, and dark "dressy" jeans into my messenger bag. I hadn't worn the sweater since last year. This was usually the sort of moment that would make me smile: sweater weather was here, along with leaves changing colors, crisp morning bike rides, and apple season. But the day's events wouldn't let me delight in the small things that usually made me happy.

My hands paused. Life would be easier if all my stuff lived together, along with me, but the current setup worked. The status quo felt comfortable.

Before I walked downstairs, I tried calling my dad again. This time, he answered on the third right.

"Hi, Pumpkin. What's going on?"

He was silent after I finished telling him about the day's events.

"Dad, are you still with me?"

His voice was measured as he spoke. "Are you sure running a coffee roaster is a great idea? It seems like you could find something safer. It's not too late to become a nun."

"Dad, I'm not Catholic."

"I know, but I can dream. Let me know if there's anything I can do. Since you're involved, I have to stay away from this case. But I'm here for you, of course."

"I know."

"Dinner next week?"

"Text me the times that work best for you," I said.

We said our goodbyes, and I slung my bag over my shoulder. I was glad my father was now in the proverbial loop. Even if, as he said, he couldn't be involved professionally.

As I climbed down the stairs, I heard footsteps on the front porch, followed by the door opening. Plus the sound of voices.

I smiled. Two specific voices: my brother Jackson's, and his girl-friend Piper Lacey's. They'd been law school sweethearts, but Piper had taken a job on the other side of the country. She'd transferred back to Oregon, and they'd slowly gotten together, meaning they'd clearly been into each other. But it took three months to admit they were dating and a few more months for Jackson to use the word "girlfriend" in casual conversation.

My brother smiled as he walked inside, bundled up in a gray wool trench coat, Bentley on his heels, followed by Piper, who rocked a retro striped jacket. When I finally feel grown up, I aspire to be like Piper, who manages to toe the line of uniquely herself, yet ef-fortlessly hip. And inside, she was brilliant and hilarious.

And as a US attorney, she represented the opposite side of the courthouse, except she focused on white-collar crimes. But she and my brother made it work.

"Here's trouble!" Piper said when she saw me. Jackson turned from unclipping Bentley's leash and glanced my way.

"It can't be that bad, can it? At least Jackson was there when I talked to the police this time." I shifted my messenger bag so it nestled against my hip.

"Did you just hear yourself?" Jackson asked.

"Give your little sister a break. It's not like she chose to fall over another body."

Another body. Soon, I'd be the Sweeney Todd of baristas, except for the cannibalism aspect. And pies. But rolling out fancy pie crust has never been in my skill set.

"Are you off to Bax's?" Jackson asked as Piper and Bentley headed back toward the kitchen.

I nodded.

"Sage," Jackson said as I opened the door. I paused and looked at him. "We do need to sit and talk."

"Should I stay?" A serious note in my brother's voice made a tiny antenna in the back of my brain ping.

"Nah, later this week is fine. Maybe lunch on Friday?"

"Text me to confirm, but that sounds great."

"Fine, I'll text you and make an appointment." Jackson whistled an old-school rock song as he headed in the direction of his girlfriend and dog, and I turned my bike toward Bax's house.

The mid-century modern–inspired drapes featuring pops of red and yellow in the front windows of Bax's house had been pulled closed, but lights were on behind them. After I locked my bike up in the garage to the side of Bax's bungalow, I climbed up the stairs to the cheery red front door and let myself in.

"Bax?" I called out. But the cushy sectional couch, perfect for marathon gaming sessions, was empty, and the TV mounted on the wall was turned off. The short hallway to the two downstairs bedrooms was dark, so I headed into the kitchen. What I saw made me smile.

When I'd first met Bax, the back deck of his inner–east side bungalow looked over a rectangular yard of mostly grass with a tree in one corner and a small playhouse in the other. After Kaldi, the orange cat, had adopted us last year, Bax fully enclosed the back porch to make a world-class catio. It was pretty much every indoor cat's dream, with a climbing structure on one side and planks around the perimeter so Kaldi could watch the world from up high. There's an outdoor love seat on one side and dining set on the other for the humans.

Not to be outdone, Bax had also upgraded the playhouse in the yard for his son, Niko. He added a covered front porch with a matching Adirondack chair. Niko had found a miniature charcoal barbecue at some point and set it up on the porch of the playhouse, although his dad had never let him light it. Which hadn't stopped Niko from inviting me over for a barbecue, although he'd asked me to bring snacks.

Bax was sitting on the outdoor love seat with a red plaid fleece blanket over his lap, with Kaldi purring loudly from a perch on his shoulder. A couple of Warhammer figurines, clean brushes, and small vials of paint were on a tray on the table in front of him. But he hadn't uncapped the paints. Bax had turned the small portable heater on, so the patio was warmer than outside. But I could see why he'd brought out one of the blankets usually kept in a bin next to his couch.

"Looks like your fleece cat trap isn't working," I said. Kaldi chirped in response. When I sat down next to Bax, Kaldi jumped on my lap. He landed with all four paws on my thigh like he was aiming for an invisible bull's-eye. He chirped again, presumably crowing "Success!" I rubbed his head, and he shoved his head back into my hand. I'd once heard a joke that all orange cats share the same two brain cells, but Kaldi defied the "orange cats are dumb" stereotype yet met all the benchmarks on the friendly criteria scale. Kaldi had adopted me at a music festival and loved life at Bax's house. I'd named him after the goatherd credited with discovering coffee, and it fit him.

"Did you get everything you need for the next few days?" Bax asked.

"Yep. Including for the meeting tomorrow." I told the small butterflies that fluttered in my stomach to chill out. I had this. And if the meeting failed, it wouldn't be the worst thing that had ever happened to me. Or to Ground Rules. It wouldn't be the end of the world.

"Today was . . ." Bax's voice trailed off.

I put my hand on top of his. "Robbie's death wasn't your fault."

Kaldi meowed loudly like he agreed.

"It doesn't feel like it happened, but I have this overwhelming sense of horror reminding me it did." He slid his hand out from under mine and put his arm around my shoulder. I leaned my head against him, feeling like an emotional support human.

"At least we can face this together," Bax said.

"Team Ground Rules Sasquatch," I said.

"I'm sure I can take on the world with you by my side," Bax said. "Although I'd probably spend the time following in your wake."

"Don't you know it."

We chatted for a while, then headed upstairs.

Tomorrow would come soon enough.

Chapter 7

My phone buzzed and woke me up bright and early, and I dislodged Kaldi from his spot twined around my head when I reached to shut off my alarm. Kaldi made a sad mewl as he moved across the bed to curl up on Bax's stomach.

Opening the Ground Rules cart on weekdays was still a point of pride for me. Plus, it let me keep an eye on the cart's stock levels and overall cleanliness. Thankfully, my baristas rarely required any corrective feedback. We functioned as a well-primed espresso machine.

This was good since my legs felt full of lead as I got ready. Grief always reminds me of when I broke my wrist as a child. I didn't want to move it else I'd feel a shooting pain. Remembering yesterday made me feel sick. Instead of reliving the past twenty-four hours, I tried to make my thoughts face forward.

Bax was still asleep as I left, freshly showered and dressed in my autumn coffee cart unofficial uniform of jeans and a long-sleeve T-shirt topped off with a hoodie. I'd packed my version of a business outfit in my bag for the big meeting later in the morning.

My bike ride to the cart took me through sleepy streets. Ground Rules was the first cart to open in the mornings at the Rail Yard, but a light was on inside Eggceptional Bagels. I caught the refrain of a popular rock song as I rolled the gate to the food cart pod back into place and locked it. I'd leave the gate open when I was ready to sell coffee unless the bagel cart got there first and opened a half hour early, as they sometimes did. It was nice to have company instead of being the only cart open in the morning. It was just an added bonus that I sometimes swapped a whole-milk latte for a fresh-from-the-oven onion bagel with scallion cream cheese.

The rest of the carts were dark. Since I'd initially opened Ground Rules, about half of the vendors in the pod had changed over. Taco Cat had left to open a small shop in the 'burbs, which was garnering excellent reviews, and the Burrito Bomb cart had taken their place. Cartography was still here, although they were only open on the weekends now that it was autumn. The Déjà Brew beer cart was still going strong, but it had new owners. They now focused on a rotating selection of the city's best microbreweries instead of selling their own craft ales. They'd also taken over scheduling the small center stage and had a robust calendar of bands and, occasionally, stand-up comedians.

Getting the cart ready to brew felt like second nature. Like my body and hands knew the rhythm and didn't really need to involve my brain. We had lucked out and had plumbed water, so I didn't need to deal with filling water tanks like I did with the second, smaller Ground Rules cart we used for festivals and events. Sophie had closed last night, and she'd scrubbed the cart down well before leaving. She'd updated our "need to buy" list with a few notes, so I planned to swing by the grocery supply store to replenish our oat milk, whole milk, and sugar supplies later today. And I needed to make a new batch of vanilla simple syrup once I regained access to the kitchen in the roastery.

Our pastry order showed up, and after I stocked the display case, I got the order window ready. I popped the awning open and set up the sugar and creamer station.

My final step before putting our sandwich board out on the sidewalk always fills me with happiness. I set up the suspended coffee board, which still had three unclaimed coffee drinks from yesterday.

Customers can preemptively buy drinks and pastries for people down on their luck. We're known by some of the local homeless as a place they can drop by for a hot cup of coffee and maybe a latte or mocha. Plus, one of the former food cart owners of the Rail Yard who left to start a vegan energy company drops off a box or two each month for us to hand out. It's not going to change the entire tide of homelessness, but it's a small gesture we can make and hopefully bring a small amount of hope to someone's day. Caritas.

One of my first customers was a man I recognized from the neighborhood. I was pretty sure he lived in a tent in someone's backyard. One of my regulars told me a couple of homeowners had looked out for him for years. Still, he wouldn't accept help other than the occasional night inside someone's garage during cold snaps. He always repaid acts of kindness by window washing. He also washed windows for a couple of local businesses for small amounts of cash, and always seemed like a combination of vague and kind.

"Would you like a hazelnut raspberry muffin? They're fresh from La Bake and smell amazing. There's one available on the suspended coffee board."

He shook his head and put a five-dollar bill on the counter in front of me. "Black coffee and banana, please."

I poured a large coffee for him and grabbed a banana from the fruit basket on the back counter. After I gave him his change, he headed to the table in the corner of the lot.

My regulars trickled in to buy coffee and then head to the bus stop on the corner or back to their cars parallel parked on the street outside the Rail Yard. The early morning coffee orders were steady and started to pick up close to 7:30. I smiled when I watched a twentysomething woman with copper hair hustle up. Sophie, aka my newest barista.

Sophie's hair was held back by a set of chopsticks, the sort you get with to-go meals. A few tendrils had escaped and framed her face with gentle curls. She looked like a Donatello painting come to life. The backpack she stored in a cubby by the cart door looked heavy, so she was probably heading to class once she was done with her shift.

Both of my baristas are graduate students, and I'll be sad to lose them someday when they go off to great things.

"Busy morning?" Sophie asked, her Newfoundland accent giving the words a soft, almost Irish note.

"Steady," I said.

We chatted for a bit, but a steady stream of customers kept our chitchat to a minimum. We sent coffee and tea drinks out to the world, clutched in the hands of commuters, guarding them against the perils of the morning commute. Or maybe giving them the courage to face rush-hour traffic or a crowded morning bus.

"You know, I've had a few customers ask about pumpkin spice lattes," Sophie said during a slow moment. She took a swig of water and then pulled an espresso shot for herself. One of the perks of working here is as much coffee as you can drink. Plus, a simple IRA match and as many financial benefits as we could offer.

"I'm thinking bourbon-cardamom, and maybe a spiced orange syrup are the forerunners for our November specials," I said. We had a special homemade cinnamon maple syrup available to celebrate October when Portland seems to change from summer to fall overnight.

"Those sound good, but I'm just telling you what the masses seem to want."

"I'm sure I could develop a syrup incorporating the spices used in pumpkin pie. We've had ginger syrup before and cinnamon. It wouldn't be hard to add in some ginger and cloves." Convincing Harley that we needed to offer a handful of syrups in the cart had been an early challenge since she's a purist. And honestly, I am, too. Give me black espresso or an unsweetened latte anyway, since I want to taste the unique notes of the coffee. My compromise had been making them all in-house, so they were something customers could only find at Ground Rules. Except for the sugar-free option, which I bought at the grocery wholesalers. And the cart-made syrups had turned into their own draw. One local coffee drinker Instagrammed photos of a latte with our new syrups at least twenty times every time we added seasonal flavors.

One bonus of living in a city with a robust culinary scene is the masses' appreciation, obsession, and commitment to craft like our syrups.

Sophie looked thoughtful. "Think about it. It might not be as creative as your usual ideas, but people know what they like. And pumpkin spice definitely says autumn to people."

"Good point."

"And we don't want to lose our regulars to other shops. Can you imagine if they started visiting the robotic barista downtown?"

"Wait, what?" I asked.

Sophie's face lit up as she spoke of the minimalist department store downtown that had a coffee stand inside, powered by a robotic arm.

"Was the coffee any good?" I asked.

Sophie grinned as she shook her head. "It was only okay. But we better watch out, 'cause someone's going to crack the code on how to make a latte with a robot eventually."

"Ah, we'll all be replaced someday," I joked.

More customers arrived, and we worked together seamlessly. Some things you know but don't have the words to explain, like the border between a cotton sweater and sweatshirt. Sometimes working with people is like that—you click in a way that doesn't require definitions. Even though I'm aware that, as the boss, I set the tone. And if I'm having a bad day, for example, a foul mood stops with me.

After the rush wound down, I tucked a couple of bags of coffee into my messenger bag and made a note on the sales sheet.

"Call or text if you need anything," I said.

"Just go, boss. You know I'll be fine."

I stuck my tongue out at Sophie, proving I'm manager material, and headed to my bike. This was the lightest and happiest I'd felt since finding Robbie's body.

But when I arrived at the roastery, I groaned as the weight of the world crashed back down onto my shoulders. Police tape still covered the door.

A girl in ultra-hip workout clothes that showed off her tight abs stared at me as she sauntered to the gym in the back of the building. Up-tempo music blared from one of the group fitness classes they ran most of the day. A trainer from the gym, Aiden, nodded hello to the girl, and his eyes returned my way. Like the crime scene tape was fascinating.

"Did someone really die in the building?" Aiden asked. Something about his voice caught my attention. Maybe a note of fear? Aiden took a few steps my way but stopped a few feet away before getting too close. He wore a long-sleeve gray PUMP IT PDX T-shirt over black athletic pants, and I knew from taking the occasional class with him that he was in phenomenal shape. Most of the trainers, except the gym owner, seemed to be in their twenties, but Aiden was a bit older than them, probably midthirties.

"Sadly, yes." My gaze returned to the tape. I had to stop my hands from ripping it down and throwing it away. Part of me still didn't want to believe Robbie was dead, and her death in my roastery felt fundamentally unfair. I didn't want to pass the buck along to a different place, like Bax's studios, but there was no logic behind Robbie in the roastery. Or, rather, I couldn't see the reason. Maybe if I could answer that question, I'd also be able to explain "why."

"One of the evening trainers texted that police were here, but we figured the death was just a rumor. Was it the woman who works here? Hailey?"

"No, it wasn't Harley," I said. My co-owner also took classes at the gym, and I wondered if he always called her by the wrong name. "I need to make a call."

I walked down the hallway toward Grumpy Sasquatch Studio and ducked into the studio's internal entrance. There's a collection of couches by their unstaffed entry desk, and I took a seat on a brown leather couch that toed the line between firm and stuffed. Someone had left a rubber duck wearing a tiny beanie on the front coffee table.

From the depths of my messenger bag, I pulled out a business card I wished I could light on fire.

"Is the Ground Rules building still considered a crime scene?" I asked after saying hello.

Even Detective Will's voice sounded square as he answered, "Yes, we still have some processing to complete. We should be out by this afternoon."

Dang it. "There's no chance we can use it earlier?"

"Sorry, no." But his voice didn't sound sorry. He added, "And you'll want to hire a professional biohazard cleaner to take care of the affected areas of your business before you start using your roastery again. I can text you the firm's name I've heard other people recommend to clean up crime scenes."

"Do you have any idea of when that will be? I have a business to run."

"I'm sorry our crime scene is getting in the way of you brewing coffee."

I tamped down on my desire to tell him everything we used the roastery for, making my voice sound sweeter than the syrups I make. "Keep your hair on. I just mean that I need to make plans for how to operate while the roastery is out of bounds. We're respecting the crime scene tape and all."

"Good, 'cause I wouldn't want to deal with you poking around in there until we're done. Which should be this afternoon. We're pretty much done, but I want to get a second opinion from a colleague before we release it."

"A second opinion on what?"

"Nice try."

"Hey, people rarely answer the questions you don't ask," I said, twisting my favorite phrase, "you make zero shots of the ones you don't take."

He snorted. "And they rarely answer the ones they are asked. Is there anything else, Ms. Caplin?"

"No, that's it. Please let me know ASAP when we're allowed back in."

"Expect a text from me in a moment and a second later today clearing the scene."

"Thank you, Detective."

At least Detective Will wasn't treating me like a criminal this time around. Or maybe he was acting and just trying to stay on my good side so I'd incriminate myself. Who knows, perhaps I'm a secret criminal mastermind.

While hoping I'd never use it, I saved the detective's phone number to the address book on my phone and tucked his card back into my wallet. Maybe I could light it on fire soon when Robbie's murderer was caught.

"Hi, Sage!" Kat walked by. Her ponytail was damp, and she carried a cup of coffee and a Tupperware container of something that smelled like egg.

"Are you doing okay?" I asked her. "Yesterday was traumatic."

"I'm okay. I talked to my dad for a long time last night. Now it's time for breakfast at my desk after my workout."

"A lot of you sasquatches eat here." A few weeks ago, on a Saturday, I'd helped Bax assemble a couple of standalone cabinets and cubbyholes that lined one of the walls of the staff kitchen. He'd created enough space for everyone on staff to have their own basket or shelf, so they didn't have store food at their desks.

"It's healthier than eating out, but I'd kill for a breakfast burrito right about now."

We both stopped as Kat's words hit home.

Her voice was quiet when she said, "Well, not kill. It's just a burrito. But I'd love one right about now."

"It's okay. I get it."

Kat walked off. Something about Kat's words bothered me. Maybe it was the unintentionally casual use of the word kill, which sometimes people use without thinking through the implications. Hopefully, no one would actually murder someone over a burrito.

My stomach growled, and I thought about how Bax and I should make another batch of egg cups, which are basically mini crustless quiches baked in a cupcake pan that are perfect for breakfasts on the go. But I'd finished the last yesterday. One with Swiss cheese and mushroom sounded perfect, but all I had was a vegan energy bar. I should've grabbed a bagel from the Rail Yard.

I texted Harley to tell her the roastery was a no-go. I closed my eyes and took a deep breath, then slowly exhaled. I could handle this. Keep things positive.

I made a phone call. "Hi, Tierney? It's Sage Caplin. Our roastery is unavailable this morning, so we need a new place to meet. How about the Red Leaf? It's a diner I adore. I can text you the address."

Tierney's voice told me he had unasked questions as he agreed to the change in plans, and I made myself smile as we talked. I'd once heard that a smile comes through in your voice, and I hoped it was true.

Chapter 8

I snagged the table by itself in a small alcove at the Red Leaf. But this didn't look good. We'd planned to meet at Ground Rules to show off the roastery and cup a few of our blends to show Doyle's Oregon Whiskey and its owners, Tiernan and Shay Doyle, what we could do. And now, our roastery was a crime scene. I knew Robbie's death mattered more in the scheme of things, but it was frustrating.

Doyle's Oregon Whiskey is a local distillery with Ireland roots that had a dream of creating a world-class Irish-style whiskey in Portland. While they're aging what will be their showcase blend, they'd decided to make a canned Irish whiskey cocktail. And the brothers were interested in partnering with Ground Rules.

But we hadn't signed the contract yet. The brothers had to be researching some of my competitors, so they could always decide to partner with someone else.

Harley walked in and swung into the seat next to me. "So, what's our plan of attack?" she asked. She looked close to normal, but I could see uncharacteristic shadows around her eyes.

"You okay?"

But before she could respond, two similar-looking, dark-haired guys walked into the Red Leaf. I waved, and they headed my way.

"Follow my lead," I said.

"I always do," Harley said, which made me smile. Since she's not really a follower, although she tries sometimes.

Tiernan and Shay are brothers and the sons of Irish-immigrant parents. They look similar, with dark blue eyes and sturdy builds. They'd worked out a detailed plan when they'd decided to start their distillery. Shay spent a few years working for a distillery in Ireland. At the same time, Tiernan found a property to develop near Portland and slowly got it ready for their business while working as a programmer. Along with a motley mix of his friends and family, he spent his weekends building the distillery, eventually ending up with a gorgeous, light-filled tasting room with a view of the Columbia River Gorge and a distillery. They'd made their business from the ground up, both literally and figuratively.

Partnering with them could be great for us, especially since they would shoulder most of the financial risk.

"I'm so sorry to change the plan," I said, "but because of police activity, we can't meet in the roastery."

"Oh?"

The waitress who seemed to live at the Red Leaf walked over with a coffee pot in her hand. I said, "At least we can have a cup of Ground Rules coffee while we talk."

After she'd poured us each a cup and left, I looked at the brothers. I knew honesty was the best option here, so I told them an abridged version of what happened.

"Wait, so this person didn't work for you?" Tierney asked. He was slightly taller than Shay. He'd rolled the sleeves of his plaid shirt up, and I noticed a vein popping out of his muscular forearms. His flannel was unbuttoned, showing a T-shirt with a drawing of a whiskey glass with the words *You're neat* under it. I approved of his sartorial taste.

"No, she's not one of our employees. I have no idea how or why she was in Ground Rules." I met his gaze, telling him I was sincere.

"There's no way we would've let her into our roastery without supervision," Harley said.

I glanced at Harley, wishing she hadn't shared that tidbit of information. Even though it was true. There was no reason why we would've given Robbie a key. Given her tension with Harley, I doubted we would have ever invited her inside, let alone welcome her enough to become part of the Ground Rules team.

"So you weren't a fan?"

Harley's lips pressed together in a thin line, and they relaxed a half second before she spoke. "A few months ago, we were working out in the gym at the same time. I was doing bench presses. While I refilled my water, she snuck a couple of extra plates onto my bar when I wasn't looking. I didn't notice until I tried to lift it. I could've dropped those weights on my chest and gotten hurt. Badly. But she claimed she was just pranking me. But that wasn't amusing. I mean, the time she put up 'no squats' signs in the squat rack was *almost* funny."

"Or the time she put up speed limit signs by the treadmills. Robbie was definitely a prankster," I said to smooth things over. "Don't even get me started about the pranks she pulled when I was doing motion capture for the video game."

"What's this about a video game?" Shay asked. So I explained that, too. "It's not taking time away from your coffee business?"

I shook my head, hearing a scoffing note in his voice like he questioned everything about me. "Ground Rules is my priority, and the motion capture is just a few hours per week. It's been a fun, small side gig. It's an added bonus there'll be a video game character based on me when the game is finished."

"The game sounds really cool. Do you know the launch date?" Tierney asked.

Shay shook his head at his brother. "Let's not get sidetracked. Do you have any idea when you'll be able to regain access to your roastery?"

"Hopefully soon. I did bring you some bags of coffee to sample until we formally meet for coffee cupping." I handed over the bags of coffee beans I'd pilfered from the Ground Rules cart earlier in the morning, all tucked inside a teal bag with our logo printed on the side. I explained how our medium blend Puddle Jumper is one of our best sellers, while our dark roast 12 Bridge Racer would create a bold drink. "And I included our new roast, Concrete Blonde, because while it's one of our lightest roasts, it's not short on flavor. Harley calls its more acidic flavor lemony, and it could be an interesting pairing with the right whiskey."

Harley nodded. "Irish whiskeys aren't made with one specific coffee roast, with some people claiming a light roast is best, and others preferring dark roasts. So we'll want to match the taste palate you're envisioning. It'll be interesting to see which option blends best with your whiskey."

I added, "And remember, if you give us flavor notes, Harley can create something custom."

"I aim to please," Harley muttered. Tierney smiled at her, while Shay looked skeptical. Maybe this was the key to their success: Tierney was happy with the world, with the type of energy that makes people want to follow him anywhere. While Shay's reserved, calm perspective varied between wet blanket and voice of reason.

Shay glanced at his phone. "We need to leave, but let's meet up for the coffee tasting we talked about in a few days."

"And we'll try the coffees you gave us and come back with notes on what we liked. I'm already looking forward to it," Tierney said.

They left, and Harley and I glanced at each other. "Breakfast burritos?" I asked.

"A day like today requires an eggs Benedict," she said. After we ordered, I thought about how Robbie's death threatened both Ground Rules and Grumpy Sasquatch Studio.

And the questions of how Robbie entered the roastery and why kept circling through my mind. It just didn't make sense.

It wasn't even 11:00 a.m., and I felt like the weight of the day was too much to bear.

After breakfast, Harley left to take the day off since she was still feeling the aftereffects of her migraine. And since we couldn't get into the roastery, taking today off made sense regardless. I wished my work laptop wasn't locked up in the roastery, making it unavailable to me. Still, I could access some of my files and contacts on my phone, so I made a mental list of things to do.

As I walked back to the building, I called the owner of Pump It PDX.

"Hey, Pete, it's Sage Caplin from Ground Rules. Is there—"

"I heard there was some massive drama at your business yesterday."

"That's why I'm calling. Is there any way I can check out your security camera footage?"

"You know the police already got copies of it, right? Why do you need it?"

I held in a sigh. "Sadly, yes there was a tragedy in our shared building, but it didn't involve any of our employees. I'm hoping your security footage might have caught something, especially if we get caught in a civil suit." I was trying to smooth the way with my words, but what if I was right? Would we be liable if Robbie's family named us in a wrongful death suit, even if we weren't involved because it happened in our space? I told myself to text Jackson the question later.

Maybe, since I knew the people involved, I'd see something the police missed.

Pete sounded sympathetic. "Sure, stop by, although I'm not sure how helpful it will be. I'm not in the office, but I'll text the trainers now so they know to expect you."

Pump It PDX takes up the back end of the building. The main hallway runs past Bax's studio and my roastery on one side, and a small woodworking shop and a seamstress on the other.

The gym had two double doors open to the hallway, and music with a heavy beat thudded through the air. Inside the doors, the small room in the front, the gym has a couple of benches that look like someone cut a slab long-wise from trees, added a couple of legs, and then polished them. The edges are a bit rough, but they look hip. And I'd seen the gym staff wipe down the furniture in the waiting room often. Which is good 'cause it's the main place people switch between their gym and street shoes. The gym doesn't have locker rooms, just two changing stalls in each bathroom and a handful of cubbies in the workout room for people to store their bags and jackets while they work out.

Not long after I walked in, a twentysomething woman rocking hip workout gear was setting me up in the front room of the gym on one of the computers tucked behind the welcome desk.

"Here's the hallway camera. Just scroll forward or back to check the footage," she said. She showed me how to navigate the security app and left to greet a personal training client. They headed into the gym to start warming up.

The security footage wasn't overly helpful. The hallway turned between here and Ground Rules and didn't quite catch our door. Fingers crossed, the video footage from the building's management would be helpful.

But I noted who was in the area around the time Harley had shown up. I wished I knew how long Robbie had been in the roastery before Harley had found her. A couple of women came in a few minutes before 3:00 p.m., followed by a man running like he was late, and one of the trainers, Aiden, left about 3:30. I made notes, wondering if this was helpful at all.

I'd called 911 a few minutes after 4:00 p.m., so I doubted anyone I'd seen on the security footage saw anything, but you never can tell. The gym is busier once the workday ends. So whoever had chosen the late afternoon had either been lucky, or they'd planned this well.

Chapter 9

When I left the gym, I stopped and stared at the front door of Ground Rules again.

Which was still a crime scene.

But there was something slightly productive I could do here.

Grumpy Sasquatch Studio felt subdued when I stepped inside. I caught a glimpse of Noah disappearing into the office he shared with a couple other employees. Someone had created a custom CAUTION: GENIUSES AT WORK sign in metal and hung it over their door. The motion-capture studio, where I spent most of my official time, was a door beyond their group office, versus where I spent most of my unofficial time. I headed to the back, to the office with a window, couch, and a view of the sidewalk outside. If Bax ever brought Kaldi to the office, I was sure the orange cat would enjoy watching the bustle of people going by on the sidewalk and the occasional bird or squirrel. Although I suspected Kaldi was happier at home. My brother's dog, however, would make a great office mascot.

I poked my head into Bax's office through the open office door. He was focused on his computer but looked up when I knocked lightly on the doorframe.

His face relaxed into a smile.

"I wondered when I'd see you today," Bax said. He stood as I walked around his desk, and he put his arm around my waist and leaned into me. He kissed my forehead, let me go, and sat back down, tugging me with him. But I stopped next to his chair since it felt sketchy to sit on anyone's lap in a professional setting. Even if I was subbing as his emotional support human after a traumatic event.

I ran my fingers through the thick hair on the back of his head. "I didn't want to wake you up this morning. You'd finally settled down after a restless night." Bax smelled like the citrus soap he uses, with a lingering note of coffee. Most likely from the half-full mug on his desk.

"I'm sorry if I kept you up."

"No worries. I just downed a few espresso shots, which is about as good as visiting dreamland." As long as I ignored the jitters.

Bax laughed. "I can't hear the word 'dreamland' without assuming people are talking about my video game."

"That's your dreamside quest, then," I joked. "Can I borrow a computer to check out the building's security footage? I could watch on my phone, but a bigger screen would be great, and I can't access the Ground Rules computer 'cause it's in a crime scene."

"Sure, feel free to use the one in the motion-capture booth. If it's not available, ask Kat or Noah to set you up. They'll know a spot you can camp out in."

Bax's laptop beeped, and he said, "I need to take this video call from Lindsey."

"Isn't she across the office?"

"Nah, she's working from home this morning," Bax said. He clicked and then said, "Hi, Linds. Sage is here with me."

"Hiya, Sage." Lindsey looked as tired as I felt deep inside. She wore glasses with thick tortoiseshell frames instead of her usual contacts and a baggy red hooded sweatshirt.

Her glasses gave her a severe look. Which reminded me of Robbie leaving to fix her contacts yesterday. I'd never seen Robbie in glasses, even when I'd run into her working long hours on the weekend once before a product launch. Wearing contacts must have been a big deal to her. Although she would've looked fantastic in anything, including the right pair of frames.

As Bax and Lindsey started talking through something technical, I wandered out into the office. Someone had made popcorn in the office kitchen, making the whole place smell like fake butter. The couch in the front called my name, but instead, I stayed on my feet and headed toward the motion-capture booth.

Kat was sitting at her desk in the office she shared with Wyatt and another programmer. The walls of their office were painted a light spa-like gray. Her desk was spotless, with a couple of Funko Pop figures lined up on the edge. Her metallic orange coffee mug sat on a matching coaster, with a water bottle lined up precisely beside it.

Like all of us, Kat looked a little rough now that the glow of her morning workout was gone. At some point, she'd put her hair up in a messy bun, which poked through a hole in the back of her chunky green beanie. And it looked hurried versus purposeful, while the beanie looked handmade. But her navy-and-red flannel shirt looked like vintage Kat. The shadows around her eyes made me guess that she hadn't slept much last night.

"Are you doing okay?" I asked her. Her Deadpool mousepad had the words "My bad" in a word balloon.

"I thought about calling in sick today, but I'm not ill. Just exhausted, but physically and emotionally." Kat picked up her coffee cup and tipped her head back to swallow the dregs.

"I'm guessing you could've taken a mental health day."

"It's better to save a mental health day for when I feel like I truly need it. But I did come in an hour later than normal, but it was so I could take a different morning class. I thought exercise would help me feel better."

"You slacker, coming in late," I said. Kat laughed.

Wyatt walked into his desk, looking perkier than everyone else. Which wasn't saying much. But he'd traded his usual graphic tees for a plain black shirt.

Unlike Kat's quiet order, Wyatt's desk was a mess of color. Post-it notes covered the wall behind his monitor and competed for space on his desk with various figurines and small toys.

Wyatt paused as he started to sit down. He looked at one of the Post-it notes. He stood up straight.

"Wait, Starlight?" Wyatt said. "What was I thinking when I wrote this?"

Wyatt looked around, pausing at us briefly, then walked to the door and stopped when Noah walked in. "Hey, Noah, what do you know about the back-end coding for Starlight?"

Noah's chuckle was a bit grim. "We finished that up ages ago. Did you forget to recycle a note?"

"Robbie," Wyatt said. He blinked hard as he stared at the note in his hands. "One of her final pranks."

"What's that?" I asked.

"Robbie loved messing with my note system. She could imitate my handwriting, and she'd sometimes add one of her own notes to my system." His voice sounded thick. "This isn't the first time she'd added a reminder for me to finish something I'd already done."

Everyone stood quietly for a moment. Kat stared down at her keyboard, and Noah crossed his arms over his chest.

Wyatt stepped toward his desk, his hands opening and closing, like dispersing energy would somehow make him feel better. "Robbie and her continual jokes."

Wyatt sat down at his desk with a thump.

Noah glanced at me. "Sage, so why are you here? You're not scheduled today."

"You're right. I asked Bax if I could borrow a workstation for a few minutes, and he said I could use the motion-capture booth, or if it's being used, one of you could hook me up."

Wyatt stood up, making me think he was a human jack-in-the-box and my words were the end of the music. "I'll make sure you get set up."

Noah half-smiled and leaned over to talk to Kat quietly. It sounded like work talk as Wyatt left the room and headed to the office in the back.

"So, what happened yesterday after you left the patisserie?" I asked Wyatt. He flipped on the light of the motion-capture booth. I could've done this myself, but something told me he needed to talk. He settled into one of the rolling office chairs while I chose the one next to the computer I planned to use.

"The whole day was a mess," Wyatt said. "Robbie was harping on us all day, saying we weren't as clever as her. But it's not like she was jumping to the right answer for each puzzle."

"Wasn't she angry one of you had gotten a clue wrong?" I asked, knowing I should ease Wyatt toward my burning questions—like how had Robbie unlocked the door to the roastery? Could she have picked the lock?

"And she didn't let me forget it. When I saw 'set your mind at cheese,' I thought of the cheesecake bakery a few blocks away. They just opened a tiny storefront selling direct to consumers. And let me tell you, they were very confused by our costumes and didn't know what a scavenger hunt was. I'm not sure I will ever be able to return for their tarta de queso, which might be a reason for justifiable homicide for my girlfriend. She loves their desserts."

"Tarta de queso . . . Cheese tart?" Wait, girlfriend? Wyatt hadn't mentioned her before.

"Basque cheesecake. If you haven't had it before, try it. It's basically crustless cheesecake with a blackened top."

"So you guys went there instead of the cheese shop?"

"Exactly, and it's a mistake that's easy to make since they're both within the game zone. Robbie alternated between blaming me and ripping on how it was just like Lindsey to write a clue with multiple interpretations. She said it was clear why Lindsey is the programmer while Bax handles the creative stuff. It was obnoxious." Wyatt's face slid from annoyed to sad. "It feels petty to get mad at her now."

"Was that your last clue before the patisserie?" I asked, even though I knew it wasn't.

"Nah, we also visited the sock shop and the dumpy diner a few blocks away."

Dumpy? I love the Red Leaf. "How was the refueling stop at the patisserie?"

"Their food is the bomb. But it was awkward because Robbie was edgy and stormed out a few times. I kept expecting her to throw another temper tantrum, which made the ambiance turn sour. She was annoyed we had to stay there for forty-five minutes before Lindsey would give us the next clue since you'd already left, and Robbie was afraid you'd win."

"Bax is her boss. Why would his winning be such a big deal?" I realized I should've said "was."

"Robbie is—was—a sore loser. But honestly, I suspect losing to Bax wouldn't have been that big of a deal since she could kiss up to him and tell him he's so smart." Wyatt's voice went high-pitched at the end. His voice returned to normal as he said, "But losing to you and Kat? That'd make her head explode."

"Why would losing to me be a big deal? It's not like I'm a threat to anyone here. I just provide the coffee. And it's not like someone else couldn't be hired to do the motion-capture stuff."

"From what I've seen, you're pretty collaborative. You help us troubleshoot when we have motion-capture issues, and when things get weird, like when we lost a whole day's work, you have a sense of humor. But this isn't your main gig, so I don't know if this would apply to your daily life. Kat's helpful, too—she doesn't see our work as a competition. And it's not. I couldn't do my job without Kat's code, Bax's story ideas, or Noah keeping everyone on schedule while outperforming all of us with one eye closed." Wyatt made eye contact with me like he wanted me to clock what he was saying. "Noah is, like, totally brilliant at this. I'm good, but he can do code better than all of us and help all of us be more efficient. Honestly, I'm in awe of him."

I smiled. "Noah's handsome, too." His even features would've been attractive on anyone, but something about his light brown eyes made him seem kind.

"Yes, I've noticed. Noah's not my type since I'm all about the ladies, but yeah, he's a catch. I'd introduce you, but you already know him, and you have the top dog wrapped around your finger."

"He's not wrapped around my finger," I said. Although Wyatt might have a point. But we'd see how the next six months go since I could foresee a few challenges on the horizon. Had Wyatt switched to talking about Noah on purpose? Was he hiding something?

"How was Robbie with the rest of your workgroup?"

Wyatt leaned back and looked at the ceiling. "You know, Robbie had serious issues with Kat. Losing to her would've been catastrophic to Robbie since she wants to prove she's the best."

"How did the scavenger hunt go after you left Jamulet?"

"Not much better. Even if we were right, Robbie had issues with anything Noah and I said about the clues. We went our separate ways at about two p.m. Maybe earlier?"

"Where were you when you went your separate ways?"

"We were arguing over the library clue, with Robbie insisting we should go to the local branch, but Noah said it was clearly outside the game's boundary. She told us she'd see us at the finish line when she marched off with a giant stick up her . . . you know." Wyatt looked away into the far corner of the motion-capture booth.

"What'd you do then?"

"We finally thought of the Little Lending Library around the corner. We texted Robbie when we found the clue, but she didn't respond. I never saw her again." Wyatt looked down at the floor in front of him.

I tried to study his face, but his brown eyes continued to study the floor like he was reading answers to whatever bothered him on the industrial carpet.

"By the way, Lindsey ordered a huge catering spread from the taco shop a few blocks away, and from Elephant's Deli. It's in the fridge in the kitchen if you're hungry," Wyatt said.

"I'll keep that in mind."

"Do you need help logging on?" Wyatt asked.

"Nah, I'm good."

Wyatt left the room, and I logged onto the computer using my official Grumpy Sasquatch login.

Before opening my email, I accessed the Grumpy Sasquatch Slack account to double-check the motion-capture schedule.

Slack opened to the last page I'd looked at.

Lindsey's birthday celebration.

And someone had sent me a personal message since I'd last logged on. I clicked on it.

Robbie.

My heart thudded in my ears a few times as I took a deep breath and read the message.

> *Hey, the Sage-est con artist, I mean boss lady, I know. We need time to talk! I think I know something that is going to blow your mind. —Robbie*

Con artist? The words rankled me. Why had Robbie led with that? While my mother is a grifter, I try to live as honestly as possible. Had Robbie researched my background and learned about my mother being a wanted criminal? It's not exactly a secret, as Bax, Lindsey, and Harley all know about the twist in my family tree. I'd told Bax once we'd gotten serious, dating-wise, and then Lindsey after they'd asked me to the motion-capture work. While I didn't have access to the studio's financials, for example, I wanted to be up front about having me on their payroll. They hadn't cared.

What had Robbie wanted to communicate to me? She hadn't acted like there was anything particular she wanted to tell me before the scavenger hunt started.

Although, knowing Robbie, telling me she had some sort of info I'd want could have been the lead-up to one of her pranks.

Or she really did have some sort of news to share. Could it have been significant enough to put her life at risk?

After a moment, I opened a web browser to log into the web-based version of my email.

The building manager had emailed me a link to a folder in the cloud with the security footage of the day Robbie had died. His note mentioned he'd also supplied it to the police.

Supplied it. Like it was a drug.

Or something valuable. Fingers crossed, this would answer the question of what happened so we could all move along from the shadow of Robbie's death.

I watched a group of sasquatches leave the main entrance of the building, dressed as ducks, including the trio that included Bax, Kat, and me. A group of two ducks and a goose with a striped beanie trailed behind a few minutes later.

Wyatt and Noah must've waited for Robbie when she'd run to the bathroom, holding her eye.

Harley walked out of the building a few seconds after them, her backpack over her uncharacteristically hunched shoulders. At least to someone who knew her, Harley's posture screamed migraine.

Robbie turned, facing the camera's direction, and said something to Harley, and my business partner tensed up. Harley must've said something because Robbie's smile flickered into something feral. Noah put his hand on Robbie's sleeve, and she shook him off. But then the duck–duck–goose trio walked one way while Harley, whose shoulders still looked tense, marched off a different way.

What had they said to each other?

If they were fighting, when had it started? Why hadn't Harley told me about it? I knew about Robbie's not-funny prank on Harley in the gym.

I started to make a note to talk to Harley about this and paused. I knew, with absolute certainty, she didn't have anything to do with Robbie's death. I'd known Harley since our undergraduate days. My business partner could be awkward and fond of blurting out whatever thoughts were in her head, especially when her anxiety hit, but she was fundamentally kind. Loyal. I'd never seen her be catty, even when she'd had justification. Even when our former boss, Mark Jeffries, had taken credit for Harley's work, she'd quietly plotted her own revenge.

And eventually, with my help, Ground Rules was born. Roasting her own blends and single-origin beans to excellent reviews was Harley's revenge. Along with creating the sort of company where we treated our employees the way we wanted to be treated. Harley didn't even trash-talk Mark, although I could see the tension in her face whenever his name came up.

Plus, on the practical side, if she'd decided to get revenge on Robbie, she wouldn't have used our roastery. And Harley never would've turned to violence.

I called Harley, and she answered after a few rings.

"How are you feeling?" I asked.

"Still half dead, but also half alive."

"So your coffee cup is half full," I said. "Question for you. I'm looking at the video footage from yesterday—"

"Wait, why?"

"I thought we should get copies in case we're caught up in a wrongful-death suit."

"Is that possible?"

"Possible? Yes. Probable, no idea. But it's better to be prepared."

"You were a Girl Scout, right?" Harley laughed.

"No, but I've watched that old movie about the Beverly Hills scout troop. Next question for you: Robbie ran into you as you left the building. What'd she say?"

"Nothing she hadn't said before." There was a slight edge to Harley's voice, like Robbie had been getting under her skin.

"Meaning? Did you two have a feud brewing that I didn't know about?"

"Feud is too strong of a word."

Harley's words sounded pensive, and I knew there was something going on I hadn't seen. And I kicked myself for not noticing.

"If feud is an espresso shot, what was your relationship with Robbie, then? Watered down Americano?"

"What is this, the SATs? Okay, think of a latte you'd make for a five-year-old. You'd put a bit of brewed coffee in a cup, then add a mug full of steamed milk so it's vaguely coffee flavored. Although in real life, you'd add some sugar, so my analogy is falling apart. But it was like that. Robbie wanted to make me angry, I think. She'd call me Princess or hint I'm lame, or the weakest link everywhere. Nothing I haven't dealt with before, like when I was the weird kid bouncing off the walls in first grade."

"What'd Robbie say yesterday?"

"She asked if I was playing hooky from work 'cause the real brains of the business was off playing. One of her coworkers shut her down, and I tried to ignore her."

Given the way Harley's shoulders had tensed in the video, she hadn't been fully successful, and Robbie had known it.

"How long has this been going on?" I asked.

"I don't know, ages. I generally ignored her. But it got worse since you started doing your motion-capture side hustle."

"I'm really sorry. Why didn't you tell me?"

"It's not your fault, and I think it's really cool that you're involved in the game, especially since Bax is so excited about it. I knew if I said something, you'd end up arguing on my behalf and, honestly, I thought it was better to ignore Robbie. She's not worth the energy."

"If someone hassles you in the future, let me know, right? We're a team."

"I'll let you know if it matters. Now, if this is all, I'm off to nap."

"Feel better! Ground Rules needs you firing on full cylinders, since we're nothing without you."

"Back at you. Now I'm hanging up. I'll see you tomorrow."

We hung up, and I turned back to the footage.

I fast-forwarded, returning to regular speed whenever I saw a group of ducks walk in. Given the slow but steady stream of costumed Sasquatch employees, I was sure our final clue had been for the gym.

Hmm. Maybe we would've won the whole game if tragedy hadn't struck.

A group of ducks entered at about 1:30, and I recognized Raoul's dreads. The group walked out about five minutes later, heads turned toward Raoul, who seemed to be reading something off his phone. Maybe their next clue?

At about 2:30, a couple more ducks flocked in, but they left not long after, making me assume they'd also dropped by the gym as part of the scavenger hunt. Although some of the ducks might have had a reason to stop by the studio.

A few minutes before 3:00, the women I'd seen on the gym footage strolled in, followed by the man. Then Aiden left, not looking in front of him as he stared at his phone and collided with Harley. Poor Harley; at least two people had run into her full-tilt that day like she was invisible.

Wait. I looked at the time. 3:58. I checked my notes.

Aiden had left the gym closer to 3:30, and it didn't take twenty-eight minutes to walk down the hallway.

This might be the best clue I'd found so far.

But what should I do with it?

And then I realized something important: I hadn't seen anyone in a goose costume enter the building.

Had Robbie entered the building from the street? Both Ground Rules and Grumpy Sasquatch Studio have doors from the front sidewalk into the building, although neither business uses them often. Which made sense since neither company has a lot of foot traffic. The front reception area is almost a waste.

Did Robbie have a key to the studio? Their door from the central hallway has a keypad, and it's frequently propped open during the day.

I stopped by the kitchen to refill my water bottle before leaving and saw the office manager, Elaine, loading up a plate of food.

Lindsey had gone all out. It looked like a mix of salads from Elephant's Deli, a personal favorite, plus cheese and deli meats, with bread on the side.

"Would you like some before I put these away?" Elaine asked.

I patted my stomach. "I'd love to say yes, but I'm still stuffed from my breakfast at the Red Leaf."

"Feel free to take something to go, as I'm pretty sure this will disappear pretty soon. The amount of food the staff here can go through is prodigious."

"Then it sounds like having free food around is good," I said. I snagged a lemon from Bax's precut (and labeled) small Tupperware in the fridge and plopped it into my bottle.

"I should check in with everyone. I'm sure grieving like this is new to most staff, and they can use my experience," Elaine said.

I wanted to remind her that the staff is adults, not teens, but I held the words in. It's possible that people can make it through school, including university and graduate school, without losing anyone close to them. But it's unlikely. If checking in on everyone made Elaine feel good, then who was I to complain? Besides, maybe she would notice if someone was taking the news especially hard and needed a shoulder to cry on.

Chapter 10

Kendall handed over a trio of coffee cups to a group of twentysome-things, all with impeccably trendy hair, at the cart. He grinned at them and said something, and they giggled. One of the women was blushing as they walked away. Sophie sat outside Ground Rules, eating something wrapped in foil and staring at a textbook.

"You should totally ask him out," one of the women said as they passed me. All three looked adorable in different and very stylish ways.

I walked up to the entrance of the cart. "Looks like you're making friends," I said.

"Hi, boss. Those three stop by every day for mochas. I think they work at a nearby salon."

"They all had gorgeous hair," I said. I touched my ponytail. I was overdue for a trim, but I'd been too busy. I thought maybe I should do something a bit funky, as I'd been in a fashion rut for a while.

"You know that syrup you dropped off? The bourbon-cardamom one? It's the bomb. I made it in an oat milk latte and tried it in cold brew, and it was perfect. Sweet with a bit of spice, with depth."

"Good to hear."

"Would you like me to make you something, boss?" Kendall asked.

"Coffee on the rocks, please." So he made me an iced Americano.

We chatted about the cart. Out of the corner of my eye, I noticed a guy standing at the entrance to the Rail Yard, looking at us. My eyes narrowed as I clocked him.

Late forties. Decked out in a long-sleeved plaid shirt and jeans. If he rolled up his sleeve, it'd show off a forearm adorned with an espresso portafilter alongside a moka pot tattoo, with assorted coffee imagery. His baseball cap was on-trend, and even without the Left Coast Grinds logo splashed on the hat, I'd recognize him.

Kendall touched my arm lightly. I turned, and his gaze my way was thoughtful. "I've seen that guy around a few times."

"His name's Mark Jeffries. He owns Left Coast Grinds."

Kendall nodded. "The guy you and Harley used to work for."

"Also the man who took credit for what should've been Harley's first award-winning blend at the US Open Coffee Cup." A flicker of the anger I'd felt on Harley's behalf flowed through me. I couldn't even imagine the rage that must've surged through my friend when Mark had accepted the award at the biggest coffee competition in the country. He'd bragged about "his" roast during his speech. Mark also claimed he'd created the blend in an interview with the leading coffee industry magazine. The quote about the tweaks he'd made to create the roast was especially irksome.

Mark hadn't mentioned Harley once.

Even without claiming credit for Harley's genius, neither of us liked him. But he did know how to craft a mean cup of coffee.

With "mean" being a play on the double meaning of the word.

To make things worse, he was a good enough roaster that he hadn't needed to take credit for Harley's work. And Harley wasn't the only roaster who'd left Left Coast and set up their own shop. Although Harley was the only one to go head-to-head with Mark in Portland.

Mark didn't deserve to take up space in my brain, so I turned back to Kendall. "Have I talked to you about the Harvest Festival next month at my friend Erin's family's Christmas tree farm? We'll be there with the second cart and every weekend through Christmas. Are you interested—"

A loud voice interrupted me. "Sage, I've been swinging by, hoping to talk to you."

Mark.

The little voice in the back of my brain instinctively told me to keep it cool. "Would you like something to drink? Our Grumpiest Sasquatch blend is especially excellent." I didn't mention we'd named the roast after Bax's company.

"Sasquatches, huh? A bit too cutesy for my taste."

"It has a complex flavor profile, very bold and cutting edge. Something lighter might be more to your taste." It wasn't my best put-down, but I was trying. Kendall's presence beside me felt comforting.

"Listen, I want to talk to you about adding Ground Rules to the Left Coast Grinds family."

The little voice in the back of my head laughed. But I made my voice heartfelt. Sympathetic. "So you're looking to sell Left Coast Grinds? Gosh, that's a huge decision, and you must feel gutted, having to give up something you spent so much time and effort developing. The sweat equity alone must mean so much to you."

Kendall turned away, like wiping down the back counter was the most exciting thing in the world. His shoulders shook as he held in laughter.

"What? No!" Mark held out his hand, encompassing my coffee cart. "You played at business owner fairly well, but with my expertise, Ground Rules could go to the next level and fill a niche for affordable coffee."

Years of my brother Jackson and Uncle Jimmy treating me like I was younger and more fragile than I was had long ago steeled me to people who acted like I was childlike.

"Affordable?" My voice was deadpan, and the devil on my shoulder wanted me to verbally slap down Mark. In contrast, the angel on my other shoulder argued about how to handle this.

"Left Coast has a strong reputation for excellence and impeccable quality, and it could focus on the higher-end market. I'd like to expand into quality, affordable beans under a second, more basic label. For people who expect a baseline level of quality but are on a tight budget."

Basic. Show my hand. Next, Mark would diss pumpkin spice lattes and the people who love their yearly PSLs. While they're not my preference, as I'm not really a sweet coffee fan, I support anyone who freaks out over pumpkin spice or any other coffee they love. And making an excellent sweet latte is as essential as being able to craft the perfect pour-over or straight shot.

"Ground Rules isn't for sale. So it sounds like you have work to do to start your budget brand from scratch."

Mark stared at me for a moment, like he couldn't believe I wasn't immediately following his wishes and thanking him for the opportunity to sell the company I was building.

His voice was sarcastic when he finally spoke again. "Did I hear about another person dying around your coffee again? That can't be good for your image."

I smiled, but I knew it matched the tone of his voice. "And you want to tie your sterling reputation to our bad-girl image? You know, with your impeccable top-shelf credentials."

"Think about what I said. The offer won't be available forever," Mark said. "Selling would be a better choice than struggling to survive. I mean, your next step will be selling coffee in a bikini."

"Hey, I'd rock that look," Kendall said. "Maybe a nice Speedo?"

Mark glared at us for a moment and then turned and stalked away.

I watched him retreat with my eyes narrowed. A couple of teenagers walked up, and as Kendall took their order, Mark stopped by the entrance of the Rail Yard, his eyes on his phone. As he put his phone back in his pocket, he looked toward Ground Rules with a smug smile that made me wish a meteor could fall from the sky and smite him where he stood. He sauntered away.

Instinct made me pull out my own phone and systematically check Left Coast Grinds on all of my social media feeds.

There it was. A photo of the Ground Rules cart while shuttered, so he'd taken it when we weren't open. The text read: *You know we love coffee, but we've heard this coffee kills. Talk about the wrong sort of deadly.*

My hand curled into a fist, but I made myself relax. Two could play this game.

I reposted his photo and typed in, *That's right! Our coffee slays and will leave you smiling for days. Tell our barista the code word "slays" anytime today for $1 off a drink of your choice! #OurCoffeeKillsTheCompetition.*

More inspiration hit. I grabbed a bag of our Puddle Jumper blend, one of our camp mugs, and a Ground Rules T-shirt and carried them outside to the picnic table closest to the cart. I snapped a couple photos of the items with the cart's logo in the background.

Once I had the perfect photo augmented by a flawless filter with a rainbow across one corner, I uploaded it to all of our social media channels. The caption read, *If you visit our cart, post about it on social with the hashtag #GroundRulesSlays for a chance to win a prize pack including everything in the photo, plus coupons for a week's worth of free coffee drinks!*

I then sent a quick group text telling everyone about my spur-of-the-moment promo and the reason why. I added, *Let's spin Mark's comment into something fun and make it seem like he's afraid of us.*

Sophie quickly responded via text, even though she was sitting a few feet from the cart and could've said something. *If he's smart, he should be terrified of you, boss.*

Kendall's response arrived a few seconds after Sophie. *I know I quake in my boots if the boss glares at me.*

Harley texted me individually. *How come you're the scary one?!?*

I replied with a shrug emoji and then sent a group text. *Sounds like I should dress up as the Wicked Witch of the Portland Eastside for Halloween.*

Sophie must be living on her phone since she replied back almost instantaneously. *Nah, dress up like Glinda because, think about it, she was as scary as the other witch, even if she didn't have flying monkeys.*

Sophie sent a follow-up text right away. *Seriously. Glinda sends Dorothy on a mission, even though she has the power to send her back to Kansas. She's the "good witch" in control of most of the country and comes to Dorothy's rescue when needed, but waits until Dorothy exposes the wizard before sending her home. And she's the queen of the freakin' field mice. MICE. Talk about a tiny, terrifying army.*

Kendall's reply made me laugh. *It sounds like someone is obsessed with The Wizard of Oz.*

I could hear Sophie's sarcastic tone as I read her response. *Yeah, I babysat my nieces last weekend, and they were watching the film on repeat.*

Clearly, I needed to find something for my on-duty barista to do because Kendall quickly texted back, *Ah, you have a bunch of future Dorothys on your hands?*

Sophie sent a *Wizard of Oz* gif, then texted, *Nah, they were fighting over who got to be Toto in their makeshift musical.*

I popped back into the cart. Kendall put his phone away in his apron pocket like he felt guilty for slacking off. "Mark acts like you owe him something, and he's so perfect that coffee shines out of his . . . butt," Kendall said.

I nodded. "Mark has an outsized view of his own importance, but Harley and I both worked for him at one point. If he was nicer, we'd thank him. Or collaborate or something."

"Have you ever thought of selling?"

I turned to Kendall with death-laser beam eyes, and he hurriedly said, "I mean, not to a creep like him, but in general? You have to have known someone, someday, might be interested."

"From what I've heard, a couple of the second-wave local coffee roasters did cash out to the big mermaid brand back in the early 2000s, but they all seemed to regret it. The owners all came back and opened their own cafés and have stayed pretty small."

"So, have you?"

"Harley and I haven't spoken about that, but I can't see us selling. We love Ground Rules. And the brick-and-mortar store is still going to happen once construction is done."

But Kendall was right. I should talk about the concept with my business partner, even if there was no way we'd ever sell out to Left Coast Grinds. But what would happen if a sweet deal came from a company we respected? We'd have to talk about it, even if we didn't want to sell. And our mostly silent partner, my uncle Jimmy, might have an opinion.

Mark showing up here multiple times bugged me. It wasn't full-on stalkerish, but why? Wouldn't a formal bid presented at a meeting make more sense if he were serious about acquiring Ground Rules? Maybe even have his attorney approach us since he had to know his entire presence was like nails on chalkboards to us.

Was there any chance Mark could've been responsible for Robbie's death? Had he tried to enter our warehouse at the same time Robbie had, somehow, ended up inside? It didn't sound plausible to me, but I put it on my long list of suspects. Which, so far, was a fairly short list. But he'd been hanging around when the cart wasn't open, so him walking by the roastery was also a possibility.

Something about Sophie's comment about Glinda pinged in my brain, but I couldn't quite bring the thought into complete form. But it did remind me, once again, that just because someone looks one way—intelligent, airheaded, sneaky, trustworthy—doesn't mean they are. We all have secrets hidden inside. And some of those secrets are the things people will kill to protect.

Sophie popped up into the opening of the cart.

"Why didn't you tell us someone died at the roastery?" she asked. "You saw me this morning and didn't share the news."

"What?" Kendall turned toward me. His gaze was a question in and of itself.

I let out a long breath. "Okay, children, gather round." I told them the story.

"Wait, you're talking about the over-the-top Australian?" Kendall said.

"She's kind of snotty and makes fun of my accent. She calls me 'discount Irish' even though she knows I'm Canadian," Sophie said.

Annoyance on Sophie's behalf flickered through me. "Yep, that's Robbie."

"She asked me out once. I said no," Kendall said.

"Did she stop by often?" Robbie hadn't ever mentioned being a regular at the cart.

"She stopped by somewhat regularly. She ordered a flat white the first time, then said my attempt to make one was pathetic. Which she mentioned every time before ordering an Americano or a cold brew. She always drank it black and joked it was like her soul," Kendall said.

"She told me I also sucked at making flat whites. But she never joked with me, just ordered Americanos like I was her servant," Sophie said.

A woman in a red raincoat walked up, and Sophie stepped up to the order window.

As Sophie handled the transaction, I stood back. Flat whites consist of a shot of espresso and milk carefully steamed to create silky microfoam that, depending on whom you talk to, originated in Australia or New Zealand. So, of course, Robbie ordered them. But that didn't excuse her being rude to my baristas.

"Let me know if you have any questions," Sophie said.

"Are you Irish? I love accents," the woman asked.

Sophie shook her head, making the red bun on her head bounce slightly. "Nope, I'm from Newfoundland."

"Is that near Ireland? Because you sure sound Irish."

"It's in Canada." Sophie's voice was chipper, but I could see that yet another customer asking about her accent was chipping away at her good mood.

"Whatever. I'll take a matcha."

"With steamed milk? Which type?"

"Of course with milk. Whole."

Kendall and I looked at next week's schedule, as he had a one-day workshop that meant he needed someone to cover for him. Behind us, Sophie made the drink, which consisted of ground green tea. The one-woman tea manufacturer we buy it from pre-mixes it with sugar. I'd debated using a company that sold only matcha, and we'd sweeten it ourselves, but this blend mixes quicker, making it easier to use in the cart. The sugar cuts the slightly bitter end note of the matcha. It brings out the grassy taste, especially when combined with steamed milk, both dairy and alternative.

"Here's your matcha," Sophie said. She put the drink down on the order window's ledge.

The woman picked up the drink and took a sip. She promptly spit it out and then ripped the cup's lid off. "What is this? Why is my mocha green?"

"Umm, you ordered a matcha," Sophie said.

"I most certainly did not. I don't even know what that is. I distinctly remember ordering a mocha. Are you stupid or something?"

I butted in. "We're sorry about the miscommunication, and we'll happily remake your drink. But never insult my baristas for an understandable mistake." I didn't tell her that I'd also heard her say matcha.

Sophie glanced at me, then set about making a mocha. She muttered, "Hang on your drawers."

Meanwhile, the woman glared at me. "Are you calling me a liar or something?"

"No, I assume this was a simple miscommunication. But that's no reason to call someone names." The desire to refund her money and tell her to never return flowed through me, but I wanted to give her a chance.

The woman stared at me for a moment, then turned away. Kendall cleaned up the bowl and steaming pitcher Sophie had used to make the unwanted matcha.

"Here's your mocha!" Sophie said in a perky voice as she put the drink down on the order window, then turned away and started wiping down the espresso machine.

The woman took her drink and walked off with an audible harrumph.

"Boss, you should've read her coffee grounds. I bet you could've created a future that showed that woman is always obnoxious." Kendall laughed.

"Sage can read coffee grounds? Like tea leaves?" Sophie asked.

I shook my head. "I've done it before as a joke, but it's just a game, basically." The sort of game con artists play, but I've never done it to part people from money.

"We should have a coffee grounds reading booth for Halloween. I bet people would love it," Sophie said.

"We'll consider it. Now, back to the schedule. I can fill in while you're in the workshop, Kendall, no problem, unless Sophie wants the hours," I said.

"I want the hours." Sophie pulled her phone out of her pocket. "Which day and time?"

Kendall filled her in, and I thought how lucky I was to have these two on my staff.

"So what does 'hang on your drawers' mean?" I asked Sophie as I pulled my messenger bag over my shoulder.

"It's like telling someone to take a chill pill," she said.

Indeed.

Chapter 11

I was about to swing my leg over my bike to head home to get some paperwork done when my phone beeped with a text from Bax. *No one is focused at work. We're holding an impromptu wake for Robbie at the Tav. Join me. Please?*

I texted back. *Sure. Although I question if it's a good idea if you're all exhausted and sleep-deprived.*

Then come and help me herd everyone home at an early hour.

I joined Bax and a couple of the sasquatches at the studio. After I tucked my bike into Bax's office, we caught a rideshare across the Willamette River from Southeast Portland, through downtown, and into the Pearl District. I was wedged into the middle of the backseat between Bax and Lindsey. She'd spiffed herself up from this morning, wearing her contacts again and a long-sleeve wool dress.

"Today was a bust. Every time I tried to code, my brain didn't want to cooperate," Wyatt said from the front seat.

As I texted Harley and invited her to join us, Bax said, "Grief is a funny thing. But talk to me if you feel like you need a few days off. I understand." I suspected Bax had felt obligated to come to work today as the co-captain of the ship.

"We'd much rather you take time now than break down in the future," Lindsey added. "And our benefits package includes counseling. Bax, we should send out a message and remind everyone."

"I'll add it to the Slack group later."

"Maybe we should even ask a rep from the HR service to come in and talk about bereavement and counseling options available to everyone."

They made plans to "loop" their office manager, Elaine, and the external HR service into a conversation later. Wyatt turned and looked back at me, and I raised my hands in a "what can I say?" gesture.

The loading spot in front of the Tav was empty, so the rideshare pulled into it, with the second car of sasquatches behind us. We climbed out, and Lindsey tapped at her phone to take care of paying for the rides. Lindsey taking care of the small details was utterly on-brand.

Miles, for once, wasn't in sight when I walked into the Tav. The bartender pouring a pint of beer had blue-and-green mermaid hair, while the second bartender, who was bussing tables, had bleached white spikes and a retro-punk vibe, with red plaid pants, black Doc Martens, and a black Ramones T-shirt. They were paired with a pearl choker that looked 1950s housewife but somehow worked with the rest of the ensemble.

The punk bartender nodded at me. "Hiya, Sage."

"Hey, Kage. Can you bring a couple pitchers of IPA, a club soda, and a few carafes of water to the back when you have a moment? And a large order of corn dog nuggets?" If I was going to make it through a night with the sasquatches, snacks were a must.

"Sure thing. I'll put it on your tab."

"Please start the tab on my card," Bax said, and smoothly passed over his Visa. "And can we add a second corn dog nugget platter plus a couple orders of tots?"

"How about you follow me to the bar so I scan your card, but you can keep it."

Bax followed Kage up to the bar while I joined the sasquatches at the table in the back room. A couple had stopped by the jukebox and were carefully making selections.

"Does everyone here know your name?" Wyatt asked me.

"Everyone knows Sage," Noah said. "You could go grab some random person off the street and drag them in here, and they'd know her."

"You're overstating my popularity," I said.

Bax and Kage the bartender dropped off a couple pitchers of beer and a stack of glasses.

"Just beer?" Wyatt said.

"You're welcome to order whatever you'd like on your own tab," Bax said. His slightly tart tone made me give him a second glance. Yesterday, he'd had to take a boss tone with Robbie, and I could hear shades of it in his voice today.

My cousin Miles walked past, wheeling a stack of boxes. "Sage, I haven't seen you in forever," he said as he passed us by.

"See? Everyone knows her," Noah said.

"That's my cousin."

"You know, I'm starting to think your cousin Miles lives here," Bax said.

"I promise he does leave occasionally. I mean, you've seen his house." Miles had invited us out for a barbecue last summer. My whole family seemed determined to adopt Bax as one of their own. He's between Jackson and me in age, so he's almost a bridge between us.

Bax stepped away before responding and I took a sip of my club soda. The beer tempted me, but drinking on work nights didn't help my early morning shifts at Ground Rules, so I stuck to an occasional weekend tipple.

"Bax and Lindsey sure are close," Wyatt said.

I followed his gaze to where Bax and Lindsey stood close together, speaking intently, with her hand on Bax's bicep.

"They've been friends for years," I said. I realized I should talk to Lindsey and see if she had any insight into Robbie's journey after she left Jamulet. Had Robbie gone solo and checked in about the scavenger hunt clues? Had Lindsey spent her entire afternoon at the patisserie?

A group from Pump It PDX, the gym in the same building as the roastery and Grumpy Sasquatch Studio, walked in. They were all dressed sportily like they'd come from work. Miles glared at them as they walked our way.

Aiden walked up to Wyatt and me. "I'm so sorry to hear about Robbie."

"Yeah, we're all in shock," Wyatt said.

Kage stopped by, and the gym group ordered a mix of vodka sodas, hard seltzers, and a lone IPA from the one person not, I assumed, worried about carbs. I stuck to my club soda from the bar's soda gun, which Kage had adorned with a slice of lime.

Harley showed up, dressed for indoor soccer, complete with knee-high socks and topped off with a fitted Nike hoodie. She looked fierce.

"Interesting style choice," I teased her.

"I have a ten o'clock game," she said.

"Who wants to play soccer that late on a weeknight?" Wyatt asked.

"Thankfully, we usually only have one late game per season." Harley explained that her team had eight games over a ten-week season. The indoor-soccer facility tried to spread the late games out evenly.

As Harley and Wyatt discussed the merits of indoor soccer, I drifted over to Noah.

"How are things?" I asked him.

"It's hard to believe this isn't all a nightmare," Noah said. He held a pint of dark beer in his hand.

"What exactly happened yesterday afternoon? The last I saw, Robbie stormed out of Jamulet."

"For us, the scavenger hunt started with a cheesecake fight and didn't get any better." Noah took a sip of his beer.

"I need to try that cheesecake place."

Noah half-smiled at my words. He took a sip of his beer. "Robbie stormed away from us at, I don't know, two-fifteen? Two-thirty?

When we fought over the library clue. She called us some names and stormed off."

Noah walked off to join a group of sasquatches, and I eyed Aiden across the room. I remembered his actions from the security footage. Should I ask why it took him twenty-eight minutes to walk down a short hallway?

Raoul walked into the Tav and paused by me. I glanced up at him. "Can I ask you something random?"

"Shoot."

"Did you get a clue that led you to Pump It PDX during Lindsey's scavenger hunt?"

"The dead-lifting ghosts one? Yeah, we had to go pose in one of the squat racks. The trainers thought it was hilarious."

"We were on our way there but never arrived."

Raoul flinched. "That's when you found Robbie? That's rough."

We chatted for a while, including about how Raoul's sister works for a nonprofit that focuses on affordable housing.

The final clue had been leading us to the gym. It explained why a regular flock of ducks had made their way into and then back out of the building during the scavenger hunt. But it still didn't explain why Robbie didn't show up on the security footage.

Chapter 12

Because I'd left my bike in Bax's office, he swung himself out of bed and drove me to the Rail Yard. Kaldi claimed Bax's pillow before Bax had managed to pull a hoodie on.

The streets were quiet on the drive to the coffee cart.

"Go home and try to get more sleep," I told Bax as I prepared to climb out of his Subaru.

"I'll see you later."

After a quick goodbye kiss, I let myself into the Rail Yard.

After a late-ish night, early mornings at the cart always make me feel like I'm dragging, but I persevered. The drizzly day reflected the sadness inside me. Sophie joined me for the morning rush, and her perkiness brought a much-needed spark of joy to the cart.

Then a new challenge popped up: my weekly no-drop bicycle ride with Bax and some of his sasquatches at lunchtime.

Usually, I enjoy the rides. We do about thirty miles as a group, regardless of weather, except for ice. Some weeks we even cross over the Columbia River into Vancouver, Washington. Other times, we might head into the West Hills of Portland or follow a bike trail south of the city into Milwaukie. I hadn't done many group rides before joining them, although my father, who is a regular at two different rides, joked it's in my blood. The exercise and sense of camaraderie almost make it worth seeing everyone in spandex.

The group leader rotated month each, and Wyatt was in charge today. He looked like he'd rather be anywhere else, so I wasn't surprised when he looked at the group and said, "I'm thinking of a shorter route today. How do twenty miles and fairly flat sound?"

"Amen," a voice said from the back.

Wyatt held up a package of coconut water mix. His name was printed across the front on a piece of masking tape. "If anyone needs extra hydration help, let me know."

"You know it's serious if Wyatt's willing to share his coconut water powder," Noah said.

"Be nice," Lindsey said from beside me. Her calf-length bike capris had blue flowers up the side, which matched the blue in her jersey.

The group felt subdued, and something told me it wasn't just hangovers, despite last night's informal wake at the Tav.

"Are you joining us today, Kat?" Lindsey asked.

Kat, still dressed in her usual jeans and a flannel, shook her head. "It's not for me."

"You did great last time!"

"But as I said, it was an experiment. Maybe I'll go again next spring or summer."

"I thought you said it was too hot in the summer."

"Good point. Maybe I'll stick to the boot-camp classes here in the building."

I glanced at Kat. "Oh, do you go to Pump It PDX?"

"Yes, but always before work. Then I can't get sidetracked by a project and miss the workout."

"That explains why I've never seen you there." The gym specialized in group fitness classes and personal training. They offered everyone in the building a discount on classes. I tended to hit up their sessions a few days a week.

"Their six a.m. Rise and Sweat class is a great way to wake up." Kat gave me an awkward smile and then went back to her desk.

"You know, you should make Ground Rules bike jerseys,"

Noah said. He wore a jersey repping Portland's iconic Lucky Lab brewery, complete with a black Lab on the chest.

"I've thought about it, but I haven't gotten past looking at the cost." I noticed Lindsey tucking her phone into the back pocket of her jersey.

Noah showed me his helmet. "I just picked this up. Top of the line, safety-wise."

"Safety first." I, too, had a quality helmet. Red, like Lindsey's, since the bright color feels safer when biking in traffic.

Everyone sort of duck-walked on our way outside since we use clip-in pedals. I'd gotten used to them, although I'd wrecked the first time I tried to stop while wearing them. It had taken me a moment to get my foot unclipped, and I'd landed on the hood of a parked police car. After proving I wasn't drunk, and a lecture on safe bicycle riding, I'd been allowed to go on my way.

I was midway through the group, with Bax ahead of me and Lindsey on my back wheel.

We formed our line and turned onto a bike boulevard, which is a street optimized for bicycle traffic parallel to a major city street. When we hit our first stop sign, Wyatt came to a halt. But Noah shot past him, straight into the intersection.

Directly into the path of an oncoming SUV.

As Noah crashed onto his side, the SUV's tires squealed to a halt. Noah's helmeted head bounced on the street, and a car coming the other way stopped.

The smell of burned tires filled the air as Wyatt and Bax dropped their bikes and rushed to Noah's side. I followed them, along with Lindsey.

Noah sat up. "I'm all right."

"You didn't stop." Wyatt sounded shocked.

"My brakes must've failed." Noah tried to stand up, and Bax immediately slid an arm around him.

"You can sit there for a moment," Bax said. But Noah continued to rise into a standing position. Although he looked so wobbly, I'm sure he would've fallen over without Bax, but they made their way to the sidewalk. I snagged Noah's bike and wheeled it out of the street.

Noah unlatched his helmet and looked at the dent and scratches along the side where it had hit the pavement. "This was new!"

"It's better to dent the helmet than your skull," I said. I didn't point out Noah had torn the shoulder of his jersey, and it was slowly oozing blood.

Noah turned white. Bax and Wyatt helped him to the ground.

"Should we call an ambulance?" Bax asked.

"I already called 911," the driver of the car said. Her hands shook, and she leaned heavily against her car like she'd fall over without it.

Lindsey took a few quick but awkward steps—because of her shoes—over to the woman. "Are you okay?"

"Just freaked out. He was just suddenly there, in front of my car. I almost didn't stop in time."

"You sure reacted quickly." Lindsey put her hand on the woman's upper arm. "Can I call someone for you? I know if I were in your shoes, the thought of driving now would make me feel flustered."

As they talked, I knelt down by Noah's bike. Over time, I've learned my way around basic bicycle maintenance—meaning that I clean my bike often and know when it's time to take it in for a professional tune-up. And I know how brake lines should look. And how they shouldn't.

And I could tell Noah's brakes had been cut. Cleanly, like someone had sliced them with a knife.

And no one would do that by accident.

"What's wrong?" Bax asked, and knelt down beside me. I pointed out the sliced brakes.

Was someone trying to pick off the sasquatches one by one?

Bax swore under his breath. So it wasn't just me; he must think the bicycle brakes looked sliced as well.

I pulled my phone out of the back pocket of my jersey, took a photo of the cut brake lines, and texted Detective Will. *You're looking at the cut brake line of a bike owned by one of Robbie Kayle's coworkers.*

As I slid my phone back into my pocket, I wondered, was someone trying out all of the sasquatches? Or did someone have it in for Robbie and Noah?

Noah and Wyatt kept their bicycles inside the hallway of the building, along with most of the sasquatches. (I generally kept mine in the roastery, except for the rare time I'd locked it up in Bax's office.) Could someone mad at cyclists have chosen a bike at random and sliced the brakes?

I glanced around the group. Most looked worried, although a few were checking their phones. Lila, the intern from the marketing department, looked like she was going to throw up.

"You okay?" I asked the intern. She nodded but was clearly lying. Or she thought standing meant okay even if she started shaking. Raoul was standing a few feet away.

"Raoul? Can you help Lila back to the office?" I nodded at the intern.

He glanced at her, and sympathy washed across his face. "Of course. Come on, Lila, I'll walk you back."

Raoul took the handlebars of Lila's bike and pushed both of their bikes as they slowly made their way back to the office. He talked to her in a calm, gentle voice.

Most of the group followed them, leaving Bax, Lindsey, Wyatt, and me behind. Wyatt started to follow them. He turned and looked at us. "This isn't the way I'd planned the ride going. I spent so much time planning the routes for this month."

"There's always next week. At least Noah's okay," I said. But my gaze said, *Seriously, you're complaining about not getting to show all of us the brilliance of your route while your coworker narrowly missed dying? Or at least being seriously injured?*

Wyatt had been partnered with Robbie on the day she died, along with Noah. And Noah had almost bit the dust.

Could Wyatt have sliced Noah's brakes? Or were all of the sasquatches at risk?

Or was this random?

More likely, this was the action of someone who had a beef with Noah, at least. And maybe also with Robbie? The cut brakes could've been a warning since it didn't seem like a guaranteed way to hurt someone. It was like rolling the dice. Roll a one, and Noah would've just scraped his leg. Roll a six, and the worst could've happened. And it could've happened anytime during the morning.

"I'm not sure I need to go to the hospital," Noah said.

"You need to get your shoulder cleaned up, and you hurt your head," I said.

"My shoulder?" Noah turned his head toward where his jersey was ripped. The movement looked painful.

"Looks like you should get your neck checked out, too," I said. "You can file a police report about your bike."

"There's no need to involve the police over an unfortunate accident," Noah said. He tried to stand up again.

"You're going to the hospital, and if it helps, consider that an order from your boss," Bax said.

"Okay." Noah settled back down, and a moment later, an ambulance showed up.

After Noah had left in the ambulance, Bax and I walked back to the studio.

"That could've been so much worse," Bax said. He looked like he was deep in his own thoughts, so I stayed silent next to him instead of saying anything.

I touched Bax's arm when we reached the door to the studio. "I'm going back to the roastery, but I'm around if you need me."

"Thanks, Coffee Angel."

The sasquatches headed back into their office. They usually queued after the no-drop rides to use the two bathroom stalls with showers in the back of their office. I beelined to Ground Rules, partially because we also have a single-use bathroom off the warehouse with a shower, and I wanted to change out of my bicycling clothes. And partly because I wanted a minute to think.

Harley was streaming heavy metal from her phone as she weighed out one-pound bags of coffee beans. Our newest single-origin from beans grown at a family farm in El Salvador's Apaneca-Ilamatepec region. This bourbon-variety bean was being shipped out to our monthly subscribers first. We'd agreed to let it be the featured coffee of the month at the coffee shop of an award-winning local barista. We'd pack smaller twelve-ounce bags of the beans to sell in his shop.

"I take it this bean pairs well with headbanging?" I said.

Harley jumped. She wheeled around. "You scared me."

"Sorry."

She turned the music down. "How was your ride?"

"Great, you know, feels like I hit a new gear."

She laughed at my not-that-funny pun and turned back to weighing beans.

"We ended early after one of the riders crashed a few blocks away."

Harley wheeled back around. "Are they okay?"

"Noah's just scraped up, although he's getting checked out at the hospital. His head hit the ground pretty hard."

"Yikes."

I leaned against the table near Harley. "I have something we should talk about."

"Not another death or bike accident?"

"Thankfully, no. But Mark Jeffries approached me yesterday."

Harley's shoulders stiffened. "What'd that creep want?"

"To buy Ground Rules."

Harley whirled around again. "You're joking."

I held my hands out with the palms down in a calming gesture. "Mark asking doesn't mean we'd sell, Harley."

"But you think we should talk about it." Harley's shoulders were so tight they were basically up near her ears.

"Not in a 'should we consider this offer' way but in a 'you should be aware of this' way and also 'hey, if we're getting some good buzz, Mark might not be the only company that wants to acquire us.'"

"Do you want to sell?" Harley's voice was flat like she was trying to cover up the emotions roiling inside her.

I knew I needed to reassure Harley that I was in this for the long haul. "No. I'm still intent on Ground Rules world domination. But there might be a point when you'd like to do something else. Or a dollar amount where you'd want to cash out so you could start your own solo roastery." As long as we didn't sign a noncompete agreement as part of the sale. But it's not as if a small detail like this mattered in a hypothetical future. At least, not yet.

"After working with you, I wouldn't want to go solo. I'd have to handle the customers." Harley half-smiled. "I like being able to focus on the quality control side."

"You create the product that makes us special," I said.

"But you can convince anyone to try our beans to start with."

"So you're saying we're happy working together," I said.

Harley's shoulders relaxed back into their usual spot. Crisis averted.

But then she stiffened. "What about your uncle? Would he want to cash out?"

"As long as we're profitable, I think he'll leave the decision up to us." But this was something I should talk to my Uncle Jimmy about to make sure we were all on the same page. "There's one other thing we should discuss."

"What?"

"You saw how I responded to Mark tweeting something negative about us, and I think I managed to spin it around. You know, the promo I created?" I showed her Mark's social media posts about our coffee being deadly, to remind her.

She shook her head. "He's so . . ."

"Extra."

"Exactly."

A knock at the door to the roastery made me jump, and then the door slowly opened.

"Is it okay to come in?" a deep voice asked. A head poked in. Detective Will.

"Sure, come on in," I said. The sight of the detective made the exhausted feeling, like my body was filled with lead, fill me again.

The detective walked in and eyed the coffee roaster before his gaze snapped back to me. "Would you care to explain your text?"

"Would you like a cup of coffee while I talk?"

"Sure," he said.

I blinked in surprise. We must not be suspects, or he thought we were smart enough not to poison him.

Or he'd watch to make sure I took a sip of coffee first, like an old-school cupbearer who'd taste the wine to prove it was safe before the king drank.

As I set up the French press, Harley said, "I'll take care of that," so I sat down at our four-seat table with Detective Will and told him about the ride and Noah's crash.

"I'm not an expert, but I know basic bike mechanics. His brakes were sliced."

"You don't think that could've happened while he was riding?" Detective Will leaned back in his seat and gave me his "I'm analyzing you" look.

"Not while he was going straight and didn't ride over a machete."

Harley brought over two cups of coffee, a half-and-half carafe, and a caddy of sugar packets. Detective Will picked up a cup without adding anything and took a sip.

Of course the no-nonsense detective drank his java black. Although I would've appreciated it if he'd been a four-sugars-and-cream person.

"Do you know where Noah keeps his bike?" His eyes strayed over to my bike, leaned up against the wall.

My coffee cup was warm in my hands. "You know the bike racks in the internal hallway? I've always seen Noah leave his bike there."

"Are those assigned spots?"

I shook my head. "First come, first serve. Some people on their way to the gym leave their bikes there, too."

"Is there anything distinctive about his bicycle?"

I leaned back in my chair and brought Noah's bike to mind. "Not that I can think of. It's blue, and while it's a good brand, it's not exclusive. I'd note a Vanilla bike or something difficult to find."

"Vanilla bikes?"

I explained how the Vanilla Workshop is a local bespoke bicycle manufacturer. "People sometimes wait several years for their bicycle, although they also offer less customized, but still fancy bikes—Speedwagen—with a shorter wait."

"So people are obsessed with their bicycles."

"Some people are passionate about their rides," I agreed. "But then there are moderately serious cyclists like Noah who bought a nice bike, but it's not custom. You'd probably find other cyclists in Portland with the exact same bike. I don't think he'd added any decals, but I've never looked. I didn't notice anything when I checked the bicycle for other signs of tampering."

"Is it hard to slice someone's brakes?"

"As long as you have a sharp knife, no, it's not hard. At least, I don't think it is. I've never tried."

"Let's be clear: Why do you think this is something I should be interested in, specifically?" The detective's eyes bored into me again.

"As I said in my text: Noah works closely with Robbie. It could be chance. Maybe someone just chose a bike at random to vandalize. The door from the street to the hallway isn't locked during the hours the gym is open, which is something like five a.m. to nine p.m., so almost anyone has access. But since a coworker from his group died two days ago, I thought you'd like to know."

"Good instincts," he said. "I hope those same instincts keep you away from everyone in that studio until this is resolved."

"I'm still working there a few hours a week. Although that should be winding down soon, most likely by Halloween."

Detective Will shook his head. "You should end it now. I don't trust anyone there, including the guy who runs it."

Was the detective talking about Bax?

Detective Will drained his coffee cup and put it down on the table. "Thanks for the coffee; it was excellent. You guys should sell it or something."

Will wonders never cease? The detective made a joke.

And he'd warned me about my boyfriend.

After the door shut behind Detective Will, I turned to Harley. "Has he asked you about the video footage from the day Robbie died?"

"I still can't believe you spied on me." Harley looked over her shoulder at me from her spot, filling bags of coffee beans.

"Less spying and more trying to get our ducks in a row in case we're pulled into a wrongful-death suit," I said. Harley grimaced at my words.

"Do you really think we could get sued?" she asked. She turned away from her task and looked at me with her arms folded over her chest.

"Someone died in our roastery. Like I said, it's possible, but I don't know if it's probable." I didn't tell my business partner it also gave me an excuse to stick my nose where it probably didn't belong.

"That'd just be dandy. Robbie sticking it to us one final time from beyond the grave."

The bitterness in Harley's voice didn't feel like her. "I still can't believe you didn't tell me about Robbie being a jerk to you."

"It was little biting comments, and it had just started getting annoying. But compared to my older sisters, Robbie's comments were like little droplets of rain, easy to flick off. My sisters prefer to go for the jugular when they're mad. But they're like you if someone outside the family criticizes me."

"Is there a secret reason you didn't tell me? I would've told her to stay away." Or face my wrath. Which I'm sure would've left her quaking in her designer sneakers.

"I know that. You've stood up for me before. I know you have my back when it counts. But it would have made your video-capture gig awkward, and it wasn't anything I couldn't handle," Harley said. "Plus, you seemed to like her."

"Honestly, I never warmed to her. But it wasn't until the day she died that I realized some of her pranks were mean," I said.

"Of course, Robbie was nice to you. Everyone thinks you're adorable."

Ouch. And it wasn't true. I stared at my business partner.

"That's mean of me," Harley said.

"Plenty of people hate me."

"Sometimes I feel guilty that I'm jealous because you're so much better with people than I am."

"But I don't have your roasting skills."

"You might be able to learn, though. I keep trying, but I'm always awkward."

I shook my head. "No one cares. We like you for who you are."

"Is that a royal 'we'?" Harley half-smiled, but it felt like her mood had started to lighten.

"I meant 'we' as in the people who know and love you. But sure, feel free to curtsey when you see me."

Harley laughed.

We talked for a while, and we'd regained our normal equilibrium. Although Robbie's death threatened to linger over Ground Rules, and our future, leaving us in her perpetual shadow.

Chapter 13

Grumpy Sasquatch Studio felt subdued. I glanced into the room Noah shared, and his desk was empty.

But Kat was at her desk, and she waved me over.

"Did you hear? The trailer for the video game is done," Kat said. "Along with the opening segment the first time the player launches the game. I don't know if these are final yet."

Nerves flickered through me. What if everyone hated the trailer? And hated me as the main character? Bax saw me as the character's inspiration and wanted that to come through, but I knew he should've hired a professional.

"No, I'm sure gamers will fall in love with this trailer," Kat said. "We still have a least a year's worth of production work to make them playable, maybe longer, so I don't know when this will be posted online."

"So I have time to freak out."

"No need to freak out. Here, watch the opening segment. It's fantastic," Kat said.

She handed me a pair of over-the-ear headphones, and once I'd settled them on my head, she pushed play on the opening for *Falling Through the Shadows*. I watched the video game version of myself staring out from the computer screen.

The character looked like me but also didn't. The character was taller, and while it wasn't as extreme as some games, she was bustier than me, with lean hips. Her lips were fuller, and her eyes took up more real estate in her face. Her white-blond hair had red tips, and she rocked a leather jacket over jeans and chunky motorcycle boots. But something about her reflected me. I wondered if this was how Bax saw me or how he'd wanted me to look.

Video-game me turned from the camera and swung her leg over a cherry red motorcycle with angel wings painted on the sides. She spoke, and I heard my voice come through her lips. "One day, I woke up. I can't remember where I came from or who I used to be."

The woman rode a motorcycle down a highway alongside the ocean. The setting sun shone orange in the sky over the water, and sometimes the clouds and shadows looked like owls, ghosts, and a mix of images that ranged from dreamy to nightmarish. "But while there's a lot I don't remember, I do know one thing: I have a purpose. Something inside me draws me to people with problems only I can solve. And I have faith that, as I make the world a better place for everyone, I'll solve the biggest mystery of my life: who I am and what happened to me."

The character pulled up in front of a dive bar. "And I can smell dive bars," she said.

Okay, the dive bar reference was very on-brand for me.

I'd recorded the lines ages ago, along with about twenty pages of dialogue.

When she moved or spoke, I could see echoes of myself in her micro-expressions. It was like acting into a funhouse mirror and ending up with a video game.

I pulled the headphones off.

"And then, the user will be able to explore the bar and start solving the first mystery," Kat said. "It's fun. The user gets to walk around and talk to different people, including a leprechaun and a jackalope."

I laughed. "I'm so glad you worked a jackalope in," I said. I pictured the mythical Oregon hybrid of a jackrabbit and an antelope rumored to attack the shins of people who'd annoyed it.

Kat continued. "And when they've collected all of the clues, they can head back to their motorcycle and start investigating in town."

"What happens when they solve the mystery?"

"The fun part is that there are different solutions depending upon which clues you decide to follow. So you can take a couple of different paths with different plot lines as you make your way through the game. Each path ends up with a different final outcome, so users will have the incentive to come back and play the game again and again to find the different storylines."

"It sounds complicated."

"It is. The storyboarding behind it is intense. But I think this might be the best game Bax has ever come up with, and I was totally obsessed when *Dreamside Quest* came out," Kat said. She referred to the bestselling and award-winning game that had turned Bax and Lindsey's company into a small but mighty contender in the video game world.

"Did you work on it?" I asked.

"No, it came out when I was in college, and all I wanted to do was play the game, but I had finals to study for. And my parents would've disowned me if I'd failed school to play a video game. But it made me look into game programming when I finished my computer science degree. When I saw Grumpy Sasquatch was hiring, I almost didn't apply because I wanted to work here so badly and what if they laughed at me? Or I ended up hating them? But then I met Bax and Lindsey, and as you can see, it all worked out."

I caught a glimpse of the vulnerability Kat sometimes showed. The one that made me guess she didn't feel like she always fit in, like she was a half step off from everyone else. I felt the urge to tell her we all feel that way, at least part of the time. Or at least I do.

"I'm glad you're happy here," I said.

"Don't get me wrong. It hasn't always been . . . how's a good way to say it . . . smooth sailing? Some days remind me of making pelmeni with my mother when all I wanted to do was anything else."

"Pelmeni?" I asked.

"You know, dumplings. But I'd put my head down and get it done, even if it was boring, and she never made my brother or little sister help out. But it was okay in the long run because I had pelmeni to look forward to."

Kat's words of devotion rang true, but it made me wonder. If she thought her job here was under threat from Robbie, what would she have done to protect it?

"Is there anything I can do to help make things easier?" I asked. "I can always suggest something to Bax."

Kat smiled. "No, I have no complaints anymore, not really. Robbie was the bad apple, but now, it looks like the bushel is healthy again. Although . . ."

I looked at Kat as her voice trailed off. "Although what?"

"Something is not quite right. In a way, it feels like everyone can breathe again. But something is off. I can't really explain it in detail. It's just something I feel in here," Kat said, and patted just below her sternum.

I wasn't sure if she meant her heart or gut was telling her something, or maybe the two were combined into one powerful spidey-sense.

"Maybe it's because we all wonder what happened to Robbie," Kat said.

"Maybe."

"If this was a video game, we'd know how to keep playing to figure out what happened. But this is different. We need to figure out how to continue without following a preplanned script." Kat seemed to understand grief.

"Did you work with Robbie much?" If they'd worked together closely, Kat would feel Robbie's loss deeper than I would.

"Only a little. I do development, and Robbie was part of the de-sign organization, but in a group that works closely with development because she was a programmer, not an artist. But she wanted to get the project manager role. If she had been chosen, it would have meant I would've been a step under her on the org chart, but Noah was chosen instead."

I tried to visualize all of this in my brain.

"She sure was mad at Bax when he didn't promote her," Kat said.

"What's this?"

"You didn't hear? Robbie full-on screamed at Bax when she found out they'd promoted Noah."

"No, go back. They were up for the same position?" Was this the reason someone had targeted both Noah and Robbie? Had there been a third person up for the role who'd gotten jealous over being passed over?

"It's like this. Noah works in development with me, but he's been here longer. As I said, Robbie is part of the design group with Wyatt and Raoul, and others. What we do is complementary and managing our deliverables affects them, and vice versa. Without us, the game doesn't work, but without them, no one would want to play the game since they take the graphics and integrate it with our work, and it looks like a movie. Are you with me?"

"I think so."

"Robbie liked to see herself as their leader. But honestly, if anyone had been promoted from their area, it would've been Raoul. But he's happy with his current job. He says he does not like herding cats, which is silly, as most of his group are clearly Chihuahuas. When the old project manager announced she needed to resign, Bax and Lindsey took résumés from anyone who wanted to be the new project manager. They talked about hiring from outside. But they looked inside first."

"And they promoted Noah?"

"Exactly. And everyone seemed happy about that. Well, everyone except Robbie. She yelled at Bax that, of course, he'd promoted the white guy. She ignored that Noah's way more experienced than

she is. I mean, more than she was. And everyone loved the old project manager and was sad she and her husband were moving. So it's
not like Bax and Lindsey only hire or promote men."

Kat looked sad for a moment. "Plus Noah was already involved
on the deliverable side, and he's really calm and excels at the big-
picture stuff. He'll be a good project manager. Hopefully, things go
back to normal."

Maybe everything still felt a bit off in the office to Kat because of
guilt. Not necessarily the guilt that she'd killed Robbie, but, I suspected, the relief in knowing she never needed to deal with Robbie
again. I suspected Robbie had been cruel to Kat, but subtly. I'd ob-
served a few digs, and who knew what happened when no one else
had been around?

"Who else was up for the position?"

Kat lifted her shoulders in a slight shrug. "No idea. Bax and
Lindsey try to keep staffing changes like that private until it's official,
to not embarrass the people who weren't promoted. I only know because of Robbie's tantrum after the announcement."

And I wondered if the police had known about Robbie yelling at
Bax. Since Kat had heard, I expected there would be more witnesses.
While I knew there was no way my boyfriend would've hurt Rob-
bie, investigators would have questions and their own suspicions.

"Robbie sure was jealous of you," Kat said.

I quickly glanced at her. "What?"

"She had a thing for Bax, or at least, she once did. But he's never
looked at anyone in the office that way, from what I can tell. Even
one of the new hires, I can't remember her name, was clearly really
into him and kept dressing like she was going to a club instead of
here. We're more about substance than style here."

Wait, what new hire?

Kat continued. "And you're easy to like and never freak out on
anyone. I think Robbie wanted to be like you. But she was too intense. She pretended to be carefree, but she just wasn't."

In other words, Robbie had been too type A for the breezy
surfer girl façade she'd tried to pull off.

"What did you say about a new hire?"

Kat laughed. "I can't remember her name, but she was only here about four months before moving to LA. And that was maybe two years ago? Around when you opened next door, Bax was trying to find reasons to talk to you. She took a job working for an animation studio, I think. You would've loved her. She was hilarious."

Considering how warmly Kat spoke of other employees, something told me it had just been Robbie she'd had a beef with.

Wyatt showed up, and his hair was sticking up even more than usual. He looked at me. "Ready to film? We have a long list of dialogue to tackle."

"Let's get to it."

I followed Wyatt back into the motion-capture booth, set my bag in a cubby outside, and got ready to work.

Which meant I changed into the motion-capture suit in the privacy booth and then got down to business.

After filming with Wyatt, I glanced into Bax's office when I was heading out of the studio. He was engrossed with his eyes on his laptop and headphones over his ears, so I backed away. We'd chat later.

Lindsey waved at me as she walked my way toward her office, carrying a bottle of water. She'd adorned her purple water bottle with a *Dreamside Quest* decal.

"How was filming?" Lindsey asked.

"Good, we got right down to work."

"No pranks or silly stuff?" Lindsey leaned against the wall. I clocked the exhaustion in her eyes like she hadn't been sleeping well.

"Wyatt was ready to get down to work, and we finished in record time. Hey, have you heard anything about Noah?"

"From what he texted, the ER doctor is worried about Noah being a little weaker on one side than the other. He's getting a CT scan to rule out a serious head injury. But, unless something turns up there, he's okay."

"Fingers crossed."

"Yeah, the world doesn't need to lose Noah. He's a good guy."

Part of me wondered what Lindsey's unfiltered comments on Robbie had been, but I couldn't bring myself to ask. "Hey, can you send me the scavenger hunt photos from Tuesday? I'd like to make a timeline of where everyone was."

"Sure, but it's not like anyone here would hurt Robbie. Or had a key to your roastery."

"The same thing goes for Ground Rules."

Lindsey and I locked eyes, and the ambiance felt weird. She let out her breath in a whoosh.

"Gosh, I'm tired. I'll upload the photos to a folder for you when I have time," Lindsey said.

"Let me know if you need anything," I said and walked out.

Chapter 14

The next morning, after opening the cart and leaving it in Sophie's more than capable hands when the morning rush winded down, I headed to the roastery. I had some calls to make and distillery owners to finesse.

But first, I needed to check in on someone. I stopped by the roastery, brewed a fresh coffee batch, poured cups into two of my favorite mugs, and carried them next door.

Bax looked exhausted when I dropped a cup of coffee at his desk.

"As always, your timing is impeccable." His smile held a note of relief, like he was glad I'd shown up, and not just because I'd brought him coffee.

"This is our newest 'Taste the PNW' blend. Harley raves about its hazelnut, brown sugar, and berry notes," I said. "Tough morning?"

"Tough week, as you know. Can you hang around for a bit? Robbie's sister emailed. She's coming in to collect her sister's things. She'll be here any moment."

"And you'd like some moral support?" I took a sip of the coffee I'd brewed, my brain mentally cataloging the tasting notes. Instead of berry, we should say blackberry when we sell this blend to give it an NW vibe.

Flying from Australia to handle your sister's final details must be incredibly exhausting. The last time I'd flown home from the other side of the world, the jet lag had hit me like a ton of bricks, and I hadn't added grief to the equation. I asked, "Did Robbie's sister fly in from Australia?"

"She didn't say. Her email just said that she would drop by about ten a.m." Bax took a sip of the coffee. "Hmm, you said hazelnut, but I taste sparkle and rainbows."

"Goofball."

"Maybe I'm biased by the person who brewed it."

He reached and put his hand on my hip like he needed the connection. Then he stood and took my hand.

We walked out to the rarely used main door facing the sidewalk together, passing by some cubicles on the way. I saw quite a few people focused on their computer monitors with their heads down. Raoul's black dreads. Noah's buzzed sandy fuzz and Wyatt's perpetually spiky brown hair. The intern from the marketing department, Lila, gave Bax a shy smile as she carried a tray of pastries in her hands with her tablet precariously tucked under one arm.

"Noah's back?"

"We tried to get him to take the day off, and we'll insist he leaves by lunch. His CT scan came back clear, so that's a relief."

The studio's main entrance looks like a typical business, with a couch and coffee table in the small lobby and a receptionist's desk. It's rarely used, although I'd seen people sneak in and use the desk or the couch if they wanted a quiet spot.

A woman with glossy brown hair cut into a simple bob stood by the door to Grumpy Sasquatch Studio. She glanced at her phone and then at the logo on the door.

Wrangler Jeans. A blue flannel shirt that looked authentic versus hipster chic. Brown day hikers. Nothing about her felt flashy or memorable. She didn't feel anything like her sister.

She also didn't look like she'd hopped off a long series of flights to get to Portland, so maybe she'd arrived yesterday. Although she did feel sad, I could almost see the grief floating around her.

Bax opened the front door. "Ms. Stryger?"

I hadn't heard Bax sound quite so formal before. But Robbie's death was new ground for him and hadn't been something he'd planned on when launching his company.

"Please, call me Ivy." Her voice sounded as straightforward as her sense of style. "Are you Lukas Baxter?"

"Everyone calls me Bax." They shook hands.

Something about Ivy struck me as wrong. It wasn't just because she didn't feel anything like Robbie, although that was part of it. Ivy's eyes were a rich brown versus Robbie's green. Their face shape was similar, as was the almond shape of their eyes.

Wait a minute. Ivy's voice sounded wrong because of what I didn't hear.

Ivy sounded just like me. She had the same Pacific Northwest accent as Bax and my family. And I'd read that while Pacific Northwest English is close to the generic General America accent, it subtly has its own characteristics. I was so used to it that it didn't sound like anything to me, even though logically, I know everyone has an accent.

"You're from here, but your sister is Australian?" I asked. Then mentally kicked myself.

Ivy's smile was tinged in sorrow. "We both grew up in Wallowa County," she said. She referenced a remote, rural, and gorgeous county of less than eight thousand people in the far northeast corner of the state where Oregon meets Idaho and Washington. "Robbie was an exchange student in high school and came back with the accent. She thought it made her sound, I don't know, more unique than a small-town girl from the middle of nowhere."

"Do you still live there?"

"Yeah, I bought my parents' farm from them when they wanted to retire."

"Do you farm?"

"Sort of. I co-own an estate brewery and like to say I grow beer."

"You're a person after my own heart. I co-own a coffee company."

We chatted about how Ivy grew most of the ingredients she needed for her brewery. She specialized in saisons and Belgian-inspired brews. She also produced a few Pacific Northwest standard ales, like an award-winning IPA I'd seen at taprooms around town.

"We turned the old barn into a brewery and started canning our ales before it became cool. We can't grow everything we need, but that's easy to source. But our rhubarb golden beer won big at the last Oregon Beer Awards, and we grew the hops and rhubarb ourselves."

Robbie hadn't mentioned her sister was a big player in the Oregon beer scene, and it's the sort of thing she would've wanted to brag about. But if she had, she would've needed to admit she wasn't Australian.

What else had Robbie lied about? Then I realized the question was, at its heart, what had Robbie told the truth about? Because she'd lied to all of us repeatedly. I hadn't suspected Robbie wasn't Australian, but it wasn't something I'd really thought about. Although looking back, maybe this was why she sometimes felt off to me? Or perhaps I was seeing everything through a new lens.

"I need to visit my sister's apartment once her desk is cleared out," Ivy said. "Would it be too much to ask if someone came with me?"

The words sounded painful, like asking them hurt. Maybe because it meant Ivy's sister was going home for the final time.

Or maybe Ivy wasn't the type of person who liked to ask for help.

"If you can wait until after my meeting, I can go with you," I said.

"Sure."

"Elaine and I can help you clean out Robbie's desk while Sage has her fancy coffee roaster meeting." Bax looked like he wasn't sure what to do with his hands.

I half-smiled. "It's not fancy. But if you'd like a cup of coffee before you start, Ivy, let me know."

"I'd love one."

Bax and Ivy followed me next door, and I filled the gooseneck kettle with water, set it to boil, and then pulled out my favorite Kalita Wave filters.

"It smells great in here," Ivy said, and she closed her eyes like she was focusing on the scents. Then she opened her eyes, looked around again, and froze with her eyes on the roaster. "Wait, is that where . . . ?"

Her sentence ended abruptly like she couldn't get the words out.

"I'm so sorry. I didn't even think about that," I said.

"So that is where . . ."

"That's where we found Robbie."

Ivy walked over and stood by the roaster for a moment. I loaded beans into the grinder but waited for Ivy to turn after finishing her moment before flipping it on and filling the air with the sound of grinding beans, along with the familiar aroma.

We were silent as I brewed Ivy and Bax cups of coffee, but Ivy seemed to enjoy checking out the roastery as she glanced at the bags of beans degassing and our stash of beans for sale.

"Thank you," she said as they left.

Bax mouthed "Coffee Angel," and followed her.

I watched them go.

Robbie wasn't Australian. The hearty, over-the-top attitude had been an act, making me wonder how actual Australians would've reacted to her.

It also made me wonder what else Robbie had lied about.

After cleaning up the roastery's kitchen following my coffee-making session for Ivy, I set up everything we needed for the upcoming coffee cupping. I glanced around. Harley should be here, so I sent her a quick text. *Where U?*

I could have started on some paperwork, but instead, I sat down in the small, rarely used front entrance that faces the street. Like Bax's office next door, we'd furnished this space with a couple of club chairs facing the built-in reception desk. This was an excellent block of time to check the Ground Rules social media accounts.

I devote a few hours per week setting up a week's worth of content to post over time and then add spur-of-the-moment photos or quips if it feels right. Usually, at lunch and again at the end of the day, I also spend a few minutes checking our accounts in case anyone asked us a question or tagged us in something we should share with our followers.

One of my fellow business food cart owners from the Rail Yard had forwarded me a post from Left Coast Grinds, featuring a photo of a latte in one of their signature mugs with their logo on the side. *Drop by our shop for the best, freshest cups of joe in town, and you're unlikely to be a victim of a violent crime, unlike a certain coffee cart. Their body count is up to what, three?* And he'd included a *#rulesforgroundcoffee* tag.

Why had Mark decided to come after us again? And why now? Was it just because I'd turned down his offer?

I uploaded a rainbow-filtered photo of a mocha with a heart in the foam and the Ground Rules Cart in the background. The perfect words clicked into my mind, so I typed in *I've heard rumors about our coffee being fatal, but don't worry: you won't actually die and go to heaven; it just feels that way when you drink it.*

Tierney showed up at the front door not long after I'd posted the image across our platforms. So I unlocked it and ushered him inside, then relocked the door.

"My brother will be here soon," Tierney said. He looked around. "This was really the site of a violent crime?"

"I still have no idea what happened, or how, and why," I said. "It feels like a nightmare."

"I can't even imagine," Tierney said.

"Would you like a cup of coffee?"

"What do you got?"

"What do you want? We have, like, fifteen different ways to make coffee."

"Truth be told, I have simple tastes. I tend to go for a simple cup of black coffee."

"You're a man after my own heart. I'm a purist, although I do enjoy the occasional caffè latte."

He followed me into the roastery. Tierney glanced around again as I cracked out the same filter and kettle I'd used for Ivy for another pour-over of Taste the PNW. The roastery looked clean and smelled of coffee beans. It was like heaven if you're obsessed with java.

"I saw some tweets from Left Coast Grinds about Ground Rules," he said.

I kept my voice light. "Once upon a time, Harley and I worked at Left Coast Grinds."

Tierney's half smile made me think he'd guessed part of what I hadn't said. "It must be hard seeing former employees strike out on their own and become the scrappy up-and-coming competition."

My next words felt like an instinctive response to the undertone in Tierney's voice. "Truth be told, Mark has offered to buy Ground Rules, but we're not interested."

Tierney laughed. "So what's he trying to do, turn the court of public opinion against you? Does anyone really turn social media activism into real-life boycotts?"

"For big corporations, definitely," I said. "Or really egregious behavior."

"You know, we talked with Mark, and a few other local roasters, around the same time we first talked with you."

"Really." I wasn't surprised, but they hadn't told me they were interviewing other roasters.

"You seemed the most receptive and, frankly, enthusiastic. You felt like your business would be a partner, not just someone who dropped off some beans and didn't help with marketing. You have some experience bartending, right?"

"I spent part of my early twenties barbacking at the Tav and only did a little bartending."

"The Tav? I love that place. It's like old-school Portland."

"My uncle owns it," I said.

"Do you think he'd be open to hosting the launch party for our canned whiskey drinks?"

It was my turn to laugh. "Considering my uncle is a financial backer of Ground Rules, I'd guess yes. But I'll have to ask him. I can facilitate the discussion."

Tierney's eyes narrowed slightly, and then he smiled. "A financial backer?"

"Think silent partner who wants to make sure our accounting is up to snuff and helps problem-solving when asked. I'm fairly sure the money would've been my inheritance if he hadn't invested in Ground Rules." Not that I expected anything from my uncle. His help with my college education alone was priceless.

"I have this idea of holding launch events throughout the Pacific Northwest and in select areas countrywide."

"That's a great idea!" I said.

And then Tierney was off and running. His excitement was infectious, and I chimed in with a few ideas.

Something told me that, if you compared his distillery to Ground Rules, Tierney played a similar role to mine, while Shay was the resident Harley. Except with a brooding intensity on Shay's part instead of Harley's endless nervous energy.

A knock at the front door made me head back into the small entryway to let Shay into the roastery. Within a moment, I was setting up a coffee cupping for them. The friendly vibe between Tierney and me had shifted into a more brusque, businesslike feel with the addition of his brother. I set up a coffee cupping of our standards, Puddle Jumper and 12-Bridge Racer, along with our Concrete Blonde, Taste the PNW, and a single-origin from Guatemala.

To properly cup coffee, you freshly grind beans and then add nine grams of coffee grounds to a special bowl-like cup designed for cupping. We boil the water to a precise two hundred degrees Fahrenheit and then add one hundred fifty grams of water to each bowl. I encouraged Shay and Tierney to take in the aroma of the now wet grounds. After four minutes, I showed Tierney and Shay how to break the top crust of the bowls, using a clean spoon for each cup so we wouldn't cross-contaminate the samples.

"You're really serious about not cross-contaminating this?" Shay asked. I suspected he was testing me.

"Would you want to mix a shot of Laphroaig with a shot of Maker's Mark?" I asked. I referred to a Scotch brewed on the Island of Isley known for peaty smokiness, and a USA-made bourbon known for notes of caramel and vanilla and considered an excellent option at the price point.

Tierney laughed. "Good point."

I showed them how to use two spoons to scoop out the grounds from their cups. "We'll want to let these cool for a few more minutes so you can fully taste the various notes of each bean."

"What'll you do with the spent grounds?" Tierney asked, and motioned to the container we'd use to discard the grounds.

"Compost, although I've thought it'd be fun to use the used grounds in either a body scrub or coffee candles. But that's a different product, so I haven't done anything other than play around at home," I said. "But if you'd like to keep the grounds, did you know you can use them to deodorize your fridge? Coffee excels at soaking up the odors around them, which is why it's so important to keep your coffee bags sealed shut. But you can put dried used grounds in a jar and pop it into the back of your fridge. It'll help keep things smelling fresh inside unless you have something severely spoiled."

"Good to know." Tierney sounded like he was telling the truth.

"The coffee should be ready to sample now. You want it to spread over your tongue to taste the entire range of flavors of each blend. Be sure to really slurp the coffee. And note how the flavor profile will taste subtly different as it cools."

Tierney took me at my word and slurped loudly while Shay was quieter. They both had intense looks of concentration on their faces as they sampled the Concrete Blonde.

"This might be too light for the canned cocktail," Shay said. "Something darker might bring out the notes of our whiskey more."

"But this lighter flavor wouldn't overwhelm the whiskey," Tierney said.

"Let's keep tasting." Shay wrote down notes, then moved on to our medium Puddle Jumper.

"I love how everyone reacts differently to the coffee, depending upon their individual taste," I said.

"Whiskey is the same way. What one person finds bold and creative, another person finds boring. And don't get me started on peated whiskeys," Tierney said.

"The peat flavor comes from drying malt over peat fires, right?"

"Exactly! People tend to either love or hate the taste."

We'd discussed the merits of all five of the coffee options when Harley walked in. She seemed sedate, without the manic energy usually flowing through her and popping out regardless of whether or not it was the right time.

And she was several hours late. Usually, this wouldn't be a big deal, but we had a meeting.

"What'd I miss?" Harley asked.

"Not much," Tierney said. "Sage has been taking us through some of the options for the Irish whiskey drink. I think your Taste the PNW roast might be the winner."

When we finished sampling coffee, Tierney smiled at me. "I love everything Ground Rules makes."

"I'm glad to hear it."

"We'll let you know our decision soon, but you're definitely the front runners in my book."

I escorted the brothers out the front door, then walked back in. Harley stood, staring at the cups and everything we'd used and needed to clean up.

"What's going on with you?" I asked.

"At least I didn't blurt out during the business meeting that I'd been questioned by the police again."

"What's going on?"

"Detective Will showed up and asked me to go to the station. My first reaction was to call your brother, and he had me go to his friend's office. I came as soon as I was done. Hey, so I now have a defense attorney. Should I make T-shirts? Do you think they have coffee-roasting positions in jail?"

"I read the women's prison in Oregon has a coffee cart and gives inmates barista training." Amusingly, the prison was named Coffee Creek.

Harley looked at me in shock.

"Sorry, that wasn't the right time to break out that factoid. I know being a murder suspect feels horrible, especially when it feels like you're going to be arrested for something you didn't do." Not being a murder suspect almost felt weird this time around, even if it was almost a relief. But we needed to figure out what happened to Robbie for all of our sakes.

"I feel helpless."

"Listen, I need to take care of something. Let's talk later." And maybe this task would shed light on what happened to Robbie.

Chapter 15

Like so many of the new apartments that had sprung up in Portland, Robbie's east side apartment along a bustling street felt like a modern take on a shoebox. One wall of the living room was a galley kitchen. The limited counter space was spotless, with just an empty dish drainer next to the sink and a stainless steel teakettle.

As I put down the stack of boxes ready to be assembled that I'd carried up, I glanced around again. There wasn't space in the room for a full-sized couch, which Robbie hadn't even tried to work in. Her computer setup dominated the room. Three screens were mounted on the wall over her metal desk, and her silver gaming chair had a race-car feel. The small white library cart tucked under the desk held a couple of controllers, keyboards, and a grid notebook. A teal velvet love seat and small coffee table were tucked in the corner, like a touch of whimsy in an industrial warehouse. A plate with a fork on top, the remnants of what looked like egg yolk, and a half-full water glass sat on the table. Like Robbie ate her meals there.

Given the general air of cleanliness in her apartment, I bet Robbie planned on cleaning up the breakfast plate when she returned home from work. But she'd never returned.

The walls were bare, with no artwork or photographs other than a single postcard from Sydney, Australia, propped up on the windowsill. I picked it up and noted the yellowing around the corners. The address on the back showed it had been sent to Robbie at Oregon State University, and the message was simple. *Miss you, Boo,* and it was signed *Rebecca.*

I walked down the hallway and peeked into the open door of the bathroom. Her teal bathroom towels matched the rug in the middle of the tiled floor and a shelf with neatly lined up skin and hair care bottles. I recognized the brand of the leave-in conditioner; everything they sold had a beach theme, and it looked like she had everything they made. Her makeup in a light plastic bin also had a surfer-girl vibe.

Hmm. I wondered if Robbie had taken a California surfer girl persona when she'd visited Australia.

At the end of the short hallway, her bedroom felt like it belonged to another person, one who'd spent a lot of time browsing the intersection of romantic and whimsical furniture on Pinterest. The faded white iron bed frame looked like a modern take on a vintage concept, as did the vanity and matching bedside tables. The yellow-and-pink quilt on her bed looked handmade by an expert.

"My grandmother made this for her," Ivy said softly, and touched the yellow star pattern on the bed's quilt. "I'm glad she kept a reminder of her past."

"It's lovely."

"My grandmother sold quilts in a local shop. 'Talented' is an understatement," Ivy said. "Do you have any ideas on what I should do with the furniture? It's lovely, but I don't need it."

"I can recommend a couple of resale shops. Or a charity that helps out single mothers setting up households after fleeing abusive situations."

"The charity sounds easiest, and it'd do some good," Ivy said.

"I'll text you their name."

Ivy walked into Robbie's bedroom and slowly sat on the bed. She looked around while one hand patted the quilt beneath her. "My poor sister never knew who she wanted to be. I didn't even recognize her the last time I saw her. She even changed her eye color."

I turned and looked at her. Ivy's face was downcast.

"What's this about her eye color?" I asked.

Ivy looked up and made eye contact with me. "Robbie had brown eyes like everyone else in the family. But she started wearing green contact lenses when she was in college."

I remember Robbie holding her eye the day of the team builder. I'd thought it was a generic contact lens issue, but maybe she'd been trying to make sure no one knew about her natural eye color.

"I'm not fully sure why Robbie felt the need to change everything about herself. Our parents always supported Robbie with everything she wanted to do. They paid for her to be an exchange student in high school. They paid for our college as long as we went to a state university. But nothing was ever enough for Robbie."

Ivy pulled out her phone and opened up a picture. "This is one of my favorite photos of us together." She handed it over. "It was my mother's birthday, and to celebrate, she hired a photographer to come out and take photos of the family at the ranch. Robbie was fifteen."

The sisters stood together. Ivy looked like a younger version of herself, with the same steady gaze. Although her hair was longer, just brushing the shoulders of her dark green dress.

Robbie's brown hair was lighter than her sister's and not as glossy, without the blond highlights she'd worn when I knew her. Her green dress matched Ivy's. And her eyes were a medium brown. She was sturdier than the Robbie I'd known, but she looked healthy.

Ivy tapped the screen to scroll to the next photo. "The rest of our relatives came over, too. My mother had decided we should be color-coded by family."

An elderly couple sat on a hay bale in the very center of the photo. Ivy, Robbie, and her family stood to one side. The family on the other side of the couple—two girls younger than Ivy, two teenage boys, a man, and a woman holding a baby—were all in navy. It looked staged but fun. It felt like the sort of family most people dreamed of having. The kind of family that probably threw homemade Christmas dinners and made snowmen during the winter.

But appearances can be deceiving. And sometimes, when your role in a family is defined, it can be hard to break out of the mold.

"Where are all of your cousins now?"

"Both of the teenage boys in the photo went into the Marines. One of the girls is a student at the University of Oregon. The other girl lives in Joseph and works at a coffee shop, but she's pregnant, so we'll see how long that lasts. The baby is in high school, which I can't believe. Life changes so fast."

"It looks beautiful. I'm surprised Robbie wasn't proud to grow up there."

"She acted like it was embarrassing. She told me once that she wanted to immigrate to Australia. She hoped her tech background would open some doors. After a few years working here in Portland, she'd be valuable enough for a company to sponsor to get whatever the Australian version of a green card is. And she was socking away money to make it happen."

Ivy looked down at the quilt again. "When she wanted to, my sister could move mountains," she said.

"I'm surprised she became a programmer," I said. Wait, socking away money? I thought of the way Robbie had always dressed on-trend. She'd favored a couple of stores that weren't cheap. That said, they weren't high-end couture, either. But maybe she'd been a thrift-store shopper or had saved money in other ways.

"Robbie always excelled at math. She dreamed of being an actor and tried out for school plays but kept getting invited to be a stage manager." Ivy shook her head fondly. "She decided to go the video game route 'cause she thought they were hip. And she enjoyed playing them and thought she'd be cooler than most people in the industry."

Part of my mind snorted. Some of the sasquatches were the most interesting people I've ever met. Lindsey is one of the coolest women on the planet. And Bax is in a league of his own.

But I'd heard horror stories from Lindsey about sexism in the in-dustry and how she and Bax were focused on making sure their company was inclusive. Lindsey had told me that while work can never be a safe space, it can be free of jerks and racists.

Yet Robbie had been a complicated person.

"Let's get started in the living room," Ivy said. "You know, this place makes me feel claustrophobic. I can't imagine living here, but I'm used to seeing mountains from my front porch."

Even if her end goal had been Australia, I wondered why Robbie had stayed in Oregon. She ran a higher risk of someone finding out the truth about her small hometown.

Oregon, though, is the most affordable of the West Coast places, which led to some of the famed California tech companies opening up offices in Portland, so maybe that was why.

After a quick discussion, I boxed up the food in the kitchen while Ivy started packing the dishes. There wasn't much. A box of Portland Breakfast tea from a local teamaker, a store-brand box of mint tea, and a green tea. A half-empty bag of steel-cut oats from Bob's Red Mill, another local favorite. The fridge showed a similar sensibility, with half of a block of Tillamook Cheddar, an opened bag of baby carrots, two bags of ready-made salad, a large container of nonfat plain Greek yogurt, an almost empty carton of eggs, and a quart of nonfat milk. I dumped the food into the compost bin and cleaned out the containers for recycling. Maybe she'd relied on takeout. Or, considering Robbie's physical changes from Ivy's photos, perhaps she'd kept strict control over everything she ate. My doctor had told me once about everyone having their own unique set point for weight, and something told me Robbie had fought hers. Even though she'd been beautiful before.

At least she'd supported local companies. I'd halfway expected all Australian imports. And a big jar of Vegemite. But she didn't even have a package of Tim Tams.

Once I'd finished the groceries, I started picking up the small items in Robbie's living room. The grid notebook called to me, and I flipped it open. An index card fell out.

I scanned it. The card listed multiple user names and passwords, plus a couple of Gmail accounts for user names that were nothing like

Robbie's. I frowned at it. Had I found Robbie's list of sock-puppet accounts? A glance at Ivy told me she was engrossed with packing up a set of coffee cups. I took a photo of the crib sheet, tucked it under the front cover of the grid notebook, and then opened it.

Robbie had kept a running to-do list with items crossed out. Most of it was mundane. *Buy groceries. Plan Lindsey's birthday surprise. !!!!*

What was the "!!!!"? Did Robbie have a prank she hadn't had the chance to pull off?

One page listed the steps for moving to Australia. It looked like Robbie had submitted her paperwork for a visa just last week. Sorrow filled me again. Robbie must've been close to realizing her dream, and she didn't deserve what had happened.

"Are you sure you'll be fine?" I asked Ivy. I'd already bagged up all of the opened products in the bathroom, with one bag ready for recycling and the other destined for the garbage cans outside. I'd put anything unused into a separate box for donating.

"I'm sure. Thanks for coming with me. I'm glad I didn't walk in alone."

I could tell from Ivy's face that she needed to be alone. Being in her sister's apartment must bring up a whole secondary level of grief.

"Text or call if you need anything. And I'll get you info on the charities I mentioned."

I heard Ivy lock the door behind me as I left.

As I walked out of the apartment building, I came face-to-face with Detective Will.

"What are you doing here?" he asked.

"I accompanied Robbie's sister, Ivy, to Robbie's apartment. I metaphorically held her sister's hand," I said. "Ivy's still inside."

Detective Will studied me like he was trying to lock in on the truth under my words. I held his gaze.

"You knew the victim better than I ever will," said Detective Will. "Did you notice anything that struck you as weird in the apartment?"

"Good question. Let me think about it."

Aspects of the apartment had felt like the Robbie I knew, but parts felt like a different person.

"Robbie had a lot of facets, and quite a few were fool's gold," I said. "She was smart, but so much of her persona was a façade. Like the fake Australian accent. It's hard to get a handle on who she was versus who she wanted to be."

We all have those shades of self. The sides we try to keep hidden. Robbie had taken everything to an extreme.

Which might be the truest description of her anyone could give. She was always the extreme. She always wanted to be the best. The most noticed; the star in the limelight that everyone else orbited around. But her strengths—like math and coding—weren't the sort of easy-to-showcase traits that led to social media likes.

A few thoughts clicked into place.

"I don't know if Robbie even knew who her real self was," I said. Which might be the saddest thing I'd ever heard. She never knew who she wanted to be, and now she'd never have the chance to figure herself out. Maybe she would've figured it out someday. And even if she hadn't, that was her business. She'd deserved her shot at life like we all do.

"Can you explain that?"

I told Detective Will about how Robbie had changed everything about herself—accent, hair color, eye color, and her origin story. Something flickered in his eyes.

"You knew she wasn't Australian," I said.

"I knew she had an American passport," the detective said. "An accent isn't proof of citizenship. Look at the Dreamers."

"But back to your main point. Robbie's house reminded me of her: a clash of tech with a surfer vibe and a bit of hidden romanticism." The bedroom decor probably showed the dreamer side of Robbie. "The only thing I didn't expect was the list of passwords saved in the notebook on her desk."

"You left the passwords, right?"

"Yes, they're still there." I didn't mention I'd photographed them before sliding the card back into place.

"And I don't need to lecture you about hacking into other people's accounts?"

"Would it be hacking if I had the passwords?" I asked. His eyes narrowed at me like he was trying to determine if my words were in earnest. He was treating me differently from the last time I'd gotten tangled up in one of his cases, but part of me wondered if he was playing me, going for a good-cop sort of vibe. "For real, I'll leave it up to you to invade what's left of her privacy."

He shook his head at me and started to walk into the apartment building.

"Detective," I said. "Was Robbie murdered? Could it have been a weird accident?"

He paused and looked at me. "Are you sure you were with Lukas Baxter during the whole afternoon?"

The detective couldn't seriously suspect Bax, could he?

"Bax and I were together for all but a few minutes, like when one of us went to the bathroom." If I'd known, I could've followed him around everywhere, like Kaldi when it's dinnertime.

"You didn't get sidetracked and lose sight of each other?"

"We were working together on the scavenger hunt. Kat was with us, except for a while at the patisserie, so you don't have to take my word for it."

Wait, how long had Kat been gone? She'd disappeared for a while.

Detective Will stared at me with his inscrutable look. "Mr. Baxter was with you the entire time?"

"Yes, except for a couple of short bathroom breaks. Bax never had enough time to walk to the roastery and come back."

Detective Will's face was unreadable. "See you around," he said. He walked into the building, and I stood in the front doorway, wishing there was something I could do to fix this.

I'm sure, if she wasn't beyond such petty concerns, Robbie would feel mortified to know her secrets were coming to light. And I had to wonder if there was a secret that had caused everything to come tumbling down somewhere in that house of cards she lived in.

Did Detective Will honestly suspect Bax? Had he heard about their argument over Robbie not getting the promotion she'd wanted?

And Kat had disappeared for a little while. Could it have been long enough to go back to the building, get into an argument with Robbie, and return like nothing had happened?

And how would they have gotten into the Ground Rules Roastery? Bax didn't have a key. Although he was on the list of people I'd trust with one. But he didn't have a reason to need one.

Bax did have access to my keys, but it wasn't like he would've swiped them to make a copy.

Something told me the next few days would be a roller coaster of bad news.

Chapter 16

Robbie's apartment was across the river from downtown. Thankfully, it wasn't too far from the bike boulevard on SE Ankeny Street, so I headed down it in the direction of the Willamette River. The local bike boulevards aren't bicycle exclusive, but they're prioritized for bikes and parallel major roads and have minimal stop signs.

Leaves were starting to fall, and the sidewalk was covered with orange and yellow as I zoomed downtown. I crossed the river, navigated downtown, and took my bicycle up to Jackson's office since I knew he wouldn't mind if I parked it in his lobby.

Jackson's practice focuses on child advocacy. His office isn't fancy, even though he rents space in a building seeped with faded art deco charm and the world's slowest elevator. But it's always clean, and Jackson keeps the kitchen well-stocked with snacks sure to help break the ice with his young clients.

His part-time assistant wasn't in the reception room of the office when I arrived. I left my bicycle next to a gold velour couch Jackson had found at a resale shop that he claimed matched the ambiance of the building. It did echo the building's faded glamour. A bookcase stuffed full of board games and children's books lined one wall, and the low table was perfect for coloring.

When I stood in the doorway of Jackson's inner office, he held up a finger to tell me to wait, then turned his gaze back to his laptop.

Since I had a moment, I checked Ground Rules's social media accounts. I had plenty of laughing emojis in reaction to my "heavenly" coffee joke.

And someone with a user name from a local alt weekly paper said he wanted to talk to me. The last thing I wanted was to speak to the media about Robbie's death, so I deleted his comment.

"I'm ready." Jackson stood from his desk, and I noted he was dressed down in olive khakis and a black sweater versus the suit he wears if he's going to court. And I knew he had a spare suit stashed in the corner of his office in case of an unexpected need to head to the courthouse. The emergency cases are always some of the hardest emotionally on my brother, although he tries to stay stoic.

"Busy day?" I asked as he pulled on his waxed canvas jacket.

"Not too bad, to be honest. Manageable."

We left the office, took the stairs, and walked to the food-cart pod a few blocks from Jackson's law office that has a row of fantastic carts lined up on the edge of a parking lot. Jackson went with a Czech-inspired pork schnitzel sandwich served on fresh ciabatta. I ordered drunken noodles, extra spicy, from a Thai cart.

Once we had our food, we found an open picnic bench nearby.

"So, what's up?" I asked as I popped open my container and unrolled my fork from a white napkin.

Jackson unwrapped his sandwich. "I wanted to let you know that Piper is moving in."

Internally, I pumped my fist in the air and danced a few steps. But my body was otherwise still as I asked, "Are you going to make it official?"

"If you're asking if we're engaged, no, not yet. We're going to see how living together goes first."

"I'm happy for you. Bentley is going to have a mom!" I joked.

"That would cast you as his . . . pesky older sister?"

"Cool aunt, obviously, as you're not my dad." Even though Jackson sometimes tries to act like he hasn't received that particular memo. But he had spent time as a college and graduate student working as basically my babysitter when my dad worked late, including nights.

"I also wanted to let you know that you don't have to move out when Piper moves in. We wouldn't ask you to leave even if you were around full-time. There's room for all of us. So don't feel like you need to rush out and find a new place to live."

"Picture this: you, thirty years from now, still living in the house you inherited from your grandparents with Piper, me, and a couple of dogs."

Jackson laughed. "There are worse futures. Will Bax still come over and play video games?"

"You could arrange playdates."

We ate in silence for a moment.

Jackson broke our comfortable silence. "Do you have any plans about where you're planning to live in the near term?"

"No, I hadn't planned on making any changes. But if you were just being kind and would like the house to yourselves, I can figure something out."

"No, I was serious about you being welcome to live there for the rest of your life. But I also wondered if you were debating taking things to the next level, so to speak, in your own personal life."

"Well, he hasn't asked me to move in, and I don't want to force anything."

Jackson half-smiled like he knew something I didn't. Or at least thought he did. So I asked one of the questions I always wondered.

"Is it awkward to date someone on the other side of the aisle, legally?"

"You make it sound like I'm a criminal," Jackson said.

"Well, you are assigned to adjudicate cases as a public defender in juvenile court."

"Look at you, throwing out terms like 'adjudicate.'"

"Hey, I've picked up some of your lingo. Like how kids commit delinquent offenses, not crimes. And if they're found to have committed an offense, after adjudication, they go to a dispositional hearing to find out what treatment, service, or placement the judge feels is in the child's best interest."

Jackson smiled as he shook his head. "You know, you could've followed me to law school."

"I'll guess my question is a sore spot. That's why you didn't answer." Piper was a federal prosecutor, so I knew they were unlikely to face each other in court.

"It helps that Piper specializes in white-collar crime. But it was awkward when she was indicted—one of the biggest donors to the Youth Justice Fund," Jackson said. He referred to one of the nonprofits he partnered with.

"Wait, did that really happen?"

"It's ongoing. It's one of the topics we don't talk about. But it shows people are complicated. Someone can commit while-collar fraud while seeing the value in supporting kids who need help."

My brother's phone beeped.

"Speak of the man. It's Bax," Jackson said. He answered his phone. "What's up? Sage and I are just finishing a late lunch."

Jackson's posture suddenly tightened.

"And you're on your way to the police station now? Haven't you learned anything from me?"

Jackson closed his eyes for a moment.

"Good, you're not in a squad car. Tell them to meet you at my office. I'll text the address. They can question you there."

My heart started to pound. Did the police want to arrest Bax?

Jackson turned and faced me. "Bax wants to know if you can pick Niko up from school. Bax is supposed to because Laurel has a meeting, and she's supposed to pick Niko up this evening."

"Yes, I can." Niko's mother, Laurel, and Bax had added me as an approved adult to pick up Niko from school, although I'd never needed to.

"Don't say anything until I get there. I'm on my way."

Jackson slid his phone back into his pocket.

"Was Bax arrested?" I asked. Surely not, if he could switch to holding the meeting at Jackson's office instead of one of the local police stations.

"No, but they want to question him further. Why would the police think Bax killed Robbie?" Jackson had slid into his blunt lawyer mode. Focusing on the facts helped the nerves inside me settle.

"First off, Bax was with me all day, so he couldn't have. As far as reasons, I didn't witness it, but Bax and Robbie did have a loud argument at work. She was up for a promotion, but someone else got it."

"Anything else? Did they have a personal relationship outside of work?"

"Not that I know of." If Bax had spent time with Robbie without me knowing, he'd done an excellent job of hiding it.

"Okay. I'm off to my office. I'll call when I know anything, but don't worry."

Jackson strode off, but I kept alongside him.

"What?" he asked but didn't slow down.

"My bike is in your office."

"Keep up, then."

Even though I wanted to wait to hear about Bax, I headed across town since I didn't want to be late picking up Niko.

Niko's elementary school is in close-in Eastside Portland, not too far from Jackson's house, a school known for parental involvement. The parents even fund a chef to cook fresh lunches. The kids grow some of their produce in their meals in the school gardens and sometimes help prepare food in age-appropriate cooking classes. It's in a bike-friendly neighborhood, and I wasn't the only parent rolling up on two wheels. Bax and Niko usually bike together. I joined them a few times, amazed at Niko's ability to chatter while cycling.

I was a few minutes early, so as I waited outside as a crowd of parents slowly grew, I texted Niko's mother, Laurel. *Long story, but I'm picking the kid up today.*

I noticed a group of women, presumably moms, eyeing me speculatively. I wondered how they reacted to Bax when he picked up Niko.

On the street, cars started lining up on the curve. Most of the drivers followed the arrows around the school that directed traffic like a chaotic ballet. But a few cars drove the wrong way down the street, and when one stopped, the parents yelled at it to keep moving.

My phone beeped. Laurel. *Thanks for letting me know! I knew there was a reason we put you on the list!* ☺

One of the moms from the group sidled up to me, bringing along a scent of hairspray and vanilla lotion. "Did you just move here? Do you have a new kid in school?"

She must be the designated welcoming committee, provided "welcoming" meant "pump the potential new mom for information."

Niko zipped up to me with a woman holding a clipboard in his wake. "Sage!"

"Your dad had an unexpected meeting, so I agreed to pick you up."

"Hi, and you are . . . ?" The woman caught up. She looked skeptical, which I assumed was good since she didn't know me.

"This is Sage. She's picking me up today!"

"I'm on his official pickup list," I said.

"Can I see your ID?"

"I can promise she's not using a fake license!" Niko bounced beside me. If someone could harness the kid's energy, they'd be able to power all of Portland.

I handed over my driver's license.

"Niko's talked about you before. If he hadn't, I would've guessed you were Laurel's younger sister," the teacher said. She scanned a sheet on her clipboard. "There you are. Niko, you're free to go."

She handed my ID back, and I barely stopped myself from asking what Niko had said. Her comment about Laurel and me looking like sisters slightly hit home since it's the truth. Except Laurel's taller and absolutely gorgeous.

"Once, I told my class about how we hiked on Mt. Hood and I put my sandwich down, and ants crawled on it," Niko said.

The thought of Niko talking about me to his class made me feel a bit warm and slightly terrified.

"I'll see you tomorrow, Niko," the teacher said before leaving.

As I attached Niko's backpack to my bike's rear rack with a bungee cord, he told me about his art class. "And then, Alex dropped a whole jar of red paint on his shoes!"

"So now he's the walking red?" I said.

Niko paused, then shook his head. "I don't get it."

"I can explain it as we walk home," I said.

Niko's steps were jaunty as he walked alongside me and my bicycle and I explained there was a TV show called *The Walking Dead*, which he thought sounded cool. "Can we detour to the cake store?" he asked out of the blue.

The cake store, aka the dessert and espresso shop in the middle of Jackson's neighborhood, had turned into Niko's favorite spot when he'd discovered its existence.

"We could get a samosa or something," Niko added, reminding me the store had more savory items than desserts, defying the word "dessert" in their name.

"Or we could bake something for your dad, and you can take some home for your mom," I said.

"Can we make brownies?" Niko asked.

"Sure, I think we have all the ingredients," I said. Baking would be an excellent way to not focus on the stress of the day and the work things I should be doing. And, more importantly, fear over what was happening downtown.

"Look: rhino!" Niko pointed to where a plastic rhinoceros was tied up to a horse ring alongside the sidewalk. The city of Portland had preserved the historic horse rings and even added new ones when fresh sidewalks were poured. All were a throwback to when people used horse-drawn carriages to transverse the city. Thanks to the Portland Horse Project and its fun social media outreach, locals tethered plastic horses to the rings, plus the occasional dinosaur, unicorn, tiger, or other animals, including rhinos. Rumor had it that at least one couple met and was married due to the horse rings. It definitely fits the "Keep Portland Weird" narrative.

Niko chatted to me about his day over the twenty minutes it took to walk to Bax's house.

Kaldi met us at the door with a trill, then followed us to supervise. Niko continued talking as I cut up an apple as a snack, adding a tablespoon of peanut butter to the side of the plate before handing it over. The kitchen was quiet for a few minutes, but the chatter started back up as we made brownies.

Kaldi sat on a dining room chair, watching us intently. Presumably, making sure we didn't drop any chicken or other deliciousness.

"And then, Abby said Alex was dumb, but really she was just mad that he'd gotten red paint on her smock," Niko said. The paint debacle was a huge deal in his world.

Niko carefully stirred the brownie batter. "Is this ready to go in the pan? You said not to stir it too long so the flour wouldn't form protein bonds."

"That's right," I said. Niko's words reminded me of how much of a sponge he was. He heard everything.

After Niko poured the batter into the waiting pan and I put it in the oven, he headed into the living room for his reading homework. Which involved him pulling his beloved beanbag chair out into the living room from his room and nesting inside. Kaldi quickly joined him and helped him study by purring loudly. Niko intently read a graphic novel, and then later told me everything that happened.

Niko supervised when the timer on my phone dinged, and I tested to see if the brownies were done, then set them on the stove to cool.

My phone finally dinged with a message from Bax. *On my way home now.*

See you soon, I typed back.

A knock on the door made me jump. Niko perked up from his beloved beanbag chair on the living room floor and raced me to the door. He glanced through the window next to the door, then un-latched the door and threw it open.

"Mom!"

Laurel stood on the front porch. We're both blond, with similar builds, although she's five inches taller than me and her eyes are green, a trait Niko inherited. I was reminded that Niko's teacher's comment about me having the potential to be Laurel's younger sister wasn't off base.

After greeting Niko, who bustled off to pack up his things, Laurel looked at me. "No Bax?"

"He should be home soon. How's the packing for your trip going?" I asked.

Laurel followed me inside. "It's easy since I'm just taking a couple of suitcases and a few boxes of baby supplies. But figuring out what Niko can't live without has involved him writing multiple lists. I told him my brother is housesitting while I'm gone, so he can stop by to pick things up, which earned me a 'Mom' and a whole new list."

We chatted for a moment but were interrupted by an anguished "Sage, you need to help me slice the brownies!"

"You baked brownies?" Laurel asked as she trailed me to the kitchen. The delight in her voice made me smile.

I sliced the brownies and Niko wrapped them in butcher paper. He left half for Bax and me and would take the second half to his mom's house.

"I'll see you next week, Sage!" Niko said as they walked out.

"Thanks for today!" Laurel called out as they headed to her car. They waved.

I stood on the porch, feeling the cool evening air, and ate one of the brownies. Niko was spending the weekend with his mom since she was preparing to go abroad for six months, and Bax had agreed to let Niko stay for an extra two weeks. I wondered how Niko would take his mother being on a different continent for a while, including over Christmas.

I had one bite of brownie left when Bax pulled into the driveway.

"You just missed your son," I said when Bax walked up the steps to the porch. He pulled me into a hug, and the zipper of his jacket brushed against my face.

"That bad?" I asked. We walked inside the living room.

"They really think I killed Robbie," Bax said.

"So they think I'm lying? We were together virtually the whole day."

"That's the sticking point." Bax ditched his sweater for his favorite hoodie, like he needed something small to help him feel cozy.

"So, how are they claiming you did it?"

He held up his hands to show he didn't know. "Maybe they think we're in a multiverse, and one of my other selves showed up. Or I'm some sort of locked-room murder mystery mastermind and worked an impeccable plan to implement during the, what, three minutes I wasn't with you or Kat."

"Yikes."

"From something I said, I suspect the police are checking security camera footage of everywhere we went. Although when the detective asked for all of our scavenger hunt photos and route, Jackson told him to get a warrant."

"Sounds like Jackson."

"Jackson is intense in lawyer mode." Bax still looked emotionally wrecked.

"We've said his name three times, and now he's been summoned," I said as Jackson's car pulled up. He parallel-parked in front of Bax's house. Like everything he did, his parking job was precise.

"I didn't mention your brother was on his way for a war council?"

Jackson had his standard grumpy look on his face as he strode up the front walkway of Bax's bungalow. But that's his usual look.

Bax opened the front door for him. "Hello, children, let's talk," Jackson said as he walked inside.

"Will this conversation go best over pizza?" I asked.

A while later, Jackson's lecture finally fizzled to a stop over a couple of pizzas from my favorite Detroit-style place. Which mainly consisted of "don't talk to the police without me there."

A lecture he'd given me before.

"Is this tougher than your usual cases?" Bax asked.

"Well, it's more complex than the custody agreement that fell apart over organic food and essential oils, leading me to get roped in as the child's advocate."

"True, no essential oils here."

Jackson looked thoughtful. "The family cases I deal with are usually around parents losing perspective, usually lost in their own reality tunnels and, sometimes, misapplied love. The juvenile court cases are tougher."

"The family cases must be easier."

"Not always. People's home lives can be a mess, even when they look perfect from the outside." Jackson took a bite of his pizza, which had to be cold by now.

A knock at the door made us all turn. Bax went to answer and came back with Piper.

"Did you save any pizza for me?" she asked, then insisted we tell her the whole story about today.

Kaldi jumped in my lap and then climbed onto my shoulder and purred in my ear as everyone talked.

If only we all appreciated such simple pleasures, like perching on a warm shoulder.

Chapter 17

Bax looked sharp in his black suit with a charcoal gray herringbone tie. I rarely saw him dressed in anything other than jeans, but it was nice to know he cleaned up well.

Even if it was for a heartbreaking reason.

And his brown hair was getting a little bit long.

I'd paired a black sheath dress with a black blazer, tights, and ankle boots with a modest heel, with my hair pulled back into a bun. My reflection looked uncharacteristically solemn and formal. And pale, despite the light dusting of blush on my face and pink lip gloss. Which felt appropriate for a funeral.

Bax looked like he wanted to say something, but he put his hand on my shoulder instead. "Are you ready?"

I nodded and snagged my black clutch as we walked out of his house to the Subaru parked in his driveway. Ground Rules owned a similar vehicle but I left it parked at the roastery. It had a very PNW-vibe, even without the Sasquatch decal he'd added to the back hatch to differentiate it from all the other Outbacks in the Fred Meyer parking lot.

We stopped and picked up Lindsey and her wife on our way.

Robbie's family had chosen a funeral home not too far from Grumpy Sasquatch Studio, in inner-southeast Portland. Something told me Robbie would've approved of the art deco building with a retro vibe.

Bax held my hand as we walked into the funeral home together. Wyatt, Noah, and a couple more of Robbie's coworkers showed up in a rideshare.

Ivy had reserved a room, but there wasn't a casket, just a photo of Robbie on an easel, along with a few bouquets of flowers. A handful of hexagonal tables ringed the room with chairs pushed beneath them, like people could sit down and discuss why we were here. A table on the far wall held carafes of, I assumed, coffee and hot water for tea, along with a tray of white ceramic cups.

Ivy stood near the guest book with her hands crossed over her chest. Her black long-sleeved dress was utilitarian, and she'd paired it with black tights and knee-high black boots. Her light brown hair was pulled back into a French braid, and she looked washed out. Her lips were slightly chapped.

"I'm sorry for your loss," Lindsey told Ivy, and we all murmured our agreement. "Is the rest of your family here?"

"No, we're holding a second service in Enterprise," Ivy said, referring to a town in eastern Oregon. "We're cremating Robbie and spreading her ashes at the family ranch."

I stepped away as Bax and Lindsey chatted with Ivy.

"What's that about a ranch?" Wyatt asked me.

"Robbie grew up on a ranch out in Wallowa County," I said. I ended up explaining where the Wallowas were to a small collection of sasquatches who'd moved to Portland from the Midwest and East Coast.

"No, she was from Melbourne, right?" someone asked. "Not eastern Oregon."

"No, Sydney," someone else said.

"Somewhere in Australia."

"Or she was a liar," Kat said. Everyone stopped and looked at her, and she fidgeted. "What? You have to all be thinking that, too."

"But you didn't have to say it aloud," Wyatt said.

There were murmurs of agreement and a few dissents.

"Kat's right," Wyatt said. "If this is Robbie's sister from eastern Oregon, where they were born and raised, claiming she was Australian is a lie."

"Maybe it was going to be some sort of epic prank. One day she would've walked in and made fun of us for believing her." Noah looked almost angry.

"Or she was simply making fun of us," Kat said. She wore black pants and a charcoal gray sweater over a white button-down shirt. It made her look slighter than normal, like her usual flannel was body armor.

"Maybe we should talk about something else." Elaine's voice was sharper than usual. Everyone stopped and stared at her. "I know I'm the office manager and not HR, but picking Robbie apart seems inappropriate, considering why we're here."

Kat turned and walked away, but I heard her say, "It's not like you liked her, either."

I stared at Kat for a moment, struck by the bitterness in her voice. Come to think of it, I'd never seen Kat and Elaine interact. Was this par for the course for them?

"We need to remember that we're professionals, even if we're not on the clock due to this tragic circumstance," Elaine said. She reminded me of a mother trying to lecture a bunch of bored teenagers.

I turned and followed Kat as Elaine continued to drone on.

"Are you okay?" I asked Kat.

"I should not have come. I do not feel like dealing with Elaine today. She treats me like a child, and it is obnoxious."

"I'm sorry."

"What's worse is that, while she acts like we are all kids, she favors the male members of the staff. I feel sorry for her daughters."

"Ouch."

"True, I should not say anything."

Wyatt walked up. His eyes focused on Kat. "Looks like someone's feeling emotional today."

"This is a funeral, not a funhouse."

"Kat, it's not like you even liked Robbie." Wyatt crossed his arms over his chest. He'd gone the dark sweater and dark pants route like Kat.

"I can feel bad she died even if I did not like working with her." Kat took a sip from her cup, which had the string of an orange tea bag hanging out of the side.

"But you won't shed a tear."

"Are you crying?" Kat asked. "I do not see any tears, but maybe I am blind."

"Okay, you're right. I'm not going to miss her, either. Although I'm not looking forward to us having to pick up the slack for her."

"Like you didn't pick up the slack already," Kat said.

"That's unfair. Robbie was an excellent programmer when she wanted to be."

"But she wasn't opposed to getting you or anyone else to do her work if she was bored. But yes, as you said, she was a good programmer when she wanted to be."

A couple of guys, including Aiden, walked up, and I recognized them from the gym in the roastery's building. Hopefully, they'd break up the weird undercurrent between Wyatt and Kat.

"Who should we give our respects to?" Aiden asked me. I directed him to Robbie's sister.

Bax joined us. "Thanks for coming, guys. I know your weekends off are important."

The chat turned basic and rather unemotional considering where we were.

The sound of a spoon on a water glass caught my attention. Ivy stood at the front of the room.

"Thank you, everyone, for attending. It means a lot to my family that you came out to pay respects to my younger sister, Robin."

Someone muttered, "Wait, I thought her name was Robbie."

Ivy continued. "Lindsey Barlow is going to say a few words now."

Lindsey looked a tad tense as she stood in front of the room.

"As Ivy said, thank you, everyone, for coming today. I know this has been a shock to us all. Robbie lived brighter than anyone else I'd ever met. She loved to prank people, to make people laugh. And that's the sort of emotion we're all missing right now. She'll leave a hole in the office, and we'll never forget her. To Robbie." Lindsey held her hand in the air.

"To Robbie," about half of the room responded.

"Thank you."

Lindsey rejoined the group, and Ivy invited others to speak. Elaine stepped up.

"I know you think of me as the company mom, and let me continue the family analogy. Robbie will always be the mischievous little sister we lost, but we'll never forget her."

A few more people spoke, and then everyone sort of scattered. I walked to the coffee station and poured a cup. Lindsey joined me.

I took a sip of the coffee. Fairly weak-tasting medium blend.

"How's the timeline you're creating?"

"I need to get started on that. Thanks for sending the files over."

One of the trainers from the gym laughed loudly, which sounded shocking in the quiet room.

The interesting thing about the gym staff: they were onsite when Robbie died, maybe teaching a class. Maybe doing a solo training session.

Maybe hanging out in the hallway, out of sight of the cameras? Could they have followed her into the roastery?

Could Aiden have followed her in?

But why would someone from the gym hurt Robbie?

Chapter 18

"Are you sure going to a bar is the best idea?" I asked Bax as he navigated into a parallel-parking spot not too far from my uncle's bar. Lindsey and her wife murmured in the backseat.

"The crew wants to go to the Tav, and I feel like we should make an appearance, even if we don't stay long. I'm driving, so I'm just going to have iced tea."

So, of course, when we walked into the bar, instead of a quiet moment, we ran into a pirate pub crawl.

And, of course, they were singing a shanty with gusto. I could almost see the words echoing off the polished wood of the bar, rebounding off the stained glass windows to fill the entire space with the rousing chant.

The work is hard and the wages low.

"Want me to grab you something?" Bax asked.

"Club soda," I shouted back over the sound of pirates singing.

Leave her, Johnny, leave her.

I followed in Bax's wake through the sea of pirates, who shifted over to let us through. A guy in a striped blue shirt with a stuffed parrot on his shoulder winked at me. Then the bird twisted his head, and I realized he had a live parrot.

"That has to be on the wrong side of health codes," I muttered.

I think it's time for us to go.

Bax ordered from Kage, who nodded at me before turning and grabbing a couple of pint glasses. Like usual, Kage was rocking an eight-ies punk vibe, complete with a Dead Kennedys T-shirt and red sus-penders.

The rats have gone and we the crew

Bax glanced at me, and I shrugged my shoulders, feeling hemmed in by the pirates and their hearty chant.

A couple of living dolls sat in the corner, watching the pirates hoist their mostly empty pint glasses in the air.

I think it's time that we left, too.

The pirates all turned and left, filtering out the doorway in an ebbing flow as some pulled on jackets from a booth by the door. Others strode out, clearly warm enough in their black coats.

The sudden silence felt jarring, like all of the air in the world had left with the pirates. The sound of a busser grabbing a batch of pint glasses on a nearby table made me jump. The pirates had left behind an impressive number of empty beer glasses.

"One of the guys had a real live parrot," I said.

"You missed him trying to share his beer with it," Kage said as they handed over my club soda adorned with a slice of lime, and Bax's iced tea. Bax left a couple dollars on the bar, which disappeared into Kage's pocket in a flash.

"You two are rather fancy today," Kage said.

"We came from a wake," I said. I took a sip of my club soda.

"That sucks. I'm sorry. Was it like an elderly relative?"

"Sadly, one of Bax's employees."

Kage and I chatted for a moment.

"Wait, the blond Australian? She came in here occasionally. I'm sorry to hear about her."

A guy down the bar said he needed a whiskey, so Kage turned his way.

Bax turned and clocked the dolls, then looked at me. "Pirates and dolls in one night?"

"It's like Roald Dahl said, 'Those who don't believe in magic will never find it,'" I said.

"Explain, please," Bax said. We made our way to the back quadrant of the bar, aka our usual table.

"Pirates, dolls, cosplay in general. People are looking for their own sort of magic. Their own small group to bond with against the force of the bigger universe. Maybe dressing up makes them feel like their true self," I said. And wondered if that was how Robbie felt. If she thought her persona was who she was meant to be versus an American girl from a small town in the NE corner of Oregon. Or, if she'd hated herself so much, she'd tried to buy into her façade.

How actively had Robbie been trying to move to Australia? I pictured her on a beach in Sydney, acting like a one hundred percent California surfer girl.

In a way, Robbie's Australian cosplay was no different from the dolls or pirates. Except neither of those groups tried to trick people into believing they were, for example, a doll brought to real life, à la Pinocchio.

"So, what's your magic?" Bax asked.

"Coffee?" I said.

He looked thoughtful, but Kat walked up carrying a highball glass of amber liquid before he said anything. She'd ditched her sweater and looked business casual in her button-down shirt and black pants.

"Are pirates a celebrated thing?" Kat asked. "Or are they just fans of *Pirates of the Caribbean*?"

"Being a pirate seems romantic if you ignore scurvy and being stuck on a ship for who knows how long," I said.

"It's nice to see you out of the office," Bax said to Kat.

"You just saw me earlier, and when I was dressed as a duck."

"My comment still stands."

A couple more sasquatches came in, and Bax joined Lindsey and chatted with them.

I glanced at Kat.

"You don't have to answer, but is there a reason you tend to skip the social stuff, like happy hour?" I asked Kat.

"I rarely drink, and I frequently need to get home to help out. My mother isn't well."

"I'm sorry. I hope she feels better."

"It's MS, so she will never get better. Now, we're just trying to keep her comfortable. She's been sick a long time."

"That must be tough."

"Luckily, my younger sister is a carpenter and has built ramps and adaptations to the house. But now the end is near."

"If there's anything we can do, please let me know. If you need time off or flexible hours, I can help you smooth-talk Bax."

"Yes, I bet you could because he is putty in your hands. But work is my oasis. I get to focus on creating a game that takes people to another world. Places where diseases like MS don't exist, except for that accidental pandemic with *World of Warcraft*, but that's not one of our games. I need it. And it allows me to help pay for nurses and aides who have the skills to care for my mother."

"Still, let me know."

Wyatt walked up, carrying a pint glass. "I saw a bunch of pirates walking down the street. Is there a term for pirates? Like how a group of crows is a murder?"

"A mutiny of pirates?" I suggested. Noah joined us.

"Plus the dolls." Wyatt nodded his head in their direction.

"A stuffing of dolls?"

"China dolls aren't stuffed, are they?" Wyatt asked. "I wonder if I could pick one of those dolls up tonight."

I tried not to grimace.

"Not the time, Wyatt," Noah said.

"I thought you had a girlfriend?" I asked.

"We're not exclusive."

"That's not making your comment any better, bro," Noah said.

Elaine and the marketing intern, Lila, joined the larger group. Once again, Elaine looked like she didn't quite mesh with everyone. It was hard to pinpoint why, exactly. I guessed she was in her forties and at least one of her children was in college, while another was in high school. Which gave her a few more turns around the sun than the average sasquatch, who seemed to range from their midtwenties into their late thirties, although she wasn't the oldest. One of the illustrators was in his sixties. One of the game testers was a woman in her fifties who regularly rocked graphic tees and clunky Doc Martens, and had major DGAF energy coupled with kindness. Age didn't make them stand out. All of the sasquatches were dressed nicer but more sedate than usual. Elaine had ditched her regular capris, tunics, and clogs for a black suit that I bet she'd originally bought for job interviews. So Elaine didn't stand out fashion-wise.

But she always acted stiff, like she can't unbend to become part of the team versus overseeing everyday details. I couldn't tell if she was just out of sync with everyone, operating on her own frequency, or if she honestly didn't fully like anyone, even if she talked about being the staff mom.

Or maybe she was just always uncomfortable. Some people never become comfortable in their own skin.

Kage swung by with a round of drinks, and Elaine snapped her fingers at them.

"Oh no, you didn't," Kage said and walked away.

Elaine stared at Kage's retreating back. "I wanted to order a glass of wine."

"Maybe try asking one of the bartenders nicely," Wyatt said.

Lila stopped by me. "Who snaps at the waitstaff?" she muttered.

"It's embarrassing," I said.

"It's just so sad to lose such a vibrant, unique member of our work family," Elaine said. Her voice boomed out. I almost wished the chanting pirates would come back.

"You sure didn't say that when Robbie switched out your Diet Coke with full sugar," Wyatt said.

"She was just high-spirited. I admired that about her," Elaine said.

A loud laugh caught my attention, and I turned to see a human doll in a red dress and cat ears clapping her hands while her laugh echoed everywhere. Kat was standing with her and three other dolls.

Including a Sally doll, who wobbled as she walked away past me in the direction of the ladies' room.

I instinctively followed her. Something about the wobble made me worry.

"Are you all right?" I asked her when we were both inside the bathroom.

"Fine, why?"

"You looked unsteady."

"I'm just feeling a bit stiff." She walked into one of the stalls.

"Were you at Jamulet last Tuesday?" I asked.

The toilet flushed. She reappeared a moment later. "Why?"

"Just curious. I thought I saw you there."

"Yeah, a group of us meet up weekly. Jamulet is one of our regular spots."

She washed her hands and walked out.

When I exited the bathroom a few minutes later, I noticed Kat and the Sally doll were talking intently by the bar. Then the doll left, and Kat walked back to her coworkers. She made a beeline for Bax.

"It was nice seeing everyone, but I am going home now," Kat said.

"See you on Monday."

Kat left to a chorus of good-byes. Bax and I followed about ten minutes later.

I found myself humming the pirates' sea chanty as we walked

out. *The rats have gone, and we the crew. I think it's time that we left, too.* It was definitely a good exit line. On any other night, the words wouldn't have felt as poignant.

After we'd walked back to Bax's car and started the drive home, I asked, "What's the story with *World of Warcraft* and a pandemic? Kat mentioned it earlier."

"Ages ago in the video game world—2005, I think—*World of Warcraft* introduced a blood corruption spell that was supposed to have a short-term impact on the character's health status during a special event raid. But due to a glitch, any player with a pet in the game carried the disease with them after the raid and started infecting players around them. If the players weren't strong, they'd erupt into blood, die, and turn into a skeleton. But the exciting part was how people reacted. Blizzard, the game developers, tried to encourage people to socially distance as they fixed the bug. Instead, people ignored them, traveled around and spread the disease, and a bunch of conspiracy theories developed, targeted at Blizzard and players in the games with pets. It showed a dark side of human behavior."

"You know a lot about this."

"Some epidemiologists actually wrote a paper about it because they guessed it would model real-world behavior. Laurel read it in one of her grad school classes and talked about their paper for ages," Bax said, referring to his ex, Laurel. "Eventually, they had to reset the game to before the supposedly short-term spell was introduced. It was like everything that occurred after the spell in the game never happened, and people traveled back in time."

"If only life could be reset as easily as a video game."

Chapter 19

Sunday felt slow, which felt like a relief after Saturday's wake. Bax stopped by the party supply store with me, and I picked up Halloween decorations. Pumpkin lights called my name, as did a few small cheerful skeletons, while Bax checked out the costumes.

"Hmm, we could be Mario and Princess Peach?" Bax said as I joined the line to check out with my decorations.

"It depends, can I be Mario?"

I dropped the decor at the Rail Yard, which had a steady stream of lunch-goers, although Ground Rules wasn't open on Sundays until next summer. I locked the decorations inside my cart, and we grabbed lunch.

Eating at the Rail Yard when Ground Rules is closed makes me a bit unbalanced. But Cartography was open. Even though one of their owners is Argentinian and the other is American, they had Colombian-style chicken and rice as their daily special, so I had to buy a plate. They focus on cuisine from all over the world.

"How's the translating going?" I asked Diego, one of Cartography's owners. He works in the court system three-fourths of the year.

"Too busy, as always," he said. Talking about everyday Rail Yard issues was like a brief return to normalcy. This was something easy to understand.

We headed home after a trip to Bax's favorite comic book store and the grocery store to stock up for the week and Niko's impending arrival.

"Our last weekend evening of freedom for six months," Bax said as the afternoon shifted into the evening, referring to Niko's arrival on Tuesday evening. His mom, stepdad, and half sister were flying out early Wednesday morning.

Wait, Bax said "our." The word made me feel fuzzy.

"Should we have a big night out or stay in?" I asked.

"As much I'd love to go out after everything that's happened, let's stay in. But let's get tacos delivered."

As Bax took care of ordering our food delivery, I paced in the living room.

"It would be easier to move forward if we knew what happened to Robbie," I said.

"We could try to solve it together," Bax said.

"We'll be like a cocktail-swilling, modern-day Nick and Nora Charles, although honestly, I feel you're more like a Hardy boy, and I'm Nancy Drew."

"That's an idea for a joint Halloween costume. What do the Hardy Boys look like again?"

Bax had been on the hunt for a joint costume but hadn't found the right idea yet.

"All-American boys, I think, while Nancy has strawberry blond hair, or titian, depending upon the book."

"Never heard of that."

"It's based on an Italian painter who liked to paint redheads."

"Hmm." He touched my naturally blond hair, which was currently on my shoulders.

"Don't even think about suggesting I dye my hair. Let's not get distracted: could we first figure out what happened to Robbie?"

Bax continued to tangle his fingers in a lock of my hair. "Let's create a storyboard. I'll show you how I'd solve this if this was a video game. Come with me."

Bax let go of my hair and led me to his home office in the back corner of the house. He grabbed a pack of index cards from his desk, pulled a corkboard out of the closet, and set it up on an easel.

"How many of those corkboards do you have?" I asked.

"Seven, I think, so I can work on different projects without having to remove the cards. Lindsey likes doing all of this electronically, but I like to brainstorm on paper."

"Or on index cards."

"I like to create a storyboard before creating the flowchart, which we then use to write the script. It helps to define the characters first. So let's start there."

Bax wrote *Robbie* in even block letters across a card. He paused. "So, what do we truly know about Robbie?"

"That's the key question. Robbie's façade kept everyone from seeing her true self. But maybe if we could figure out who the true Robbie was, we'd be able to solve what happened."

As we discussed Robbie, I wondered, once again, who she'd been deep in her core. But maybe that didn't matter. Possibly one of the façades had led to her murder.

"Who would've benefited from Robbie's death?" I asked.

"What do you mean?" Bax asked.

"Would it help anyone at work? In crime novels, they always look at someone's estate."

"It'd be sketchy if I checked if Robbie had signed up for the studio's life insurance policy, right?"

"You offer life insurance? Is it good?" That wasn't one of the perks we offered Ground Rules employees.

"Yeah, but it's not really worth killing over. It just matches a year's worth of salary. Our HR service convinced us it's a good bridge for families in case something bad happens. Not that one year's salary will set Niko up for life, but it'll give Laurel a chance to make plans."

"I heard Robbie was up for a promotion? With her out of the picture, does that open any new job opportunities for someone else?"

"Not really, since we promoted Noah instead of Robbie. But it wasn't really a contest. Not that Robbie agreed."

"I heard she took exception." So much so the police had heard about it, too.

"If by 'took exception' you mean she screamed at me in the office, yeah. I'm sure people told you about that. She was so loud I bet everyone in the gym overheard, even if they were blasting music."

"That sounds miserable."

"You know, it was a surprise. Robbie acted overconfident when she interviewed, like the interview was a formality. Like, of course, we'd want to promote her. When we originally interviewed her, she felt enthusiastic and confident but not cocky. She was like a different person when she wanted the promotion."

"Was it ever a contest between her and Noah?"

Bax paused, then slowly said, "We took the time to compare their achievements. But no, I don't think we ever considered her the better candidate. Noah's experience trumps Robbie's, and he's shown more leadership over the years. I'd hate to lose Noah, while Robbie's skill set is easy to replace."

"When did you make the decision?"

"We announced Noah's promotion the day before Lindsey's birthday."

"Wait, so she screamed at you the day before she died?" Kat had mentioned it, but the timing hadn't fully sunk in.

Bax nodded.

No wonder Robbie had acted a bit over the top, even brittle, as we got ready for the scavenger hunt. I remembered her cozying up to me. She must've been trying to annoy Bax.

"When you talked about the potential promotion, did Robbie's pranks come up?"

"That was a concern, even if they never crossed the line into harassment. We want to keep a happy workforce, and that includes feeling safe in the studio. We debated having the HR service talk with Robbie, even if her actions were harmless."

"I wonder if all of Robbie's pranks were as harmless as you think."

"What do you mean?"

"We sort of talked about this on the scavenger hunt. It seems to me that while most of Robbie's pranks seemed silly, she was mean to a few people. But the harmless pranks basically provided cover."

I didn't share my next thought with Bax: with Robbie gone, whose day-to-day workplace would feel kinder, less like they were waiting for a jack-in-the-box to pop up at any moment?

Kat, definitely. But maybe Wyatt, too. Or Noah? And maybe there were other people in the studio, like one of the interns.

"Did anyone check out Robbie's laptop? Could there be something there about her plans the day she died?" I asked.

"Someone does need to scroll through her work email, although Noah is checking for immediate-action items," Bax said.

"We should create a timeline on a different board with the scavenger hunt photos," I said. So we spent the next hour printing the photos on Bax's rarely used home black-and-white laserjet and adding them to the board.

I stared at the photos for a moment. "You know, we don't know where Lindsey was during the day, other than reigning at Jamulet for a while." Bax looked at me, and I added, "I'm not saying Lindsey did it, but what if she can alibi someone?"

"I'll text her."

Bax laughed a moment later and showed me Lindsey's response. *What, do you think I'm the story's villain? Do I at least have a wicked cape and maybe a katana?*

"Tell her we're just eliminating her from inquiries."

Bax typed some more, then laughed. "She says, 'Thanks, *Law & Order.*'"

Bax sat down on the couch by one wall of his home office. "You know, Robbie's death helps out Kat since she'll take on more responsibility. But that might be negative to her since she's busy enough without taking on anything more. I haven't gotten the sense that Kat wants a promotion. She seems to enjoy her current job."

"I thought Kat's group was separate from Robbie's?" Given her responsibilities at home, I would bet that Kat didn't want more at work. But I could be wrong.

"Sort of, but they work closely together, and some of the integration tasks Robbie did will probably fall onto Kat. I'll need to make sure we don't overwhelm her." Bax pulled out his phone and tapped something into his notes app.

If I was right, and Kat hadn't spoken up about Robbie's pranks despite being targeted, why had she stayed silent? Fear? The desire to just put her head down and hope Robbie would go away?

Or was there something deeper? Was Kat keeping something quiet, the sort of secret that could explode her current life? If Kat had been telling the truth about her mother, she had a lot resting on her shoulders.

Could it be something from Robbie's past that kicked off now? Because one thing I've learned over the years is that the past always has its fingers tangled up in the present.

Chapter 20

Monday morning at the cart felt like a sliver of normalcy in an otherwise topsy-turvy week full of grief and a bit of anger. The anger was a mix of fury at Robbie's death coupled with fear.

But waking up early, snagging my jar of overnight oats, and heading to the cart felt like I was clinging to a tiny sliver of normalcy. Opening the cart was automatic, even comforting.

Not long after I opened, Robbie's sister, Ivy, walked up to the cart. She'd reverted to the plaid shirt and jean style that looked like it was part of her. Her hair was pulled back into what I suspected was her usual French braid. She felt like an anachronism in the city. But maybe I felt that way because I knew she really wanted to head home to the open air of the Wallowas.

And I was sad I hadn't had the chance to get to know her better.

"Hiya, Sage." She put a green Stanley travel mug onto the cart's order window. She eyed the menu. "I wanted to check out your cart before I split town."

"I'm so glad you stopped by. Are you driving back to eastern Oregon now?"

"Yeah. I packed and loaded everything I want to keep. Robbie's building manager is really nice and is helping donate the rest of Robbie's stuff. We set up a time for that charity you mentioned to drop by and cart off her stuff."

"They'll be grateful."

"At least something good . . ." Ivy's voice trailed off. She cleared her throat. "How about a pour-over."

"Guatemalan or Kenyan?"

"Let's say Guatemalan," Ivy said. "Thank you for coming to the memorial service."

"I wouldn't have missed it. Thank you for holding it. It's always good for people to have a chance to say goodbye." I'd heard people say that funerals and wakes are for the living, and getting a chance to say farewell felt important. Even if Robbie's death still felt like a shock.

"I still have another one to go since my parents are also holding a memorial service at home." Ivy turned and checked out the other carts as I ground the beans she'd chosen and slowly made her pour-over. While it's one of my favorite ways to drink coffee, pour-overs are the most time-consuming drink we make at the cart. I'm always glad when people order our house coffee when we're busy since we keep a carafe of French press ready for quick pours throughout the day.

But at least it's easy to keep an eye on the happenings outside the cart when slowly twirling the gooseneck kettle in slow circles while brewing a pour-over.

Sophie walked up, wearing her usual jean jacket, her copper hair poking out of a dark green beanie.

Ivy turned back to me. I noticed the whites of her eyes were slightly red. "I've been thinking about playing around with a golden pale ale with coffee."

"Oh?"

"Most people think coffee stouts, but I had a pale ale once brewed with oats and coffee. It was crisp with fantastic coffee notes."

"Sounds delicious."

Sophie climbed into the cart and dropped her backpack into the locking cupboard we'd set up for staff bags.

Ivy rubbed the back of her neck. "Do you think you'd have a light roast that'd make a good beer?"

I poured Ivy's coffee into a to-go cup. "Let me grab one of my business cards for you, along with a bag of our new Concrete Blonde roast. It could be a winner for you."

I put Ivy's coffee on the counter, plus a pitcher of cream, and slid one of my business cards out of my wallet. Thankfully, we still had two bags of Concrete Blonde, so I put one into a teal bag with the Ground Rules logo stamped on the side, then grabbed a flyer.

I handed the bag over to Ivy. "Here's a bag of our Concrete Blonde and one of our Coffee Club flyers inside. It talks about our different roasts and the history of Ground Rules. Ignore the prices since we have wholesale rates and special deals for business-to-business sales."

Ivy picked up the flyer. "Perfect. You'll hear from me. How much do I owe?"

I only charged her for the pour-over.

"You should charge me for the beans."

"Nah, I'll just bill it under marketing. I'd love to work with your brewery. Your farm sounds really awesome." The idea of trying to grow virtually everything she needed onsite to brew beer sounded fantastic.

Ivy smiled and ran her credit card on the cart's point-of-sale system. My inner child still giggles when I call it the POS system.

"Meeting you was one of the silver linings of my trip. Your help was invaluable."

"I'm sorry we met under such tragic circumstances."

"I've never understood my sister, and now I think I never will." Ivy took a sip of her coffee.

"Chances are, Robbie never knew herself, either," I said.

Ivy walked away, and I wished I could tell her what had happened to her sister. But maybe we'd never know.

Sophie had poured a cup of coffee and started digging through the bag of Halloween decorations I'd dropped off yesterday.

"These pumpkin lights!" Sophie said.

"Let's decorate the cart after the morning rush."

After our steady stream of morning traffic, breaking out the Halloween decorations felt like a treat.

"I wish I could decorate my room for Halloween," Sophie said. We wound the string of pumpkin lights around the Ground Rules cart.

"Why can't you? Does your landlord have decoration rules?" I asked.

"I can't afford them. Things are tight right now. I can't even afford to buy ChapStick until next month."

"What's going on? Why are things so tight?"

"Well, I'd planned on living with my sister during grad school, but that didn't work, so I found a room to rent, which is okay. But the cost of books was way more than I expected, and I had a few other expenses pop up. So I have to make every penny count. If you can give me more hours, I'll take them. To be honest, I'm debating a second job if I can find one for a few nights a week."

"When will you study?" I asked.

"Afternoons and very early mornings."

"I have one idea. Hang on." I texted my cousin Miles.

Do you need any help at the Tav? One of my baristas needs more hours. She's reliable. You'll like her.

"Have you been in the Tav before?" I asked Sophie.

"No, but you've mentioned it before. I've heard my classmates talking about it being one of the better dive bars in town. But I don't have money for eating out."

My phone dinged. Miles. *I could use someone willing to bus tables and barback a few nights a week.*

"If you're willing to do grunt work, my cousin Miles needs help at the Tav." I explained the basics of barbacking, basically doing the basics to keep the bar hustling, like refilling ice wells, washing glasses, slicing up lemons and other garnishes, emptying the garbage, wiping down the bar, and all sorts of busywork. "And you'd need to help run food out to the customers and bus tables, too. You'll be on your feet all night. But it starts a couple bucks over minimum wage, and the bartenders will tip you out, which means share a portion of their tips." Oregon state law requires waitresses and bartenders to make at least the state minimum wage regardless of tips, and Miles had told me once he kept employees longer by starting them at least two dollars over minimum wage.

"Is it a good place to work?"

"Honestly, yeah, it's good. I barbacked there during college. Miles is a good boss, and he's fair. As long as you work hard, everyone will love you. And it's not like they'll expect you to work there forever. Just give reasonable notice before leaving."

Sophie nodded.

"Oh! I forgot to mention you'll get food each shift, along with a draft beer or well drink at the end. Don't be surprised if Miles encourages you to get the nightly special. If it's the fried chicken sandwich, always say yes."

Sophie smiled. "I'd practically kill for a cheeseburger."

"It's not exactly a cheeseburger, but I can grab us food from the Burrito Bomb, and we can finish decorating for Halloween. Their Milanese torta isn't quite a hamburger, but it's fantastic."

"Get me that, and I'll love you forever."

As I picked up a torta for Sophie and a carne asada burrito for me, I thought about the benefits I offered my employees, covered in a "perks of the job" sheet in their staff handbook. Harley and I should sit down and run the numbers to see if we could afford to give our baristas a raise. They kept the cart going, and as we grew, they'd become more and more valuable if they stayed with us.

"Sage, I grilled a couple of jalapeños for you," Matias, the owner of the Burrito Bomb cart, said. He handed over a small cardboard plate with jalapeños nicely charred along the side. "Your order will be ready in a moment."

"Thanks."

"Have you heard about the new coffee cart supposedly opening up the street?" Matias asked.

I paused as I bit into a jalapeño. "What?"

"Some guy was saying a drive-through bikini coffee cart is open-ing down the street. But I don't know if that's true. And he said it was up the street, but I don't see anything."

Bikini coffee? Seriously? But the real question was, even if some-one did open a drive-through up the street, would it be competition for us? I hadn't heard of a bikini coffee known for the quality of their coffee, although maybe that was unfair. If drivers wanted to stop for Ground Rules coffee, they had to park their car; in the mornings, we ended up with many mass transit commuters who were lured by the siren song of coffee as they waited at the corner bus stop. But I'm sure some of those walk-ups were park-walk-and-return-to-their-car-customers. They'd be the most likely to abandon us for the ease of a drive-through, especially on rainy mornings.

I had faith we could go toe-to-toe with anyone in the city based on the quality of our coffee.

A couple people walked up to the coffee cart, so Sophie quit hang-ing pumpkin lights and took their orders. I asked her via hand mo-tions if I should join her, and she shook her head.

Matias handed over my order, wrapped in foil and on top of the reusable bamboo plates I'd brought over from the coffee cart, along with a squeeze bottle of avocado salsa. "Bring the salsa back when you're done, right?"

"Of course!"

Matias looked past me. "Hey, that's the guy who told me about the bikini coffee place."

I turned and saw Mark enter the Rail Yard.

"Oh yeah?"

What rationale would Mark have for making up a story like that? Or maybe he was telling the truth. Perhaps he was trying to make life uncomfortable for me? Or had he intended to imply my cart was bikini-adjacent?

I remembered Kendall's Speedo joke and grinned at Mark as I passed him.

★   ★   ★

Mark had avoided our cart but stopped by the bagel cart. I'd felt his eyes on us as he left.

By the time I left the cart, it looked ready for Halloween. The skeleton dog on the order window looked especially festive.

As I entered the roastery, I checked the time. 11:40 a.m. Bax had a standing hour-long personal training appointment on Mondays to, in his words, "start the week off right." When I had time, I liked to drop in on one of the TRX, aka Total body Resistance Exercise classes using straps bolted to the ceiling and, sometimes, the boot camp–style fitness class held during "happy hour" each evening.

When I walked into the gym, I could see Bax on the workout floor, slowly dead-lifting a hex bar loaded up with bumper plates while one of the trainers stood near him. He looked serious, like all of his focus was on lifting correctly. Very prudent, since no one wants to lose their form and throw out their back.

I glanced around for Aiden, but he wasn't in sight. Which felt strange since he practically lived in Pump It PDX.

I needed to talk to him, but I wanted it to feel casual. Natural. Not like I was showing up to interrogate him.

I sat down in the waiting area and eyed the cubbies and lockers along the wall. Bax's red hoodie was shoved into one at his chest height.

I sat, listening to the thumping music until Bax was done.

Bax's face transitioned from a focused scowl as he walked off the floor and saw me. "What's a nice girl like you doing in a place like this?"

"I am a member here," I said. "So you can't make any jokes about not wanting to join a place that would have me as a member."

"That explains why the masses are queueing up to join the gym," Bax said.

I laughed and shook my head.

We walked out into the hallway together. "Lunch in my office after I shower?" Bax asked.

"It's a date."

When I popped my head into the roastery, Harley wasn't there. But her bag was, so she'd probably popped out for lunch. Or she'd gone on one of her lunchtime runs, which she does two to three times a week, depending upon her soccer schedule.

Kat was sitting on the couch inside the studio's door when I walked in.

"You talked to my sister on Saturday," Kat said.

"What's that?"

"My sister, Nadia. She was at the Tav."

"Oh?"

"She dresses up as Sally from *The Nightmare Before Christmas*."

"That's your sister? Her costume was flawless."

"Yes, she is a fantastic cosplayer. You should see some of the clothing she's sewn. She's a genius."

"I saw you speaking with the dolls."

"They're a nice group. Very welcoming. Although I don't see the need to pretend to be a toy. But not everyone thinks designing or playing video games is good, so I'm happy to respect their choices."

"So true."

"Why did you talk to Nadia?"

"Honestly, I saw the dolls taking photos at Jamulet, and I'm curious if they caught anything in the background related to what happened later."

"Robbie was not killed at Jamulet."

"True, but I'm trying to low-key figure out what happened. Life will feel better if we get answers." And maybe this continual sense of worry would flee and let me deal with life like normal.

"Why not let the police do it?"

"I don't think I'll solve the murder, but I want to feel like I'm doing something. If I found anything important, I could pass it along to the detective in charge of the case."

"If you are free this coming Wednesday, I can take you to meet the dolls. I bet they'll show you their photos if you ask nicely. They like it when people compliment their costumes, provided it's honest. They can tell when someone is patronizing."

"Their costumes are phenomenal, so that won't be a problem."

"I'll text you about the meeting when I get the scoop from my sister on where they'll be."

"Perfect."

Was investigating with Kat a great idea? Maybe, but maybe not if she was secretly the villain behind this all. But if she was, would she be willing to introduce me to her sister? Or was she helping out so she could keep an eye on me?

After lunch with Bax, I worked on a few marketing projects for Ground Rules, then headed back to the studio.

Wyatt and the crew weren't ready for me to start filming, so I stowed my bag in a cubby and sat down in the unused cubicle by the motion-capture booth. I knew I shouldn't do it, but I logged onto Discord using Robbie's crib sheet's user name and password.

MonkeyBiz38-972_5 seemed like a weird user name, although the account name was Derek, according to Discord. The avatar showed an illustrated face with a buzz cut and black aviator glasses.

Grumpy Sasquatch Studio has its own server on Discord and individual servers for its games. Users can log on and discuss game strategy, get technical help, and chat about various topics within the server on separate pages. Bax's company had disabled the voice channels, meaning users had to type in answers, and on a few pages, users mainly seemed to communicate with gifs.

I searched the "Derek" user name, and my eyes widened at the posts.

Lindsey had a visible role in the server, engaging with video game fans and listening to their jokes and concerns. The Derek account was rude to Lindsey virtually every time she posted. The comments were vague enough that they could be written by someone who didn't realize they were being abrasive, but if you looked at them as purposeful, they were mean.

And the meanness was always directed at Lindsey. The social media manager for the company was also active all over the server, and Robbie's account was friendly to Derek.

Was there any chance this was Robbie's account? Could she have swiped the login details from someone else?

Derek also claimed to be a video game influencer and lobbied for free stuff. T-shirts. Games and quests, including for games that weren't designed by Grumpy Sasquatch Studio. The social media manager's responses were always kind, but it looked like "Derek" hadn't scored any swag.

I clicked on the direct messaging icon. Three unread messages. The first was from a small group talking about how to get free stuff; Robbie's account betted they'd be able to get a T-shirt by the end of the month.

Trust me, they'll do anything to get me to chill, the account bragged. *Or else I'll bring the whole company down.*

"Sage, we're ready!" Wyatt summoned me, so I logged off Discord and then the computer and focused on the task for the day. Although the direct messages bothered me.

Did Robbie know something terrible about the studio? Or was she just making stuff up to impress the "friends" of her Discord troll persona?

"Something on your mind?" Wyatt asked me.

"How often do you use Discord?" I asked.

"If Discord is getting you down, just walk away," he said.

"I'm just curious."

"Well, I have a server with my college friends 'cause it's a great way to meet up, talk, and play video games, and I belong to a couple of video game servers. But I'm not a power user or anything. If I didn't work here, I'd probably have my own Twitch account to stream video games. But the last thing I want is to focus on developing a curated Twitch stream when I spend all day here."

"Does working here mean you play fewer video games?"

"Nah, I still get in a few hours every night. But I only play to relax."

Playing video games after coding one all day wasn't quite my idea of relaxing, but it was like me visiting coffee shops in my downtime, which I loved to do. And I did enjoy my occasional video game session with Bax, who played often but not quite daily.

We got to work, but one thought did keep bugging me.

Did Robbie know something bad about Grumpy Sasquatch Studio?

Chapter 21

After my usual coffee cart routine on Tuesday, and after spending time at the roastery, I dropped by the studio's kitchen on my way to the motion-capture booth. The intern who joined us for the weekly no-drop bike ride was there. The microwave was counting down.

"Hi, Lila," I said. She looked fit, with a thin build and curly brown hair she usually wore pulled back into a bun. She'd told me once that she's a senior at a local university.

"Hey." Lila popped open a can of grapefruit sparkling water.

"That's the best flavor," I said. I motioned at her can.

"I agree, but blackberry is a close second."

"How are you doing? The past week must feel a bit traumatic. This hasn't been the work experience you'd planned on."

"I can't complain. This internship is way more interesting than most of my friends'. And it's not like the accident happened to someone in my department, which sounds harsh, but I feel separated from it."

"Did you work with Robbie at all?" Lila referring to Robbie's death as an accident caught my attention.

"Rarely, thankfully."

I raised my eyebrows at her.

"Robbie was the sort of person who loved to find out people's weaknesses and then exploit them," Lila said.

"Did she pick on you?" I asked.

"I'm in recovery from an ED," Lila said. She must've read the question in my eyes. "Eating disorder."

"And Robbie used that to hassle you?"

"I'm pretty careful with food. I make sure I eat enough and work out, but I avoid triggers that make me obsess. Like when Elaine suggested some of us do a healthy living challenge that involved counting calories and steps, that was a big no for me."

"Makes sense." No one in the studio had seemed particularly jazzed about Elaine's idea, and it had fizzled out.

"Considering how serious Robbie was about counting the calories of everything she ate, she should've been sympathetic," Lila said.

"Oh?"

"You didn't notice her meal prep? Robbie usually brought her lunch and snacks in and mainly ate salads with tuna or chicken or Greek yogurt. Plus lots of celery and carrots. She bragged about how she was regimented, but that's a warning sign for me. So I asked if she was okay, and that's when she figured out I was in recovery. So she'd tell me how many calories I'd probably burned during the weekly bike rides, and when she saw me take a third piece of pizza, she texted me the estimated calories. It was cruel, but it was subtly cruel, usually. Most people probably wouldn't have noticed, but it was like she was poking at my biggest insecurities."

"I feel so bad that I didn't realize she was bullying multiple people like this," I said.

"She probably hadn't figured out how to play on your insecurities yet, but I bet she was looking," Lila said. She sounded bitter so Robbie must've really gotten under her skin.

Could that have been the reason Robbie had ended up in the roastery?

Lila half-smiled. "I mean, she tried flirting with Bax a few times

when you were around, but I don't think either of you really noticed. Neither of you seemed to react, anyway."

"Really?"

"Oh yeah." I remembered once when Robbie had talked intently with Bax one happy hour, subtly pushing her way to stand
between us while maintaining eye contact with him. Bax had responded by edging around her and pulling me to his side, instinctively, while Wyatt and I had talked about the novel *Dune*. Robbie
had offered to grab a drink at the bar for Bax, and Wyatt had joked
that Robbie never offered to buy a round.

"And she subtly patronized your coffee, but no one ever com-
mented. So she changed tactics."

"This makes me wonder if Robbie ever tried to antagonize
Bax," I said.

"Robbie was way too strategic to antagonize him," Lila said. "But
I bet she was looking at ways to subtly chip away at Lindsey. From
what I've seen, some women here are really supportive. I mean, look
at Lindsey. Or Kat, who spent an hour one day helping me with tech
specs so I could finish a project. They're encouraging and like to
build others up. But if Robbie had seen me drowning, she would've
stood on my shoulders if it would've helped her."

"Harsh."

"Maybe. But I'm still pissed about the pizza incident because it
was deliberate. I remember the look on her face when she saw me
read her text. And that makes me feel guilty because Robbie's dead,
but my therapist said I should work through my anger without feeling guilty."

"Why do you think she was targeting Lindsey?"

"Jealousy. Oh, do you mean, like, proof? I heard her say she
knew how to get Lindsey's goat and had a prank in mind. I assumed
she meant something more than a rubber chicken in a desk drawer."

Robbie's actions on Discord flashed to mind. Had she done anything in person? And if she had, how had Lindsey reacted?

"It's always the ones who make a point of being 'not like the other girls' that cause problems," Lila said. "Like there is one way girls are supposed to act. But whenever someone claims they never get along with other women, they're always the problem."

"I hope everyone else has been nicer."

"Everyone in my department is fantastic, and like I said, Kat has been a huge help. Raoul and his wife invited me over for dinner the night of Noah's crash. I love it here, overall. I have my fingers crossed that a full-time spot opens when I graduate since I'd love to stay on. And it gives me a ton of cred with my little brothers because they love the games we make."

Lila removed her lunch from the microwave and took it and the sparkling water back to her desk while I headed toward the motion-capture booth.

When I'd helped Ivy clean out Robbie's kitchen, I'd guessed Robbie had eaten most of her meals out. But maybe one way she'd exerted control over her life was through a limited diet. Like Lila had said, that is a sign of an eating disorder, and I'd always heard that, for teenage girls, limiting their food intake is an example of the few things they feel they can control, even if it's an illusion.

Finally, we were done with motion-capture filming for the day. I'd spent most of the day following a series of choreographed steps with a bright blue prop knife.

I found Wyatt and Noah sitting with the designer who managed the motion-capture booth.

"Everything's looking perfect," Wyatt told me. "Our Q&A testers have really been enjoying the game so far."

"Maybe they'll enjoy it even more when they can get into the knife fights," I said.

"One of the best things about this game is there are ways through every conflict without fighting, as long as the gamer wants to take them," Wyatt said. "And the choices the end user makes affect the storyline's eventual outcome."

"But you know everyone will prefer knives," Noah said.

I wondered if the option for a lack of violence was appealing after losing someone you worked closely with.

"Are you heading to the boot-camp class today?" Wyatt asked. When I nodded, he said, "Me too. I'll walk over with you."

Why, 'cause I'd get lost in the few hundred feet of the hallway? But I smiled and headed to the women's bathroom.

After changing into my workout gear, I stopped by the entrance to the office kitchen. Wyatt was shaking a water bottle with his usual bag of dried coconut water mix in front of him.

"You know you can just drink water when you work out," I said.

"Nah, this tastes way better." Wyatt put his drink mix, labeled with his name, back into the cupboard. He held his water bottle in his hand as we walked out to the hallway, past the Ground Rules office, and turned to follow the last bit of hallway to the gym.

The music thumped like always, and I wondered if the regular employees sometimes used earplugs to prevent hearing loss. A couple of regulars I recognized were stashing their gear in the cubbies in the front room or stretching near the wooden benches. I nodded hello, and signed in at the highly official spiral-ruled notebook on the front counter. I stepped onto the mats and chatted for a moment with a woman who worked at the nearby leatherwork shop.

The trainer—Aiden—started the class, and I followed along with the dynamic warm-up. Wyatt was on the other side of the room, looking a mix of solid and gangly. Fellow gym-goers tended to give him a wide berth when he swung his arms.

Partway through class, during a water break, Wyatt and I reached the shelf near the gym floor, where everyone stashed their water bottles.

I flipped open the top of my water bottle and took a swig. Wyatt did the same and then grimaced.

"You okay?" I asked, and put my bottle back on the shelf.

Wyatt looked at his bottle. "It tastes funny. Maybe the mix has gone off." He put it down, then started to step away. He suddenly leaned over and started gasping.

"Are you all right?" I asked. One of the trainers showed up by my shoulder.

"Allergic reaction," Wyatt gasped out, then sat heavily on the floor. I knelt with him, wishing I could do something other than hold his hand.

"Call 911!" the trainer shouted over his shoulder.

The woman from the leather shop raced by and came back with a thin box. "I have an EpiPen."

Wyatt looked at her and gasped. He was struggling to breathe.

"Should we give you a dose of the EpiPen?" I asked.

Wyatt nodded, and the woman pulled it out of its case and uncapped it. She took a deep breath and then stabbed it into Wyatt's leg. I flinched as it entered his thigh muscle.

Wyatt's breathing seemed to ease, although it still sounded rough.

A few minutes later, paramedics rushed in. Wyatt was still breathing, and they took over his care. I stepped back and sat down on one of the wood benches in the lobby. I watched them load Wyatt onto a stretcher and bustle him off. I wished I could do something versus sitting there feeling ineffective.

When they left, their voices echoed in the hallway, and then silence descended.

Until a whiny voice asked, "Can I get a refund? The class finished early."

"Umm, let me grab my boss."

I glanced around and realized most of the class had left, including the woman from the leather store. I should have gotten her name and info, since EpiPens aren't cheap.

As the whiny-voiced person talked with Pete, the owner of the gym, Aiden walked up to the spot where Wyatt had collapsed. He sprayed the spot down with the orange-scented cleaner they always used. Aiden started to pick up the water bottle Wyatt had left behind.

"Wait, we should save that," I said.

Aiden turned to me. "Why?"

"Whatever is in there caused Wyatt's reaction, so I'm sure he will want to know what's in it."

I didn't add, "And what someone must've added to it," although the thought crystallized in my mind. Wyatt drank his coconut water often, and I'd seen him drink some just a few days ago without a reaction.

But someone could've added an allergen to it. Lindsey had made a point of ordering a vegan pizza for Wyatt, and he'd talked about how dairy wanted to kill him.

I took the bottle from the trainer and retreated back to my bench. I pulled my cell phone out of my bag and sent a quick text message.

Another sasquatch is in the hospital. I think his water bottle was poisoned.

I sent a second text. *If causing a person to go into anaphylactic shock counts as poisoning.*

Detective Will responded quickly. *Where are you?*

At the gym next to the Ground Rules roastery.

There in five.

As I sat there, Aiden stood up from where he'd wiped down the floor, removing any lingering Wyatt-cooties. As he stepped toward the free weights, presumably to wipe them down, he flipped the spray bottle in his hands and the cap fell off, dousing him in whatever cleaner was inside.

"Darn it," he said and pulled his black T-shirt off as he walked past me to the cubbies. On a different day, maybe I would've noticed his back muscles, or his sculpted biceps.

But the combined bicycle-and-compass tattoo on his lower back, disappearing under his shorts, caught my eye. Someone had told me about a tattoo like this recently.

Miles's voice came into mind, along with the words "intimate place."

I wouldn't have really called a lower back tattoo intimate. But in a place like the Tav, with a strict "you must wear a shirt" dress code, it could qualify. Although if Miles had viewed all of the tattoo—including the bottom, which I suspected went quite low—maybe it would qualify. And it would definitely be something I wouldn't want to see in my bar.

I let myself into the roastery and carefully pulled Wyatt's water bottle out of my bag, trying to barely touch it.

I looked at the final text from Detective Will again. *There in five.*

Well, thank you for the kind words, Detective. I pulled my hoodie on and sent Bax and Lindsey a joint text detailing what had happened.

Bax FaceTimed me back. "Seriously? Wyatt collapsed?"

"He's on his way to the hospital. Did you guys see the ambulance?"

Bax shook his head. "I didn't, but I had headphones on, and as you know, my office faces the street."

"We were able to give him an EpiPen, so I hope he'll be all right."

"Do you know which hospital they took him to? Want to visit with me in a bit, if we can?"

There was a knock at the door. "Yes, to visiting, I gotta go. I can go over to the studio in a bit."

"See you then."

I disconnected and let the detective inside the roastery.

"Explain your text," Detective Will said.

"Hello to you, too," I said. The grim look on his face lessened, which I took as the equivalent of a smile. I pointed to the water bottle and told the story of Wyatt's collapse.

"I can't promise this was done on purpose, but Wyatt definitely had a reaction after drinking from the bottle. Before we went to the gym, he added a scoop of coconut water powder to that."

"Coconut water powder?"

"Yeah, he buys an organic powder from a place in Sisters. It has dried coconut with Aquamin, dried beets and oranges, and other stuff and adds it to water. He stores it in the Grumpy Sasquatch kitchen. He says it's a healthy sport drink 2.0."

The detective's nose wrinkled slightly, so I added, "It's not bad if you like coconut water."

"I'll keep that in mind. So Wyatt drinks this regularly?"

"Definitely before he works out and on bike rides. Like I said, he has a bag labeled with his name in the office kitchen."

"Do you know if Wyatt has food allergies?"

"He was pretty serious about avoiding dairy products 'cause of an allergy," I said.

Which meant, if someone added dried milk powder or something like that to the coconut water powder, they'd need access to the studio's kitchen. They'd need to know about Wyatt's allergy and the drink mix.

So they needed to know Wyatt somewhat well.

Unless someone contaminated Wyatt's drink mix by accident. Maybe they'd stolen some of it with a spoon that had been used and not properly cleaned.

"Did you empty the water bottle?"

"No, it's still full. I did touch it, along with one of the gym employees."

"I can still get the contents tested." Detective Will wrapped the bottle in plastic. "Thanks for notifying me."

The detective looked grim, and part of me felt guilty since I suspected this would move Bax back at the top of his list of suspects, although it might eliminate Harley. This reminded me of Noah's accident, in a way, given the element of chance. They had to hope Wyatt would drink it and not have an EpiPen around or someone to call for help. And they needed Wyatt to drink the mix. Granted, I hadn't seen Wyatt share any of his food, but it was possible. But if someone else had consumed it, as long as they didn't have an allergy, they wouldn't have been in danger.

Part of me wondered if it would've been better to empty the water bottle, but that would've been the wrong choice. I needed to have faith that justice would prevail and the truth would come to light.

Even if I had to drag the truth out of the shadows myself.

Chapter 22

Drizzle was falling as we walked to the small parking lot at work. Bax had one of three Grumpy Sasquatch–reserved parking spots in our building's lot; another spot belonged to Lindsey, and the third was a guest spot. But street parking was fairly easy to find, and quite a few employees took alternative means to commute to work. The nearest bus stop was only a block away, and plenty of people bicycled. Including me, but I'd left my bicycle inside the roastery to run this errand with Bax.

Bax drove us to the closest hospital to Grumpy Sasquatch Studio. He turned off NE Glisan Street into a parking garage and wound through it until we found an empty parking spot for visitors.

"This place is a maze," I said as we walked through the damp garage toward the hospital entrance.

"Last time I was here, it took me over half an hour to find my car. I'd thought I'd retraced my steps exactly, but I was a floor higher than I'd intended, and it was miserable. One of the worst parts is the map program on my phone didn't help me, since it's a parking garage. The map doesn't track individual floors."

"So you come here often?"

"There's a good pediatrician in the health center on the other side of the garage."

We made our way to Wyatt's hospital room. He was reclining in the bed closest to the door, with an older man watching daytime TV in the bed by the window.

Wyatt looked sedate, like the joy had been sucked out of his soul and left his skin paler than normal. He wore a hospital gown, with a blanket tucked over his lap, and he was sitting up. An IV dripped into his arm.

"Hi, Bax. Sage. Come by to commiserate?"

"Are you okay? You sure gave us a scare," I said.

Wyatt tried to smile. He looked exhausted. "I must have cross-contaminated my coconut water mix somehow. I'm just going to drink straight water from right now because I don't want to relive this experience. I'm thankful the leather chick had an EpiPen. That saved my life."

"Please don't end up in the hospital again," Bax said.

"Thanks for staying with me, Sage. That was terrifying," Wyatt said.

"It was scary for us, too," I said. "You should know I passed your water bottle along to Detective Will. He'll have the contents tested."

Wyatt sat up. "You did what?"

"We can't sweep this under the rug if someone tried to harm you."

Wyatt laid back down and stared at the ceiling. "I really wish you'd just let this go. I'm sure it was a mistake. It was probably my stupidity."

Bax tried to smooth things over, and our chat was desultory. Something Wyatt said didn't ring true, and it wasn't just because he felt like a faded shadow of his usual high-energy self.

"We'll let you rest. Take as much time as you need off before coming back into the office," Bax said.

"I'm sure I'll recover quickly. We're going to fall behind since we're already down a programmer."

"Still. Don't rush it. We can always push back the date of the game's launch, but it's not as easy for us to fix your health."

We left.

As we made our way back to the car, Bax glanced at me. "Do you think someone on my staff is trying to hurt their coworkers?"

"I really hope not."

"I feel like I'm living in a nightmare."

After the hospital, we had another errand of a sort: getting home in time for Niko to be dropped off.

Niko's mother, Laurel, was on her way to Trinidad and Tobago for six months to study birds, along with her husband, Ryan. Her trip had been pushed off a few times, but they were finally ready to go. Her mother was tagging along to take care of Laurel's baby daughter, but Niko would stay with his dad full-time. Although we'd been invited to visit.

Given Niko's every-other-week custody arrangement, Bax hadn't needed to do much to prepare for his son's long-term stay beyond his usual grocery stock-up. The weeks Niko is in residence are the times I tend to head to my room at my brother's house for part of the time, to give him one-on-one time with his dad.

Bax's house has a different energy when Niko is around. It's louder and livelier. But it feels intensely like home. Bax clearly misses Niko when he's not there. Even if he uses the time to work late and play hard.

I was putting a load of clean towels into the upstairs bath when Niko arrived.

When I came downstairs, Niko bounded over and gave me a hug, then asked, "Will you help me make my overnight oats?"

I blinked. "Of course." I glanced at Bax.

"Evidentially, they taste better when you help him." Bax held out his hands like this was one of life's big mysteries.

"I'm guessing it's the liberal use of peanut butter."

We grinned at each other.

"If this is all, I should be off," Laurel said. Niko turned back to his mother, and I could see her leaving was finally sinking in.

"Have a safe research trip," Bax said.

"Take lots of cool photos!" I added.

Niko ran over and hugged his mother. "We'll FaceTime often," she said.

"I know."

"Six months will be over before you know it."

"It's going to take forever."

After Laurel left, Kaldi walked over and headbutted Niko, like he knew the child needed some attention. Niko sat down and hugged the cat, who purred in his ear.

A while later, Niko chattered as I helped up set up three mason jars of overnight oats for his breakfast each morning before school for the rest of the week. We used Greek yogurt in two and milk in one, then added liberal amounts of peanut butter, a dab of maple syrup or strawberry jam, and a small scoop of chia seeds. Bax would add fresh fruit each morning for a healthy breakfast, along with a boiled egg on the side.

"How come you never help me with my oats?" Bax joked as Niko loaded his jars into the fridge. Niko arranged them carefully as he had some sort of system that included which days he wanted yogurt and which day he wanted milk.

"I'm not sure I would've eaten chia seeds at his age," I said. "At least not willingly."

"Pretty sure he's like me and does it to impress you," Bax said.

As Niko left the room in search of his sketchbook, I said, "When we have a moment, let's talk about our storyboard."

"You mean Robbie?" Bax asked. We checked, and Niko had settled on the couch with his sketchbook and headphones over his ears.

"Is he actually listening to music?"

"I'm not sure. Sometimes, I'm under the impression Niko thinks wearing headphones is part of the drawing process."

I smiled. Bax wears headphones so he can listen to music when he draws, and Niko emulates him.

I turned back to the serious subject at hand. "Think about it. Someone has gone after Wyatt, Noah, and Robbie. What do all three of them have in common?"

"You mean other than the three of them working at the same place?"

"Could they have seen something when they were on the scavenger hunt?"

"Like a mob hit?" Bax tilted his head when he looked at me.

"Something that would put targets on their backs. Maybe they saw something they didn't realize the significance of."

"So, a mob hit."

"Or someone stealing a car or something."

"That had a body from a mob hit inside? Or maybe a map to a hidden treasure that he could find if it hadn't been for those meddling kids."

"Bax, be serious."

He ran his hand through his hair. "You're right. But I can't imagine they'd see something illegal and not speak up about it. It seems too far-fetched."

"True, because someone had to know which bike was Noah's, and that Wyatt keeps coconut water mix in the office kitchen. And it's someone who knows Wyatt well enough to also know his dairy allergy."

"You're saying it's an inside job." Bax's voice was grim.

"Think of your story logic. If you made this as a flow chart, would there be any other avenues forward?" I asked.

Bax ran his hand through his hair, taking a moment to tug on the top of his head as if that would pull the thoughts he was struggling to draw out as fully formed ideas. "Their jobs aren't worth killing over. They're all talented, but there are other people with the same skill level."

"Video game development is a dream job, though." There are entire majors around creating and coding video games, and whenever Grumpy Sasquatch had a job opening, résumés flooded in.

"They don't have access to money—"

"Unless they could hack in?" They all had computer skills, after all.

"I guess they could have something sketchy saved on the servers, although that could be a nightmare. Out of an abundance of caution, I should coordinate with Lindsey to get the servers checked to ensure there aren't any surprises."

I leaned against the desk. "You know, they might not be doing anything wrong at work. Maybe they're a threat to someone at the studio who is doing something sketchy, or they know something." Could they have found out something during the scavenger hunt? Like at Jamulet Patisserie after we'd left? I tried to remember everyone who had been there.

Had they discovered something at work? Or threatened someone, even unintentionally? Robbie's pranks involved sneaking around, like when she'd left a rubber chicken inside Lindsey's desk drawer. Had she gotten into something she shouldn't have? Maybe unknowingly, her subtle taunts felt like attacks to the guilty party.

Or maybe she hadn't been so innocent. Perhaps she'd taunted the murderer, not realizing it was the sort of secret someone would kill over.

Robbie had been mean to Kat. Had Robbie known something about Kat that turned her into an easy target? Or did Kat's calm competence rankle Robbie?

"What are you thinking?" Bax asked me. But a voice from the other room called out.

"Dad! I need you!"

"I better check on him." Bax headed in Niko's direction.

I wished the security camera footage had been helpful, and I asked myself again if Ground Rules should invest in a camera over both of our doors.

What had local CCTV picked up? Hopefully, the police were analyzing it since I didn't have access to anything that could have been recorded on our route.

Unless it was posted online and tagged on social media. The living dolls in the patisserie had been photo happy. Had they picked up any duck-suited people in the background? And, maybe, one goose?

I decided to start by searching for people who'd added Jamulet Patisserie as their location on social media. My first couple of searches turned up nothing new, but then I searched Instagram and scrolled back to the date of Lindsey's birthday.

Jackpot. Quite a few of the dolls had uploaded photos. I saw a flash of yellow in the background of one image, but it was the wig of a doll versus a duck.

Someone named CherryGirlPDX had uploaded multiple photos, so I clicked on her profile, which was public. There wasn't anything interesting in her photos inside the patisserie. She'd tagged TheSweetestAngriestDollEver multiple times, so I checked out her profile.

Some photos of the group, plus several shots of cakes inside Jamulet. What else, if anything, had the dolls captured from that day?

My phone dinged. Kat. *Dolls: tomorrow at 7 p.m., The Regulars Room.*

I responded. *I'll see you there.*

Later that night, after he'd read to Niko and tucked him in, Bax collapsed down next to me on the couch.

"Lindsey checked out Robbie's laptop," he said. "There's no hidden snuff films or other disturbing videos. As far as we can tell, there's nothing to be concerned about."

"That's good." I leaned my head against his shoulder, and he put his arm around me.

"Lindsey is going to have our servers checked. Did I ever tell you someone who hacked in once stored illegally downloaded movies? It was wild. But I don't think we have anything to worry about."

"C'mon, let's go to bed," Bax said, and led me upstairs.

Chapter 23

I'd set my clock for a half hour earlier than usual, since I'd left my bicycle at work, and the official Ground Rules Subaru, which I drive occasionally, is parked in the secure lot behind the roastery. Niko was snoozing in his room, so I'd refused to let Bax give me a ride since leaving a child home alone would feel sketchy. Waking him up would be unfair to him and Niko's elementary school teacher if he were cranky from being dragged out of bed too early. After getting ready, I checked my favorite rideshare app, but there weren't any drivers circling the nearby world, waiting for fares. So I commuted old school.

I walked.

The streets were dark and quiet. A few cars cruised down the main roads and the occasional garbage or recycling truck passed by, taking care of their morning pickups. I came to a halt when an urban coyote stood on the sidewalk in front of me, but it bolted when it saw me. I read once that about three hundred fifty coyotes live in the Portland metro region, with dens in the pockets of wild areas.

Seeing the gates of the Rail Yard was like a beacon in the quiet morning. Lights were on inside the Eggceptional Bagels cart, and a voice called out, "Good morning," as I walked up to my cart.

"Good morning to you, too!" I called back.

"Any chance you can brew me a cup of coffee as soon as possible, and I'll deliver a fresh onion bagel with scallion cream cheese when it's ready?"

"For sure!"

I made a quick pour-over and carried it to the Eggceptional Bagels cart. The woman working, Alicia, smiled with relief when she saw me.

"Thank you. My coffeemaker died this morning, and I so need this."

We chatted for a few moments, then I walked back to my cart. Not long after I opened for the day, my eyes narrowed.

Mark Jeffries. Walking my way. Again.

"I came to talk about my offer," Mark said.

"My answer hasn't changed."

A regular walked up, with Sophie right behind him. Mark said, "I can't believe people still drink your coffee, considering you have a death count. How many people have died in your roastery?"

The regular glanced at Mark, then at me. He handed over a travel mug. "Americano, please."

I glanced at Mark. "If we're as deadly as you say, I can't believe you'd want to acquire us to be your premium brand."

"Budget."

Sophie glanced at me. "I'm after telling him to stop," she said.

The regular glanced at her. "Are you from Newfoundland? I always assumed Ireland, but that sounded very St. John's."

They chatted as I made the Americano, and when I turned back around, Mark had gone.

It felt like a bad omen for the day.

After leaving the cart in Kendall's capable hands, I headed to the roastery. I left my bicycle inside as I loaded up the Ground Rules Subaru with boxes of coffee beans. Today, most of my stops were with my regular retail shops, although I had an exploratory sales call with a new shop that had called and asked me to drop by.

I dropped by the new Six Impossible Things Bakery & Café in the St. Johns neighborhood about halfway through my day since it was on the route. There was a CLOSED sign on the door, but it was propped open, so I popped my head inside. They weren't ready to open, but given the cheerful yellow walls, scattering of mint green wingback chairs paired up 1:1 with funky end tables, and a few pastel-painted wooden tables and chairs with an *Alice in Wonderland* vibe, they were close.

"Sorry, we're not quite ready for customers yet," a woman in overalls with her hair pulled up in a bandana told me.

"I'm Sage Caplin. You asked me to drop by?"

"Oh, Ground Rules! Come in! I'm Maddie."

"Your café is going to be so cheerful," I said. When I walked closer, I realized Maddie was getting ready to hang framed images from Lewis Carroll's famed novels. The name and the decor made sense.

"That's the goal. We'll have fresh pastries that we bake in-house each day, along with a selection of sandwiches, soups, salads, and maybe the odd burrito. All named after our *Alice in Wonderland* theme, of course, with our Mad Hatter Tea Party menu being our true showstopper." Maddie lit up, and her energy felt like the jolt of an espresso shot. I couldn't help but smile back at her.

"Tea party?"

"Think high tea with a Portland twist. Coho salmon finger sandwiches, hazelnut petit fours, marzipan strawberries, plus some of the usual items, like scones, cucumber sandwiches, et cetera. Customers will be able to choose coffee, or tea from Stonefield Beach Tea Company, which is absolutely my new favorite tea source. All served with a whimsical flare. Just wait until you see the china we've picked out."

"Sign me up. Although I haven't heard of Stonefield Beach Tea Company." I knew where Stonefield Beach was on the Oregon coast. But I could only picture a handful of houses and no tea shops.

Maddie laughed. "That's because we're their first client. The owner is friends with my little sister, who is also one of my bakers.

And hopefully, we'll offer Ground Rules because I love the drinks you make at your cart, and I always buy your beans for home use."

"We'd be happy to supply your shop. I can send over an order form, which lists our wholesale rates."

"Perfect. Want to try a scone while we talk business? My sister made a test batch earlier."

We talked logistics and discounts over apple cinnamon scones with cups of pear green tea from Stonefield Beach, which Maddie brewed in a vintage teapot she'd found thrifting.

"You're right. This tea is out of this world."

"I'll text you her card. She's going places." Maddie paused. "You know, the owner of Left Coast Grinds showed up the other day and tried to pitch his product. Mark told me your coffee was more likely to put me under the ground versus impress me, which is when I decided we should officially order our coffee from you."

Mark? I kept an even expression on my face, then a thought made me smile.

"Is it okay if I take a photo of your shop and post about you on our social media feeds?"

"Please do. We open on Halloween, so please mention it in your post. Anyone wearing a costume will get a free 'white rabbit' or 'queen of hearts' sugar cookie, and we'll hand out candy in the evening for kids."

"Sounds fantastic."

I took a couple photos of the interior, taking a moment to set up the vintage teapot on a table in one of the shots, along with a Ground Rules card. The teal of the card matched the shop's ambiance. I wrote the caption carefully. *On Halloween, come jump down the rabbit hole and check out your new favorite coffee shop in St. Johns! Fresh pastries and an Alice in Wonderland theme make this a place you won't want to miss. Our apologies for when all of your friends discover it and the lines are out the door.*

Under the ground, indeed.

But why was Mark chasing down small accounts on his own? He

should have a sales staff, and when I'd worked for him, he'd aimed for the big shots. Like expensive hotels and large chains that'd order in bulk. He wouldn't have turned down a café dripping with quirky energy, but he wouldn't have gone out of his way to pursue it.

Maybe he'd been in the neighborhood?

Or maybe Mark was desperate.

But why?

Chapter 24

After dinner with Niko and Bax, I headed to the old-school dive bar on Division to meet up with some dolls.

And Kat.

Thankfully, the hip area on Division, a street in SE Portland, was a short bicycle ride from Bax's house. Bax had offered to loan me his car, but I'd pointed out that by the time I'd found a spot to park, it'd take me as much time to walk to the bar as it would take me to bike. But I'd promised to call him if I needed him to pick me up.

As I walked up to the Regulars Room, a tiny flicker of annoyance made my smile turn fey.

"What are you doing here?" I asked my brother, Jackson, who was standing near the bar's front door.

"Piper and I are getting some of the bar's iconic chicken and jojos," he said.

"You just happened to choose tonight?"

"Bax thought you might like the backup. And honestly, Piper and I love this place. We come here weekly."

"Hi, Sage!" Piper's voice sounded from behind me.

As Piper kissed my brother hello, I could tell she'd come from work since she wore a dark gray suit and an off-white shirt with thin black stripes underneath, with a camel coat over her arm. Her dark brown hair was styled in its usual sleek bob. Jackson's usual grumpiness faded from his face, but it snapped back into place.

"This is a surprise," I said.

"Really? Jackson said you'd love for us to join you here." Piper furrowed her brows when she turned and looked at my brother. He had the grace to look embarrassed as he explained that Bax had texted him earlier.

Piper turned back to me. "Do you want us to leave?"

Part of me wanted to say yes since my brother should've trusted I could handle the dolls on my own. As should Bax. But part of me was pleased he was giving up an evening 'cause he cared, even if he was getting dinner at one of his regular haunts out of it.

"No, you can stay, but don't slow my roll."

"What exactly does that mean?" Jackson asked.

"Let me talk to the dolls without scaring them off. And if you're really regulars here, come in for the chicken."

"Oh, good, I've been craving their chicken since Jackson mentioned it earlier today."

We walked in, and Piper and I snagged a table in one corner while Jackson went to the bar to order on our behalf.

My phone buzzed in my pocket, so I pulled it out and scanned it. Kat. *Running late.*

"So tell me about why we're here," Piper said. I told her about the dolls who'd been at the patisserie the day Robbie died.

"I love the tarts at Jamulet," Piper said as Jackson brought a trio of drinks to the table: a pale beer for him, an IPA for Piper, and a lemonade for me. He put a holder with the ace of hearts on the table's edge, visible to the bar.

"Supposedly, the dolls will show up here tonight. I'm hoping they will share their photos with me."

We chatted for a while, and the food arrived. I snagged a piping hot jojo off Jackson's plate. He gave me a narrowed-eye look.

"Me stealing your jojos is your own fault. You chose to follow me here."

"I'm not sure that argument would hold up in court."

"What, in the food court? Will the case come up right after the hearing on how this fry sauce is deadly?" I dipped my jojo into the special sauce on Jackson's plate and bit into the breaded potato wedge. It was crispy on the outside, and the potato inside was soft. It was seasoned just right. If the chicken matched the quality of the jojo, I could see why Jackson and Piper were regulars.

I was fairly sure Piper enjoyed our conversation as she bit into one of her broasted chicken pieces.

A group of five dolls walked in, and Jackson's eyebrows rose when he saw them. "You know, you said dolls, but I didn't realize how authentic they'd look."

Three of the dolls had gingham dresses with stiff petticoats, and two looked anime-like, with exaggerated eye makeup. But no Sally.

A few more dolls trickled in, and they set up shop on the other side of the bar.

Then Kat walked in with the Sally doll who had to be Nadia. Kat motioned to us, and they walked over. I could read questions on their faces as they glanced from Jackson to me.

"This is my brother," I said. "Long story. He's just here for dinner."

The Sally doll spoke. "So you want to see our photos? You know, you could've just asked the other day at the Tav."

"I'll keep that in mind in the future."

"Come over, and I'm sure everyone will happily share their photos. Just remember to fawn."

"Let us know how it goes," Piper mouthed at me.

Nadia and Kat were right: the dolls were happy to pull out their phones and share their photos from Jamulet.

"You see what I did with my eyeliner there? I practiced

for days," one of the dolls told me as she showed a close-up of her face.

"Your hand sure is steady," I said, remembering the advice to fawn.

"It just takes practice. I'm lucky that my sisters let me practice on them all the time when we were younger. But I've always had a steady hand. Although no one can beat Nadia's straight lines."

"You know, when I stepped outside that day for a vape, I saw two women arguing," an anime doll said.

"Oh?"

"One of them had a white bird costume. Not a very good one, kind of like a onesie. No real artistry—I mean, there weren't even fake feathers. But I thought it was weird. 'Cause I'd seen a few people in yellow onesies, but she didn't match."

"Was the white goose arguing with a yellow duck?" I felt like a demented Dr. Seuss.

"No, the woman was dressed like my mom."

Based on the scoff in Anime Doll's voice, I suspected she was barely old enough to enter the bar.

"Didn't we come out and do a photo while you were vaping?" one of the gingham dolls asked.

They scrolled through some photos, and one of them showed me a picture. Robbie in her white goose costume in the background was turning away from a woman in business casual.

And not just any woman in business casual. Robbie had been talking with Elaine.

But Elaine had left long before Robbie had arrived. Or, at least, she'd said she was heading back to the office.

Maybe she'd come back?

Or maybe she hadn't left the patisserie at all?

Or she could've been waiting to talk to Robbie. But why would Elaine choose the patisserie as a place to confront Robbie? Unless she didn't want the sasquatches to see her at the office. But, if anything, she'd be more conspicuous outside the office. Inside, Elaine could always claim the employee needed to refill out a form as an excuse to talk to them.

I'd need to check Lindsey's logbook of when people had arrived, eaten, and left. Fingers crossed, Lindsey hadn't deleted the info.

Elaine had said she was heading home. But it's not like anyone had walked her outside, right?

Had she hung around, waiting to confront Robbie?

And Robbie held something red in her hand, but even when the gingham doll zoomed in, I couldn't tell what it was.

When Robbie had walked into Jamulet, had she carried anything? She'd worn a yellow-and-green-striped beanie. Maybe her costume had pockets? The duck suits had shallow pockets that barely held a phone; maybe Robbie's goose costume had them, too. And Robbie had to have carried her phone at least.

More importantly: what was going on with Elaine?

After a while, I ended up standing with Nadia, who told me about the different costumes she'd developed over the years, and mentioned how she turned into Kat's tailor over the years, taking in her shirts to fit, even if the clothing, according to Nadia, was unexciting.

"Your sister is truly unique. And patient," I said.

"Kat isn't a fan of being pushed around," Nadia said. "She seems calm, but she'll run out of patience eventually. But she respects people who respect her. She's pretty much my idol."

"Is it okay if I ask why you dress up as a doll?" I asked.

"Because it makes me happy. It's a fun escape for a few hours with my friends."

I couldn't find fault with Nadia's words. We all find our ways to escape real life for a few hours. Some people use body paint to show their love for a sports team. Others use it to create a fictional, doll-like version of themselves.

Another doll joined us. "I heard you want to see photos?" She held out her phone and scrolled through them with me, of the dolls in meeting places, but not on the day I wanted.

Something told me I'd found out everything I could, and it was a doozy. Elaine had been skulking around.

Now, I just needed to find out why.

And I'd see if my brother and his girl wanted to give me a ride home.

Chapter 25

Thursday morning chugged along like normal, and I left the cart in Kendall's hands before heading to the roastery. I had some overdue tasks to handle and payroll to submit to our service.

But I dropped into Grumpy Sasquatch Studio to thank Kat for taking me to see the dolls.

"It was no problem. As I said, the dolls are happy to share their photos with anyone who would enjoy seeing them." Kat looked perkier today than she had for a while, and today's flannel shirt was a blue plaid that worked nicely with her hair.

"You said one of your sisters is a carpenter?" I asked.

"Yes, Nadia, you met her. The Sally doll."

"Really?"

"Yes, she is good at visualizing things. And dolls can build things, too, as you can see."

"Your sister said something interesting yesterday," I said.

Kat looked up at me. She brushed a loose strand of hair out of her eye, tucking it behind her ear.

"Did you get into trouble, or something, as a teen? And did Robbie know?"

Kat's shoulders hunched. "How do you know?"

"Nadia said something about you running out of patience."

"Some girls were very mean to Nadia when I was in high school, and she was in eighth grade. So I stopped their meanness."

"What does that mean?"

"It means I told them I would beat them if they were mean to my sister, and when one girl continued, I punched her. I was suspended but thankfully not expelled."

"So why would this matter to Robbie?"

"She must have spent an evening researching me online and found out I'd been arrested. I was under eighteen, and I wasn't convicted or anything. The girl's parents dropped the charges when they found out their daughter was bullying Nadia. But I had to agree to anger management counseling. Which I did for six months. But it was bad. And Robbie said Bax and Lindsey wouldn't trust me if they knew. No one trusts people with anger issues."

"Kat, you should tell Lindsey about it, or Bax. I think they'd understand. And then you wouldn't worry about the past wrecking your future."

Kat looked down at her desk. "That is not all."

"Oh?"

"Robbie caught me researching death with dignity one day."

"For your mother?" Sympathy washed through me. Oregon had passed a Death with Dignity Act in the 1990s. We'd made the news again over twenty years later when we'd broadened the law to open the act to anyone willing to travel to the state and able to meet the act's requirements.

"Yes. Robbie said she would tell people I wanted to kill my mother. I'm not even sure if Mother would qualify for the act, and she might have been asking out of frustration. She feels like a burden, but we love her. But Robbie said no one will like me if they find out."

"I think everyone here would mainly feel compassion for you. I do. Your family is in a tough situation."

"Thank you for saying that, Sage."

"I'll keep everything you told me private, but you shouldn't feel like you have to hide any of this. I'm not saying blab about it indiscriminately, but it's nothing you need to be ashamed of."

Kat had a reason to dislike Robbie, even hate her, considering the continual subtle bullying. But could she have killed her?

But another thought pinged in my brain. Kat fought back when her sister was bullied; had she done the same thing to Robbie, but it had gotten out of hand? Or did Kat only get aggressive when she defended people she loved, like her sister?

After talking with Kat, I was going to see if it was a good moment to say hi to Bax, but I detoured into Elaine's office. Maybe I could ask her about Jamulet Patisserie. Although perhaps I was just grasping at straws and should leave all of this interviewing to the professionals.

As I entered Elaine's office, I scanned it again. It looked pretty much the same as the last time I'd been in. Her wall of locked file cabinets always makes me smile, since this is an office that tries to use zero paper, but she insists on keeping hardcopies of certain files. Elaine also has a board, similar to ones I've seen in hotels and doctors' offices, holding a variety of pamphlets. Except instead of health or tourism, hers are for work-related issues, like a brochure with explanations of insurance benefit terms, the counseling service, retirement 101, and other benefits offered by the company.

"This is interesting." I motioned to Elaine's collection of pamphlets.

"Originally, I had them in files, but this makes it easier if someone wants info on one of our programs but is hesitant to ask me."

I noticed a brochure on domestic violence awareness alongside one that listed local resources for people fleeing abuse.

"Some of those are valuable to people who don't want their spouse to see what they've been researching online."

But the brochures on one side were for local attractions, like The Grotto and the historic Heathman hotel.

"I love The Grotto. It's where I go for peace." Elaine's fingers tapped on her keyboard, but her eyes were watching me.

"It's beautiful." I tried to picture Elaine walking around the sixty-two-acre shrine to the Virgin Mary on Portland's outer east side. I could see why someone would make it a regular stop to help find balance within themselves; after all, that's the whole point of The Grotto.

I sensed Elaine was about to ask me why I was here, so I made my voice casual and asked, "Did you enjoy Jamulet the other day?"

"I was barely there," Elaine said.

"Really? Because I thought I saw you around the patisserie a while later."

"Not me," Elaine said.

"That's weird, 'cause I saw you in the background of a photo from one of the dolls. You saw them, right? Their costumes are amazing."

Elaine eyed me for a moment, and I returned her gaze. I had the sense she felt exhausted, deep inside, from her posture. Like she was barely holding everything together. Something told me a lot of the sasquatches felt that way.

Elaine half-smiled when she spoke. "Oh yeah, I'd forgotten about that. I left Jamulet to finish something here, then realized I needed a slice of their opera cake. I finished my workday at my kitchen table, scarfing down the cake in private before my kids got home from school. Along with a few macarons because I have no willpower where Jamulet is concerned."

"Those macarons are legit. I sometimes dream about them."

Elaine closed her eyes for a moment, like she was looking back in time, then she locked her gaze on me again. "I did see Robbie outside Jamulet. That girl was spitting mad."

"You pride yourself on knowing what everyone's up to," I said. "What was going on with Robbie?"

Elaine shrugged. "She was such a hoot, but she wanted to be taken seriously. Robbie thought she deserved the promotion she interviewed for. I counseled her to be patient, that her time would come since the hiring decision was fair, but she didn't want to listen.

She wanted to formally complain to the HR service that she didn't get the promotion due to gender."

"How do you think the HR professionals would've reacted?"

"As I told Robbie, even if they investigated, they wouldn't have found any wrongdoing. The interviews and eventual decision were well documented, including multiple glowing yearly reviews for the person who got the job. The studio regularly hires strong female candidates and promotes them across the company. The last place I worked only had women managers in HR."

"Really?"

"HR is a rather female-dominated field. I read somewhere seventy percent of the industry is female." Elaine looked at me again. "So why did you drop in?"

"Good question. Why did I come in here? I had a question about staff management that I thought you might have insight into, but I can't remember it now."

"Feel free to come back when you remember." Elaine's eyes went back to her monitor, and I walked out. Chances were, she'd known I'd come in to ask about Robbie. And she hadn't acted like it was a big deal, or that she had anything to hide.

Elaine spoke highly of Robbie, so they must've had a good rapport. Maybe Elaine thought she could take the faux-Australian under her proverbial wing.

Bax was busy, but we made plans to meet up at lunch, and I headed to the roastery. Harley was in fine form, roasting a new batch of beans, and I set up at my desk and popped my headphones on. After all, this paperwork wasn't going to finish itself.

By the end of the day, I simply felt frustrated. Like everything was covered by a giant thundercloud and lightning could strike at any moment.

But there's something that always cheers me up and turns that frown upside down.

A good workout. I changed into the workout clothes tucked into my messenger bag and snagged my running shoes from my old-school locker in the Ground Rules office that was precisely what it looked like: a set of vintage high school lockers we'd found in a re-sale shop and thought would make fun employee lockers/storage area.

I dumped my keys into the drawstring bag I stored in my locker, filled up my water bottle, and put on my game face.

I signed into the suspension class and spent the next hour using TRX cables and my own bodyweight to squat, do push-ups, and per-form other exercises. The class wasn't as pulse raising as boot camp, but the mixture of strength training, balance, and focused movement made the frustration melt from my body. Everything annoying me would work out, pun intended.

After I was done, I stopped to pick up my bag and saw Aiden sit-ting on the benches, alone.

I paused by him, and he looked up. He tried to smile. "Hi, Sage. Did you have a good workout?"

"I always love the TRX class. Are you doing okay? You look down."

"Just taking a break."

I put my foot up on the bench and stretched, but I kept my eyes on the trainer. "Were you close with Robbie? It was nice of you to attend her memorial."

Aiden looked away and fiddled with his water bottle. "She was a client, and my boss thought it would be nice if some of us attended in solidarity. But we didn't have a personal relationship."

His words rankled me, but I made my voice sound sympathetic. "Are you lying to yourself, or to me? Just a client? You made out with her at the Tav after a Thorns game."

Aiden groaned and leaned his head into his hands. "You saw? I'm so embarrassed about that."

"Quite a few people have gotten a bit drunk and done something they shouldn't," I said. Granted, my mistakes are usually ordering necklaces on Etsy, leading to a more extensive collection of sunstone pendants than one person needs. But I didn't need to fill in any details given the look on his face.

"I doubt my wife would approve."

"Oh." For a simple word, "oh" can mean a lot based on the inflection. Aiden nodded, acknowledging the mess he'd created.

"Did you fight with Robbie afterward or something?" I asked.

"We argued when we left the Tav. Being drunk didn't help. But I was smart enough to catch a ride home instead of going to her place," Aiden said.

"Did you argue with her again later? Say, in my roastery?"

Aiden looked at me with wide eyes.

"Wait, I didn't kill her," Aiden said. "A few days after the Tav, Robbie talked about telling my wife. But I thought she was cadging to get a few extra perks at the gym, like free personal training sessions. I told her that if she tried to blackmail me, I'd get her banned. I've worked at Pump It for almost a decade, and trust me, Pete would've sided with me."

"It wouldn't have looked good." My voice was soft.

Aiden nodded. "True, and it wouldn't have been my finest moment. We don't have a strict non-fraternization policy like a school has, but it's highly discouraged. I mean, I try to be professional, since it's not good optics if the staff hits on the clients. We want people to feel like they're coming to get a good workout and meet their fitness goals, not walk the gauntlet in a meat market. But we've had a few relationships come out of the gym."

His words sounded like an excuse to me. "Are you sure about that? I can't imagine dealing with a situation like that at Ground Rules."

"My boss would've been annoyed with me, but I'm fairly sure he always thought Robbie was obnoxious. He was annoyed by her pranks and told her they weren't amusing and to cut it out if she wanted to continue working out here. My wife wouldn't have been happy, but I'm sure we could get over her finding out I got drunk and kissed a client."

"How'd you end up going out with Robbie, anyway?"

"It wasn't on purpose. One of my regular personal training clients had extra Thorns tickets and gave them to a few of my coworkers and me. Robbie was at the game, and we walked out of the stadium together. I'd planned on grabbing a slice of pizza and then catching a bus home. Robbie suggested we stop by the Tav for a drink, and their drinks are really strong. I'm a lightweight these days, and the alcohol hit my empty stomach. I wish I could excuse my behavior, and I'm embarrassed that anyone saw it. But like I said, it was chance, not a planned hookup. She's not really my type."

"I heard it was a bit more than kissing."

"We were in public, and once the angry bartender threatened us, we sat on opposite sides of the booth. We never touched again. Walking back into that bar again was embarrassing. At least I knew to stick to water."

"You've seemed pretty off since Robbie was found." Aiden used to seem like a sort of laid-back happy type, but his smile had felt forced for a while. Like he was trying to be his normal self, but he had a spring of tension inside threatening to unravel.

"But not because of Robbie, although to be honest, yes, it does bother me. Someone dying in this building, let alone someone I knew, does feel weird. No, I'm having other problems."

"Oh?" I switched and stretched my other calf muscle.

Aiden looked like he was analyzing himself. "My wife has been emotional since she got pregnant, and I always feel like I can't do anything right in her eyes. I guess Robbie's attention felt flattering. It was nice to pretend I was interesting instead of someone married and boring. I hadn't really thought of it that way until now."

"It sounds like you have some things to work through." Especially with a kid on the way.

"Trust me, I'm aware. Things have been a mess for a few months now."

"But are you okay? Do you need help?"

Aiden shrugged. "Things will work out. They have to."

True. The future always arrives, even if it brings outcomes and events we don't want.

"I have to ask. On the day Robbie died, you left the gym at three thirty p.m. But you didn't walk out of the building until three fifty-eight. What happened? There's no way it takes twenty-eight minutes to walk down the hallway."

"Wait, why are you asking this? Are the police going to question me about this?" Aiden turned to face me. His voice held a panicked note.

I made my voice sound sympathetic. "Should they?"

Aiden blushed like a Victorian spinster. "I didn't do anything wrong, but I don't want my wife to find out. You know the seamstress? I dropped by."

"Did you need a new dress?" I couldn't help the sarcasm. The seamstress specialized in bespoke dresses. Not exactly Aiden's style, unless he had a side to him I'd never suspected.

He looked down at the ground. "I was less interested in her designs and more interested in her. We've been spending some time together recently, so I dropped by to say hi. She's a good listener."

I barely stopped myself from asking if she was another woman who stopped Aiden from feeling old and boring. But I knew I wasn't in the position to judge Aiden's life, nor were his relationships my business.

"If you have a good reason for the time gap, then I don't think you need to worry. Did you see anything that, even tangentially, might be relevant to Robbie's death? It'll be good for all of us to find out what happened. Can you imagine if this hangs over all of us for months? Years?"

"That'd be terrible," Aiden said. "And no, I didn't see anything, and if I had, I would've told the police. For what it's worth, Robbie did her usual boot-camp class the day before she died, and afterward, we talked. She said she was working on something epic."

"Like the video game she was working on?"

Aiden shook his head. "No, it felt personal. Robbie said she was finally going to crack a puzzle that'd been bothering her for a while. But it felt different from the way she talked about work. She said people should be wary of crossing her, but giggled when she said it, like it was a joke. But it didn't feel like one. Now I wonder if she was boasting about something sketchy, maybe from her personal life. The sort of thing that would lead someone to off her."

"Weird."

Aiden stood up. "I have a client to get ready for."

"Wait," I said. I made my voice gentle, and my words were honest. "It sounds like your personal life is troubled, so I hope you have someone you trust to talk to, like a counselor." Especially before adding a baby to the mix.

"You're right, Sage, this isn't any of your business." He walked off.

Aiden's words about Robbie working on something epic rankled me. Had she been trying to pull a prank on Harley? On me?

If only I knew why Robbie had been inside the roastery. I trusted Harley had found Robbie versus letting her in. But how did this all tie together?

Could Aiden have come across Robbie breaking into Ground Rules and followed her inside? Maybe he hadn't planned it, but it had seemed like a good time to clear the air between them, especially if Aiden thought Robbie was trying to blackmail him.

I texted Detective Will about Aiden's thirty-minute walk down the hallway and added, in a second text, that the two had history.

I was picking up my bicycle from the Ground Rules roastery when the detective called, so I summarized the situation.

"Please tell me you're not playing Nancy Drew," he said. "You'll put yourself in danger."

"Please, I'm way more Trixie Belden." I didn't add that Bax, Jackson, Harley, and my baristas are all my Bob-Whites, aka my confidantes and chosen family. Although we don't have matching jackets like the fictional crew in the Trixie Belden series. Although that could be my Christmas gift to all of them.

"Do you think we haven't noticed this alleged missing thirty minutes? This is my job, after all. You should stay far away and focus on making coffee."

"Noted." The slight disdain in his "making coffee" tone made my metaphorical hackles rise, but I ignored it. For now. Given Aiden's reaction, the police hadn't asked him about it yet.

After we hung up, I headed home. Hopefully, this would be the final missing clue the detective needed to solve this murder, but deep inside, I doubted it, since the case still wasn't solved.

But maybe, clicking this puzzle piece into place might bring the rest of the picture into focus.

Or, by telling the police, I'd just blown up Aiden's life, even if he wasn't involved in Robbie's death. But he clearly had other secrets this was bringing to light.

Chapter 26

Friday morning. My last workday of the week, as Kendall would open the cart tomorrow; we didn't have any special events scheduled for the second cart. We'd decided to close Sundays between Labor Day and Memorial Day.

During the rush, Sophie joined me at the cart, and we worked side by side. I was getting ready to leave when a familiar face walked up.

"Hi, Noah," I said.

"Today seems like a good day for a mocha."

I glanced at Sophie. "He said 'mocha.'" I stopped my lips from twitching up into a smile.

"You know you heard that woman say 'matcha.'"

Noah looked at me, so I told him the story.

Sophie put his mocha down on the order window. "That woman was way out of bounds."

"Noah, have you met Sophie before? Sophie, this is my friend, Noah."

"It's nice to meet you," Noah said. "Sage, can we talk for a moment?"

"Go on, boss, I've got the cart."

Noah wanting to talk was a surprise. If anyone was going to catch me for a one-on-one, I would've guessed Wyatt.

I poured myself a cup of French press, stepped out of the cart, and joined Noah at the picnic table closest to my cart. "What's up?"

"I don't want to go to work." He looked down at his mocha. I eyed the swirl of hair in the front left of his head, noting how it would be a cowlick if he grew his hair out.

"You could take a mental health day."

"I feel like something weird is happening at work. First Robbie, then my accident, then Wyatt collapsing."

"Is there someone who has it out for all three of you?"

Noah looked up at me. His hazel eyes had flecks of green. "That's the thing. I can't think of anyone who'd hate all three of us. I thought my bike accident was a fluke, but then Wyatt ending up in the hospital really freaked me out."

Accident? His brakes were cut. I studied him.

"No one would blame you if you said you needed a day off after everything, especially considering you had a head injury. If you don't feel safe, you should listen to the feeling."

"I might be making something out of nothing, though. No one will let me live it down if I am," Noah said.

"Is there anything else you want to tell me?" I asked.

"We're super impressed by the motion-capture work you're doing, and the game will be fantastic."

We talked for a few moments longer, and I wondered why Noah had really stopped by. Unless he just wanted a sympathetic ear.

"Maybe I will take today off," Noah said. "I have vacation time, and I can log in a few hours at home this weekend."

"Isn't that the opposite of vacation?"

"I love what I do."

I could feel the sincerity in his words.

"So, what's Sophie's story? Is she Irish?" Noah asked. He looked over to the cart, where Sophie handed a drink to a man in an orange raincoat.

"She's a grad student in Public Health. She's from St. John's, Newfoundland, has a wicked sense of humor, is always reliable, and if you hurt her, I will make you feel like your recent bike crash was mild."

Noah laughed. "No one in their right mind wants to cross you."

He stood up, strolled to the cart, and started chatting with my barista. Sophie blushed slightly as she talked to him.

Maybe something good would come out of this after all.

Saturday morning dawned as a perfectly crisp fall day. Niko danced by the door in the afternoon as Bax stopped by the closet to grab their fall coats. "What's that? You think we should skip Sauvie Island and the pumpkin patch?"

"Dad!" Niko moaned, but I could tell he knew his dad was joking and had responded in kind. "The corn maze has ghosts! Ghosts!"

Sauvie Island is located about ten miles from downtown Portland on an island where the Willamette River meets the Pacific. It's known for its pumpkin patches and corn mazes, plus u-pick berry farms and freshly grown produce. The twelve-mile road circumnavigating the island is popular with cyclists. The hike to the small Warrior Rock Lighthouse on the north end has always been a favorite.

Niko and Bax had always made annual trips to pick up a pumpkin for Halloween, drink apple cider, visit the petting zoo, and spin through a corn maze. But for the first time, they were visiting the haunted maze.

Niko looked at me. "I'll protect you from the ghosts," he said. Then he glanced at his dad. "Sage knows they're not real, right?"

"Safe assumption, buddy. Hmm, Sage and I could be ghosts for Halloween."

"That's boring, Dad."

For the first time, I was joining their annual trip. We were all decked out in sweaters, jeans, boots, and new matching striped beanies that Niko had found and coerced his dad to buy. Although I suspected it hadn't taken much arm-twisting.

"You guys are taking too long," Niko said. Bax handed over his son's jacket, then put his arm into his own coat in slow motion.

"Stop teasing the kid," I said.

"Listen to Sage!"

We finally made it into the car, and once Niko was safely in-stalled in the back, we were off.

Getting to Sauvie Island involved taking a bridge over the Willa-mette River and driving down highway 30. We passed by the charm-ing Linnton sign, shaped like a curved fish, immediately followed by its historic downtown that feels like a small town, even though it's part of Portland. But that's one of the things I love about local neigh-borhoods: they frequently feel like their own small towns with desti-nation streets that feel like their city center.

Niko said, "Finally," as we drove over the bridge that dropped us onto Sauvie Island, and it didn't take long for Bax to park in the lot for the farm with the haunted corn maze.

"Maybe we should get apple cider first," Bax said, but he let Niko drag him toward the corn maze. Bax held out his hand to me, and I grasped it. We followed in Niko's wake to the booth that led us to the ticket booth, where we checked in for the maze.

"About time!" Niko said. As if he'd been waiting for years in-stead of minutes when he entered the maze.

"Which way?" I asked Niko. Niko turned his head when we heard a howl on the air, like a werewolf's, coming from the right.

"Let's go left," he said, and Bax and I followed him.

When we turned the first corner, a black figure in a cloak jumped out at us. Niko jumped and then stumbled backward into me.

"You okay, buddy?"

"Don't worry, Dad, it was just a big surprise."

The vampire stepped back into the shadow of the hay bales.

I paused. Could it really be that simple?

Niko recovered quickly, and we eventually wound our way through the maze, seeing a werewolf, a few more vampires, and a couple of ghosts along the way.

After we finished the maze, we took a hayride to the pumpkin field to pick out three pumpkins, aka one each. My thoughts were whirling. I knew what had led to Robbie's death, although I wasn't sure why.

But something told me I knew who was involved, although I couldn't prove it.

Bax nudged my shoulder. "You okay?" he asked.

I climbed off the hay bale, and he helped me off the wagon to the ground. "Yeah, just thought of something I want to chat about later. Let's get the best pumpkin ever!"

"I know the exact sizes we need . . ." Niko started chattering. I did my best to listen and stay in the moment as we picked out our pumpkins, caught another hayride back to the main farm store to drink mugs of apple cider, and then pet the goats in the barn.

"Do you think Kaldi would like a goat friend?" Niko asked.

"I've seen weirder duos become friends," Bax said.

"Maybe we could draw a goat friend for Kaldi?"

"That sounds like a brilliant idea, buddy."

"I can write a whole series of Kaldi and goat friend adventures!" Niko danced ahead of Bax.

"What are you going to name the goat?" Bax asked. I noted the laugh in his voice; he was probably thinking about how our Kaldi was named after the goatherd, so the friendship would be oddly appropriate.

"Ben!" Niko said.

I tried to stay in the moment, but my mind was buzzing.

My friend Erin texted me early Sunday morning, not long after I'd woken up and was blearily setting my gooseneck to boil for my first cup of coffee. *OMG DID YOU SEE THIS?*

And she sent a link to an article from the local Sunday paper.

Left Coast Grinds Loses Luster

Once the king of the Portland coffee scene, former juggernaut Left Coast Grinds struggles to adapt to a changing coffee scene.

I skimmed the article, which detailed how Left Coast Grinds's expansion had dramatically slowed, and a national deal had fallen through. "Sources say some of their longtime customers have jumped ship to other local roasters."

A quote from an "industry expert" caught my eye.

> Newer start-ups, like the nimble Ground Rules, have been carving their mark into the Portland coffee scene with their commitment to quality and focus on social consciousness. They not only focus on the minutiae of the science of roasting and brewing coffee properly, but they're more than fair trade. They can tell you which small farms they acquired their beans from and discuss what makes that bean or blend unique. Visiting their shops—or in Ground Rules's case, coffee cart—is an education in coffee.

An education in coffee. I smiled and screen-captured the quote to add to Ground Rules's social media accounts.

I returned to the article and read a quote from a local roaster I knew and admired.

> In the past week, Mark Jeffries has been posting negative comments that seem to imply Ground Rules and some of our fellow roasters are trash. One has to wonder if Jeffries is projecting on himself. It's mean, regardless, and lets down the entire Portland roasting community.

A tiny sliver of love slid through me. It was nice to see my fellow competitors sticking up for me and the other micro-roasters and small coffee shops in the city.

Bax wandered into the kitchen, his hair rumpled, in flannel pajama pants, as I started pouring the coffee. Niko soon followed, already as energetic as most people are after their fifth cup of coffee.

Later in the morning, Tierney texted me with the same link to the article. *You know, this explains some things.*

Oh? I replied.

He responded quickly. *For someone that acts like a big shot, he sure was disparaging when we said we were interviewing a few other roasters, including you. And he seemed oddly desperate to get our business.*

Hmm. I texted back. *Maybe Mark wants the contract to show he's still the top dog. Plus, regardless of who you choose, it will be a fantastic product.*

Expect a call from us tomorrow. Shay and I have decided and want to schedule a time with you to talk about contracts.

Kaldi meowed at me, so I picked him up and waltzed him around the room. Then I popped him onto my shoulder, and Kaldi lounged there like it was the exact spot he'd plotted to hang out in. I picked up my phone to send another text. *I'll be in the roastery (versus cart) tomorrow after 10. We look forward to working with you!*

Have a good Sunday! I'll see you tomorrow.

Of course Tierney would want the final word.

"Why're you so happy?" Bax asked. "Texting your other boyfriend?"

I motioned to Kaldi. "No, my other man is right here. That was Tierney. They've chosen to go forward with Ground Rules for the canned Irish whiskey drink."

Bax high-fived me. "We should celebrate."

"Let's save the celebration until after tomorrow."

"About that . . ."

"Yeah, let's run through the game plan again."

Chapter 27

Monday morning. If today was a chessboard, all pieces were set up to play, and I'd make the first move this afternoon. We'd know who was responsible for Robbie's death if I was right.

But first: I opened the cart like today was a typical day. My first few customers filtered in.

Sophie was chipper and jumped to work. "My first shifts at the Tav went great!"

The last thing I wanted to deal with today was Mark Jeffries, but I didn't have much choice. I looked up during the morning rush to see him bearing down on the cart.

He bypassed the three people queuing up in front of the cart and banged on the front counter.

"Please get in line if you're here to order a coffee." I looked at the regular he'd cut off. "What can I get for you?"

"A large house coffee to go, please," she said. She stepped around Mark and handed me a reusable tumbler with a law firm's logo screen-printed on it.

"Don't ignore me," Mark said.

"You have two choices: get in line or leave. If you do anything else, I'll have you removed from the property," I said. Mark must've loved the newspaper article yesterday.

Sophie brought a vanilla latte to the window for a man waiting, and he eyed Mark when he stepped forward to pick up his coffee. I stepped back and filled the woman's tumbler. Mark was still standing at the order window when I brought it back.

"Here's your coffee," I said, looking at her. But when I tried to hand it over, Mark knocked my hands, causing the coffee to douse my sweatshirt.

The customers in line gasped. I pulled my hoodie off, glad the coffee hadn't soaked through to my T-shirt and burned me.

The woman took a photo of Mark with her phone. "Good, this photo captured your face nicely," she said. She turned to me. "Have I ever mentioned I'm a personal injury lawyer? Let me give you my card, as you might have a lawsuit here."

Mark held up his hands. "I'm out of here. But don't think you're getting that whiskey contract," he said.

I smiled, even though I shouldn't have, and didn't tell him my good news, and waved. He glared at me, then turned and walked away.

"I'll get your coffee refilled," I said.

I rinsed out her mug, and as I was filling it, she said, "By the way, I don't specialize in personal injury, although I am a lawyer. I specialize in real estate."

I put her refilled mug down on the counter. "Thanks for the assist. You got him out of here, which is all I wanted."

She put her business card down on the counter. "But if you do need a witness for today, contact me. The photo I took of him does show his face clearly, although I didn't react in time to record him."

"Thanks again," I said. She paid on the tablet, and I took the orders from the regulars behind her. By the time we'd served all of them, I had all their business cards, and offers to serve as witnesses if necessary.

"Are you going to do anything about today?" Sophie asked. "What a creep."

"I think getting our company attorney to send a cease-and-desist letter might be worthwhile."

"We have a company attorney?"

"Sort of. My brother has stepped in before, although we've also started working with a lawyer specializing in business law. She's fantastic."

While Sophie took over the primary duties of the cart, I shot the attorney who would also negotiate the canned Irish whiskey contract a quick email. I asked if we could send Mark a cease-and-desist letter and request that he avoid the Rail Yard in the future. I knew the letter wouldn't be legally binding, but it would hint we were ready for further action.

I shivered in the cold morning air and pulled my damp hoodie back on. Thankfully, I had clothes to change into for my meeting later, so I wouldn't smell like coffee all day.

Something told me I'd hear from Mark again.

When two o'clock rolled around, hours after I'd spent the morning negotiating the new canned whiskey deal with Tierney and Shay, it was go time.

It was time to unmask the murderer. Hopefully the cloud of Robbie's death would quit following all of us around.

I strolled into Grumpy Sasquatch Studio like usual for my motion-capture session. But when I passed by Noah's and Wyatt's workspaces, I motioned for them to follow me. I led them into the motion-capture booth, turned, and faced them.

"Guys, we're clearing the air. I know you caused Robbie's accident in the roastery. You were trying to prank her, right? But it got out of hand?"

"Why would you think that?"

"You're the two who had the chance to do it. I'm not sure how you got keys to the roastery, but I'm sure the thought of being in there without me around was like catnip to Robbie."

"She did want to snoop in there," Wyatt said.

"I'm guessing when you heard Harley was going home sick, you realized it was the perfect day to get back at Robbie for all of the pranks she'd played on you."

"Why are you asking us this?" Noah asked.

"Because it's time for the truth to come to light."

They glanced at each other.

"You're right. We decided to prank Robbie," Wyatt said. "I'd borrowed your keys one day while you were filming, and Noah made a copy of the Ground Rules keys."

"You stole my keys?" I should feel angry, but if anything, I felt hurt. I'd thought these two were my friends.

"You always leave your bag in a cubby, so I snagged them one day when you were getting ready in the booth. I wouldn't have given them to anyone else, and we wouldn't have let Robbie into your roastery alone. But it seemed like the perfect way to set up a prank. We didn't expect anyone to get hurt."

"What happened on Lindsey's birthday?"

"When we split up and Robbie stalked off, we realized it was a perfect time. We texted her and acted like this was our way of apologizing to her. Noah went inside, and I met Robbie on the sidewalk and let her into the roastery."

I glanced at Noah.

"I was waiting inside, wearing a mask, with the lights off. Robbie said they should mess with your roaster as a prank and I jumped out from behind it. She screamed and slipped. When she fell, she hit her head on the roaster." Noah looked at his hands.

"Robbie was dazed at first, but when she sat up, she started screaming at us. Said she'd get us both fired." Wyatt looked at Noah.

"So I bolted, with Wyatt on my heels. We went to the hallway and into the studio, debating what to do." Noah stared at the wall above my head.

"You just left her there, alone?" I asked.

"I was going to go back and see if she needed help, but when I walked into the hallway, I saw you were already there." Noah finally made eye contact with me.

"You came to the Rail Yard to talk to me about how you were afraid. Like you thought whoever was after Robbie was also trying to harm you." I glared at Noah.

"I wanted to talk it through with you. I couldn't tell you I was responsible for Robbie's accident, but I was concerned. I didn't spike Wyatt's coconut mix, but I wasn't sure I believed him when he told me he didn't slice my brakes. I thought he was warning me not to talk." Noah continued to make eye contact with me. The feeling in my gut told me he was telling the truth.

"You're still lying about the coconut water?" Wyatt asked. He turned to Noah, starting to posture like he wanted to fight.

But Noah continued to face me like Wyatt wasn't there. "I started to feel like Robbie's ghost was haunting us."

"Did the ghost want justice?" I asked.

Wyatt's posture slumped. "Are you seriously claiming you didn't poison me?"

Noah turned his head to look at Wyatt. "I swear I didn't. I'd never injure someone on purpose."

The door opened, and Detective Will walked in, followed by Bax.

"I want to talk to both of you about this assault on Robin Kayle," Detective Will said. "And I want to know which of you suffocated her."

Chapter 28

"Suffocated her? Neither of us touched her," Noah said.

"We only meant to scare her," Wyatt said.

"We can sort this out at the station." The detective's face was stony as he stared at them. Wyatt looked like he wanted to puke, while Noah fidgeted like he wanted to run away.

If he was telling the truth, he had a history of running away from hurting people.

"I want a lawyer," Noah said. He glanced at Bax. "There's some sort of legal services coverage in our benefits, right?"

Bax nodded.

"I'm pretty sure there's a brochure for the legal services in Elaine's office. I can go grab one," I said.

"I'll give you five minutes to get that brochure before I haul these two off." Detective Will stared at Noah and Wyatt like his glare would make them confess their misdeeds, including who had ultimately killed Robbie.

It wasn't like other people didn't have a window of opportunity. Aiden, for example, had spent twenty-eight minutes walking from the gym to the front door with a detour to meet up with his seamstress girlfriend. The timing was right as he ran into Harley on his way out.

Bax came with me to grab the info about the law services the studio offered for their employees, which I knew were intended to cover issues like divorce, adoption, wills, and matters that weren't criminal. But they'd be able to refer Noah and Wyatt to the correct type of attorney, and hopefully, they'd protect their rights in the short term. Because while I could see them pranking Robbie, I couldn't see them as cold-blooded killers.

I hadn't known about the suffocation aspect until today. While I could see both of them planning a prank gone wrong, I couldn't picture them harming Robbie on purpose.

When I scanned the wall of brochures, there wasn't one about the legal services offered.

"Maybe it's in here." Bax motioned to the file cabinet labeled SERVICES. It was locked when he tried to open it, so he grabbed his keys from his office.

"This should work." He unlocked the file cabinet, and something green and yellow caught my eye.

"Isn't that Robbie's hat?" I said. When Bax started to lean over to touch it, I said, "No, let it be."

I texted Detective Will. *We just found something important in the office manager's file cabinets.*

Bax glanced at me. "What's the significance of this?"

"Remember how Robbie was wearing a hat for the Australian women's soccer team on Lindsey's birthday? She was wearing it when the scavenger hunt started."

"Yes."

"Well, she wasn't wearing it when we found her."

"Did Robbie lose it?"

"But why would it have ended up here?"

"What are you two doing in my office?" Elaine's voice boomed out, scolding us like we were a couple of errant high schoolers.

Versus Bax being her boss.

I remembered a Dave Barry quote my father liked and whispered it to myself. "A person who is nice to you, but rude to the waiter, is not a nice person."

"Those are my private file cabinets." Elaine moved like she was going to shut the open cabinet.

Bax held up his hand. "These are office cabinets."

I pointed to the hat. "What's the story with this?"

But I already knew.

"I keep my spare hat in there."

"And you lock it up?"

"To keep anyone from borrowing it. I don't like sharing my personal possessions."

"And is that your blood on the hat?"

"No, I cleaned it up," she said and then froze.

Bax looked between us. "What's going on?"

"I don't know the full story, but I'm guessing Elaine saw Noah and Wyatt flee Ground Rules and come back here. So she went to check on things. Robbie was injured, but not dead. At least until Elaine left." They'd come in the street entrance to Ground Rules, then left through the interior door, and entered the studio. They'd missed being caught on the security cams.

"You don't have any proof I smothered Robbie." Elaine put her hands on her hips like she was in a position of moral authority.

"Who said anything about smothering? Everyone thinks Robbie died of a head injury."

"You two need to leave my office. I have work to do." Elaine flung out her arm and pointed to the door. She turned her head.

And realized she was pointing at Detective Will. Wyatt and Noah stood behind him.

I looked at the detective, who watched the scene with his usual skeptical look. "Looks like we found your murderer. Here's Robbie's hat, which I'm guessing might have traces of her blood on it. And maybe saliva, since Elaine needed something to help her suffocate Robbie."

Elaine moved forward like she wanted to slap me, but Bax grabbed her outstretched arm.

"Back off," Bax said.

Detective Will interceded before Elaine had a chance to react, and cuffed her.

"You murdered Robbie? You let us think our prank had killed her," Noah said. Wyatt's mouth was open as he stared at the office manager.

"Everyone here is so immature, acting like you're saving the world when you're just creating a way to waste time."

Why had she ever applied here if she felt that way about games? But I sensed something else.

Elaine continued. "I saw you two rush in the office, talking about the roastery, so I checked things out, thinking I could help. And I found Robbie sitting there, dazed, and she was rude when she saw me. She called me pathetic."

I spoke. "But that's not the only reason why you snapped, correct? Robbie could be vicious to people around her, and especially to women. I'm guessing you were an easy target." I could tell my words had struck home. From the way Elaine's eyes shifted, I knew this wasn't the whole story. "Or was there something more?"

Elaine glared at me. "That . . . brat . . . tried to blackmail me. Me. After everything I did for her. She was such a user. She took advantage of anyone she could, if she thought it would help her get ahead."

Blackmail? Work perks or money? Robbie had supposedly been saving up to move to Australia.

"What did she have on you?"

Elaine stayed quiet, but Noah spoke. "Remember a while back, six months ago, maybe, when the candy money from Raoul's son's basketball fund-raiser went missing, only to be found in the kitchen later? Robbie used to joke about someone swiping it, including when Elaine was around. I didn't put it together until now."

"You stole money from a kid?" I asked.

Elaine glared at me. "I needed gas money, and I replaced it the next day. But Robbie saw me borrow it, and she took photos on her phone."

"Was Robbie trying to make you support her claim to HR about deserving the job promotion?" Had Robbie held onto the photos for months, waiting for the right time to strike?

"She said she needed a better-sounding job title and threatened to post photos of me stealing the money to the company's Slack account. But some of us have kids to feed on a single mom's salary. Maybe I just snapped."

"You could've said something," Bax said.

"You should thank me for ridding the business of the cancer that was Robbie," Elaine said.

I had the feeling Elaine was already trying out excuses to see what would work as a justifiable reason for what she'd done.

But ultimately, this was all on her. She'd really let her children down if she'd really offed Robbie to hide a minor theft.

I did feel sorry for her kids.

And I wondered if that was the real reason Robbie was blackmailing Elaine. Maybe it was one of many transgressions Robbie had uncovered. After all, Elaine was always the person collecting money for birthdays, fund-raisers, and other events.

Noah stared at Elaine. "So you're the one who cut my bicycle tires and spiked Wyatt's coconut water mix?"

"I wanted you two to turn on each and either confess or turn the other one in. Who would've believed one of you wasn't responsible? I should've remembered to throw out the hat, or planted it in one of your desks."

The police escorted Elaine, Noah, and Wyatt out of the building, while most of the office staff watched in shock.

Later that day, Lindsey, Bax, and I ate chicken rice bowls from a local Japanese food cart.

"I had no idea Elaine hated us that much," Bax said.

"I suspected she wasn't happy here, but it always seemed like she did her job well, so I let her be, although I did remind her to respect everyone's viewpoints," Lindsey said.

"It seems like she hates video games." I took a bite of my oyakodon.

Lindsey glanced upward, like she remembered something. "I overheard her on the phone once, and it sounded like one of her kids was skipping school to play video games with a friend, which is typical kid stuff."

"You'd think she would've found a new job."

"If she had, it would've been better for us." Bax sounded grim.

"What do you think will happen to Noah and Wyatt?" Lindsey asked.

"I talked with Jackson earlier, and while he's not going to make any predictions, he said they might be charged with assault. But if Robbie was sitting up and talking after they left, it was an accident. Who knows?"

"If only they'd just called for help when it happened versus leaving Robbie on her own."

"If wishes were horses . . ." I said.

"We'd all drink strong coffee," Bax said.

"That's close enough to the proverb to count," Lindsey said.

Chapter 29

Halloween had arrived. The smell of pumpkins was in the air. Well, not really, but I loved seeing the jack-o'-lanterns adorning the front stoops of houses as Niko went trick-or-treating with a group of friends.

"Did I tell you congratulations on signing the big contract?" Bax asked as we tagged along behind the cluster of kids on a candy mission.

"I'm so glad the Irish coffee deal went through." Ground Rules had formally signed the contract with Tierney and Shay's company, Doyle's Oregon Whiskey, at 10:00 a.m. today. The attorney had also sent a cease-and-desist letter to Mark, and I hadn't seen him since everything went down.

But something told me Mark would remain the proverbial thorn in my side.

Grumpy Sasquatch Studio was recovering. Noah and Wyatt were back at coding as they worked out their legal troubles. Bax and Lindsey had taken on a temporary office manager recommended by their HR service, but they were still figuring things out. But I knew everything would come out okay in the end.

"I got a full Snickers bar!" Niko showed me, then scampered off to the next house.

Niko's costume was the height of DIY, and he'd compiled it himself: a too-big trilby he'd snagged from his dad's closet (I'd helped him stuff it with paper so it would stay out of his eyes), plus a black cape from a previous year's costume, a silver chain belt he'd borrowed from me, cargo pants, hiking boots, and a black sweatshirt. All finished with a brown canvas military messenger-style bag he used to store his candy.

I still wasn't sure what Niko was dressed up as, but he clearly loved it. We'd acquired a trio of his friends, and their costumes were store-bought. The skeleton's bones glowed in the dark, so between him, the green dragon who seemed to leave a trail of glitter behind him, and the girl dressed as Link from *The Legend of Zelda*, they were an easy group to track since we were chaperoning their candy quest.

Bax had acquired our costume for us: tunics that looked like slices of bread, one spread with peanut butter and the other with jelly, which Bax insisted I was the sweet one in our relationship. The night was warm enough that we only needed jeans and sweaters underneath the tunics; no heavy jackets were needed.

"Nice costumes," a guy said as he followed by with a couple of princesses and a toddler in a Dalmatian onesie. Our crew ran up a flight of steps to the front door adorned with pumpkins on their retaining wall and fake gravestones in their steep yard.

"We fit together like peanut butter and jelly," Bax said. He turned to me. "Maybe we should take the leap."

I turned and faced him. "You mean I should move in full-time?" He reached up and tucked a strand of hair behind my ear.

"Yes, but I was actually thinking marriage."

"Pretty big leap."

"One I'd happily make with you."

Niko's voice broke into the moment. "Dad, they gave out full candy bars!"

Bax turned. "It sounds like your lucky night."

We held hands as we walked to the next house. "I knew I should've waited and taken you for a hike to Bridal Veil Falls. I'd been debating all sorts of romantic proposals . . . and then brought it up now."

"I mean, we are peanut butter and jelly. I can see why you couldn't resist."

Bax turned to me. "Is that a yes?"

My heart thudded in my ears. "Yes."

We grinned goofily at each other while our quartet of kids trick-or-treated.

When we returned to Bax's house, the kids compared their hauls and traded for favorites. Niko swapped all of his Skittles, candy corn, and SweeTarts for Reese's Peanut Butter Cups or KitKats.

Finally, we turned off the front porch light. All of the kids had been picked up by their parents and had gone home. Niko was tucked up in bed with his bag of Halloween candy alongside his pillow.

Bax opened up a 375-millimeter bottle of Prosecco.

"I would've bought something fancier if I'd planned this," he said. He poured the Prosecco into vintage coupe glasses we'd found at the neighborhood yard sale last summer.

"I like the baby Prosecco bottles from Fred Meyer," I said.

He handed me a glass, and we looked at each other. This was official. Permanent. Nerves fluttered inside me, although this was the right choice.

Bax set his glass down on the table and then took my glass from me and put it down next to his. He then slipped something out of his pocket and took my left hand. He slid a ring onto my finger. "We can get this resized if needed, and it'll be easy to do since the jeweler who made this has a studio in SE Portland. But Harley helped me figure out your ring size."

I couldn't say anything. The ring had a brilliant blue stone in the middle, flanked by two clear stones in a platinum band twisted into the infinity symbol.

"That's a star sapphire, flanked by white sapphires," Bax added. "I know your opinion about blood diamonds."

I wanted to tell him it was beautiful, but the words couldn't slip past the lump in my throat.

"A star sapphire seemed especially appropriate, 'cause you're a star. And sapphires are considered hard-wearing, meaning they're durable, which is good for a ring you'll wear every day. And it's platinum, in case you were wondering."

A laugh wanted to bubble up in me. Bax was afraid I hated the ring, and his nervousness came out as chatter.

"Bax, I love it."

Whatever the future brought, we'd face it together.

RECIPES

Ground Rules Espresso Brownies

Ingredients
1 cup dairy-free chocolate chips
8 tablespoons canola oil
3 tablespoons cocoa
1 shot of brewed espresso or 1 teaspoon of espresso powder
1¼ cups sugar
½ teaspoon salt
1 teaspoon vanilla extract
3 eggs
1 cup all-purpose flour

Preparation
Preheat the oven to 350° F. Line an 8-by-8-inch pan with tin foil and give it a once-over with cooking spray (or otherwise grease the tin foil).

Mix the dairy-free chocolate chips and canola oil in the top of a double boiler, and melt over medium-low heat, stirring regularly. Once the chocolate has melted, remove from heat and whisk in the cocoa powder and one shot of brewed espresso or espresso powder. Put aside.

Whisk together the eggs, sugar, salt, and vanilla in a large bowl. Once it's combined, whisk in the chocolate mixture. Once it's mixed, add the cup of flour, taking care to incorporate the flour without over-whisking the mixture.

Pour the batter into the prepared pan, and bake for 35–40 minutes. When a toothpick comes out mostly clean, your brownies are ready. Note that if your toothpick comes out completely clean, you've overbaked the treats.

Let the brownies cool for about an hour before removing them from the pan. Cut into squares, store in an airtight container, and consume within a day or two.

Notes:

These brownies are fudgy. If you prefer a cake-like brownie, mix 1 teaspoon of baking powder into the cup of flour before adding it to the chocolate-eggs mixture.

If desired, you can substitute butter—vegan or regular—for the oil. The canola oil gives the brownies a cleaner taste than vegan butter; taste tests also showed dairy butter works well in this recipe.

While you can leave the espresso out, it adds richness and depth to the brownies. Feel free to stir nuts or chocolate chips into the batter before pouring it into the baking dish.

Spiced Orange Syrup

Ingredients

1 cup water

1 cup sugar

orange zest from one orange

2 cinnamon sticks

2 star anise pods

Preparation

Mix water, sugar, orange zest, cinnamon sticks, and star anise in a saucepan. Bring it to a simmer over medium heat, being sure to stir as the sugar dissolves. Simmer, covered, for 10 minutes, then remove from heat and cool. Take out the cinnamon sticks and star anise and store the syrup in a covered jar (Sage suggests a mason jar with a reusable lid).

Use in coffee, or tea, or on pancakes or waffles. Or in an old-fashioned!

This makes a great homemade tea latte when mixed with steamed milk, a perfectly brewed cup of black tea, and a teaspoon or two of spiced orange syrup!

Cinnamon Maple Syrup

Ingredients

1 cup water

½ cup white sugar

½ pure maple syrup (or brown sugar or turbinado if maple isn't an option, which would turn this into an equally delicious cinnamon-sugar syrup)

3 cinnamon sticks

1 teaspoon vanilla extract (optional but recommended)

Preparation

Combine water, sugar, maple syrup, and cinnamon sticks in a saucepan. Put on medium heat and stir until the sugars dissolve and the water comes to a boil. Reduce heat, cover, and simmer for a few minutes.

Remove from heat and stir in the teaspoon of vanilla. The vanilla is optional, but it truly rounds out the flavor of the syrup and elevates from good to excellent.

Let it cool for at least an hour on the stovetop. Remove the cinnamon sticks and store the syrup in a container, like a mason jar with a reusable lid, in the fridge. Note: the syrup will thicken as it cools, but it's not going to be thick like honey or molasses.

Use in coffee, tea, hot chocolate, apple cider, ice cream, or cocktails. Or drizzled on fresh-cut apples, waffles, chia-seed pudding, or anything that can need a burst of cinnamon-maple goodness.

Spiced Orange Cold Brew

First, you'll need to make cold brew concentrate. Ground Rules tends to use mason jars when making cold brew concentrate at home, although you can buy fancy pitchers for cold brew. Or use a French press.

Making coffee is all about the proper ratio of coffee grounds to water. To make a cold brew concentrate, you'll use ¾ cup of coarse ground coffee to 4 cups of water.

You can double, triple, quadruple, etc., this recipe; just keep the ¾ cup grounds to 4 cups of water ratio intact.

Ingredients
¾ cup coarse coffee grounds
4 cups water

Preparation
Mix four cups of water and the ¾ cup of coffee grounds in an appropriately sized mason jar, and screw on the lid. Place in the refrigerator for 12 to 24 hours.

When the coffee has brewed to your liking, strain it into a clean pitcher or mason jar.

To make a spiced orange cold brew:

Put ½ cup of cold brew concentrate into a glass, along with ½ cup of water or milk (note: you'll want to keep your cold brew to milk or water ratio at 1:1). Add a teaspoon of spiced orange syrup (or to taste, if you'd like a sweeter drink). Add ice, and you're ready to go!

Spiced Orange Coffee Soda

Ingredients
  ¾ cup cold brew concentrate
  1 tablespoon spiced orange syrup
  ¾ cup club soda
  ice

Preparation

   Mix the cold brew concentrate and spiced orange syrup in a wide-mouth, pint-sized mason jar (or glass of your choosing). Add ice to the top of the glass, then slowly pour in the club soda. Lightly mix, and your soda is ready.

Spiced Orange Tea Soda

Ingredients
the tea of your choosing (black, green, white, rooibos)
1 tablespoon spiced orange syrup
¾ cup club soda
ice

Preparation
First, you'll make your tea concentrate. You'll want to dramatically up your ratio of tea leaves to water. If you use a teabag instead of 1 tea bag to 1 mug of water, you'll add about an inch of water to your usual cup.

Brew the tea for the usual time (30 seconds to 1 minute for green, 3 to 5 minutes for black, 6 minutes for rooibos). Do not brew the tea for longer than normal—that will make it bitter. We want to make the tea stronger, not overbrewed.

Once your tea concentrate is done, and you've strained it and/or removed the bag, you're ready for the fun part!

Mix the tea concentrate and spiced orange syrup in a wide-mouth, pint-sized mason jar (or glass of your choosing). Add ice to the top of the glass, then slowly pour in the club soda. Lightly mix, and voilà! You have a tea soda.

Ground Rules DIY Fridge Deodorizer

Used coffee grounds make a fantastic deodorizer and, if you make coffee at home, you have everything you need to make one!

After you brew your next cup of java, instead of composting your coffee grounds, dry them out. One easy way: spread them on a cookie sheet and leave them to dry on the counter.

Once the coffee grounds are dry, pour them into a mason jar or a bowl, and pop them in the back of the fridge. You can leave the jar or bowl uncovered. But if you're afraid of spilling the grounds, punch holes in the lid of a mason jar and use it.

The grounds will work as a deodorizer for a few weeks. This won't help with something truly rotten, but will absorb everyday smells and keep your fridge smelling fresh.

After a few weeks, dry some fresh (used) grounds, and replace the grounds in your fridge with a new batch!

Acknowledgments

As always, I owe a lifetime supply of coffee to John Scognamiglio, Larissa Ackerman, and everyone at Kensington for their support in bringing the Ground Rules series to the world. And a giant thank-you to my literary agent, Joshua Bilmes.

Thank you to everyone in Ben's Cozy Crew and the Lighthouse Library for your encouragement, support, and taste-testing the Ground Rules recipes.

As always, thank you to Robin, Miriam, Sonja, Fonda, Bill, Jenn, Tina, Angela, Kate/Ellie, Leslie/Alicia, and all of my writer friends.

Visit our website at
KensingtonBooks.com
to sign up for our newsletters, read
more from your favorite authors, see
books by series, view reading group
guides, and more!

BOOK  CLUB
BETWEEN THE CHAPTERS

Become a Part of Our
Between the Chapters Book Club
Community and Join the Conversation

Betweenthechapters.net